Brooklyn

Kings of New York

BLUE SAFFIRE

Perceptive Illusions Publishing
Bayshore, New York

Blue Saffire/Perceptive Illusions Publishing, Inc
PO BOX 5253
Bayshore, NY 11706
www.BlueSaffire.com

Publisher's Note: This is a work of fiction. Names, characters, places, and incidents are a product of the author's imagination. Locales and public names are sometimes used for atmospheric purposes. Any resemblance to actual people, living or dead, or to businesses, companies, events, institutions, or locales is completely coincidental.

Ordering Information:
Quantity sales. Special discounts are available on quantity purchases by corporations, associations, and others. For details, contact the "Special Sales Department" at the address above.

Cover Designed by Natasha Snow Designs www.natashasnowdesigns.com
Cover Image ã WANDER AGUIAR PHOTOGRAPHY LLC.

Brooklyn/ Blue Saffire. -- 1st ed.
ISBN 978-1-941924-39-6

I can love you through time, but can time move through our love?

–BLUE SAFFIRE

PREFACE

Wedding Blast

Deja

I stand in the mirror looking at myself in my wedding gown. This is one of three. One for tonight and two for ....

I turn as Tasha places a hand on my forearm. She looks me in my eyes with concern. I already know what she's thinking.

I'm okay with this.

"I have so much respect for you. You know I love you like a sister, right?" she says as she holds my face between her hands while she presses her forehead to mine as we stand in the bridal suite the girls created for me here at the manor in Dublin.

"I love you too. I'm doing nothing you guys wouldn't do for me."

"I thought LaSalle was lying when he told me what you two planned to do. You and Brooklyn were made for each other.

"This is crazy. Balls to the wall doesn't have to be your preset. We could have handled this a different way. We still can," she replies, looking me deep in my eyes.

"What fun would that be? Besides, I know a little boy who says this is the way. I get two, one covered in red, the other in white. Irish bells toll for death, wedding bells ring on a Scottish night," I repeat the words Sammy told me.

Tasha sighs. "But the blue eyes haunt the night as she stands out of sight. Yeah, yeah, the boy was singing the same thing all last night."

"That bitch is making my ass itch. I can't wait for Misha to pull a blade across her throat," Misha's wife says.

"You and me both," Tasha mumbles.

"This will bring us closer to the end. Ya wait and see."

"This should all be over already. Enough is enough. Haven't we sacrificed enough? This isn't right," Pam says.

"Everyone will be safe. The children and our families will be protected. I have done everything to make sure everything happens as I was told," Sim says.

"I know ya have, love. Breathe, ladies. I know what I'm in for. Ye all are taking the joy out of me wedding day. Please, can we finish getting me ready?"

"Your wedding day," Tasha snorts. "How are you so calm? I told LaSalle you were crazy."

She rolls her eyes and snorts. "He laughed at me. Then he told me to think about who your best friend is."

"Hey, stop trying to act like you don't live in Crazy Town with the rest of us. You might hide it well, but you live right on our street and have tea parties with us every week," Val says from behind me as she fixes my veil.

"Shops with me often," Dean sings as she sits with a huge gift box resting on her lap.

"I know that's right," Val says.

"DJ, this is for you. Will you come open it?" Dean says, pointing to the box with a huge smile on her face.

I turn and go to sit next to her in the spot she pats beside her. She helps me slide the box into my lap. With excitement coursing through me, I lift the lid off the gift.

"You didn't think we would let you do this without the right equipment, now did you?" Dean says.

"But how—"

"I might have let it slip that you asked me for adjustments. Not to Cole, but I was talking to Val and Tasha as they made the same request and ..." Sim trails off and begins to chew on her lip.

"I'm glad she did say something. We all know you ain't shit with two Glocks in your hands."

I glare at Val and roll my eyes. I'm not even going to go there with her about this again. Not everyone can be freaking John Wick. I get things done when it counts. We all know this.

"This is your something old, something new, something borrowed, something blue," Dean says ignoring the rest of them.

"Borrowed? How is it borrowed or blue?"

Dean lifts the rifle with the airholes from the box as if weighing it in her hands. "It's borrowed because this is one of my favorites. I want it back. It's new and blue because Lovie modified the trigger. Making it old but with a little something new. It still works like a dream, trust me."

I take the rifle and examine the matte-blue-finished trigger. Lovie never fails to amaze me. This is a work of art.

"Well, I say yer ready to get married, ya are," Laoise says.

I look to Dean's mother-in-law and smile. She gets me. One is enough.

Brooklyn

"Do you, Cole O'Brien, take this woman to forever be the love of your life?" Uncle Joe says.

I grin at the words Deja and I decided to use for this night. They suit us and who we are. As I look down into her brown eyes, my heart fills with so much love for her.

"Aye, I do," I say.

If there is one thing I know for sure, it's that I love this woman standing here before me. Her wedding day is meant to be about her. Yet she's allowed us to make this evening about something else.

She says we didn't have a choice. I don't believe that. Everything leading to this day has been a choice. Some choices were right, others were dead wrong.

I'm trusting this is one of the right ones. As long as everything goes according to plan, it will be. We need to give Misha and Uri the window to bring this all to an end.

We'll catch the fox tonight once and for all. She wants my DJ. The one who got away. Someone was taken from her, and she wants to take from us.

While The Alliance is established, it's the little bullshit like this we're still cleaning up. The pieces Phoebe Romaine warned us about and the parts her grandson is still filling in. We will reign supreme.

Everything has its time and place. I have to remind myself of this constantly. One minute, we're all ready to move forward with our lives, the next, something is trying to pull us back into our past.

I never wanted our wedding to be in this place. The thought of doing this in Ireland makes my skin crawl. This manor would probably jinx us if this were the wedding we have planned for Scotland.

After all, if these walls could talk, they would tell a tale of a madman. Aye, it was me. No need to whisper or speculate about it. I, "Brooklyn" Cole Patrick O'Brien, killed Oland O'Brien's sorry ass. He deserved it.

I didn't care who agreed with it; I only wanted him dead. When I want something, I make it happen. I could tell from the look in his eyes he understood that with his final breath.

"And do you, Deja Walsh, take this man to forever be the love of your life?" Uncle Joe says, pulling me from my thoughts.

"Aye, I'll take him," she says with a smile.

Everyone laughs and my smile grows wider. I love her smart ass. We've been bantering back and forth for years.

From those days when she wore bangs and pigtails while in a softball uniform, giving me shit about how Americanized I had become. I looked forward to every summer I would get to come back. Her smart mouth was something I longed for.

"The time is now. Two minutes."

The words are spoken into my ear by the boy we're all banking everything on. I reach beneath my tux jacket and pull the two

Glocks from my holsters. At the same time, I step on the pedal beside my foot.

Smoke fills the air, giving my guys time to get into position and pull their weapons. I look around to make sure things are going to plan. At first glance, it seems to have worked like a charm; all guests who aren't meant to be above ground vanish. All except my bride and her bridesmaids. Instead of falling to safety, they all pull guns of their own.

I don't have time to process what's happening as my bride pulls a semi-auto rifle of her own from beneath her dress and all hell breaks loose as the smoke settles. A bullet whizzes by my head and an explosion goes off, causing me to snap back into focus.

Uncle Joe has already moved into action with my cousins and brothers. This is happening whether I want it or not. All the arguing was for nothing.

I should have known better. This woman will go to death's door standing right beside me, time and time again. As I glance out the corner of my eye, I have one thought.

These motherfuckers are getting more than the Alliance tonight; they have awoken the Bellas. Shit move.

"Ya will get over it, but I won't get over losing ya. Focus, Cole. I told ya, this is my world too," DJ calls at me.

CHAPTER ONE

Change of Course

Onyx

About thirty-nine years ago …

"*Net*, my brothers and sisters aren't interested, my friend."

Ian snorts as he hears the same lie I do. I peek through the crack of my hiding place. The look on Aleksandr Krupin's face confirms what my ears tell me.

He's lying and that smug-ass grin says it all. I never did trust the Krupins. I don't think Ian does either, with the exception of Lev. If you ask me, the entire family should be certified.

"Funny, when I spoke to Lev, he spoke a different story."

"*Da*, but it is my approval you seek. I say no. It is disrespect to me you go to younger brother first."

"Then why did ye come here?"

"I hear noise, I want to see who make. I like to see rat before set trap."

"Are ye threatening me?"

"No threat. Just promise. The answer *net*, and we will not allow this."

"Ye are a fool. No one is allowing us to do anything. It is already done."

"*Net*, it is not done. *Da*, I may be fool, but fool who live to see another day. You and Lev, not so much."

With that, Aleksandr Krupin gets up to leave. I take the phone in my hand off speaker and lift it to my ear as I watch Ian Black glare after Aleksandr. The tension in the air can still be felt.

"Did you hear that?"

"*Da*, I heard. One million. Aleksandr not return to Russia."

"Are you sure? This is your brother."

"*Da*, he won't stop until he kills us all. I know what I have started. I handle others. You handle him. If he returns, he problem for me. Tell Ian deal still on."

I end the call and step out of my hiding place. Ian turns to me and looks me in my eyes. I can see the rage in his face.

"Lev wants him gone. He says the deal is still on."

"Aye, ye know what to do, Onyx. I've already transferred your money. I will be on my way back to Scotland. Be safe, love."

I go to ask him about the other mercenary he sent to work with me on my last mission for him. However, instead, I nod and turn to leave. I don't bother to tell him I'm not going to follow him this time. My baby girl doesn't need this world to know about her.

Friends and enemies alike. I won't risk it. Her conception was a mistake, but it might have been just what I needed. This life is taking a toll on me.

Other than money, I have no real vested interest in any of this. Ian is on a mission. He's playing a long game.

I'm just one of his pawns. I fell into this life to survive. Ian Black became like a father figure to me—that is, when he's around.

For the most part, I've become used to being alone. I know I'm not the only one; Ian has us all over the world. I never understood his interest in me. It's not anything pervy or creepy, but I know he has my back. He looks out for me.

That's why I agreed to do that last job. Most times, we work alone, and it gets lonely. No strings, no attachments. Well, I broke all the rules and now I have consequences.

If Ian hadn't asked me to partner with that newbie, this never would have happened. It's my fault. I let things go too far.

It's okay, my little angel. It will be just you and me now. One more job and we'll find something else.

This time, maybe I'll go off-grid for good. No more jobs for Ian Black, no more missions.

***

"Room service," I sing as I knock on the room door of Aleksandr Krupin's hotel suite.

In and out, that's the plan. This cart has all the heavy artillery I need for this job. I take a deep breath as the door is pulled open.

Showtime.

"I hope you remembered steak this time," the big guy who opens the door says as he looks behind him.

I lift the dome from one of the plates and grab the gun with the silencer. Aiming at this guy's head, I pull the trigger before he gets a chance to turn back around.

I then push the cart inside and let the door click shut behind me. Swiftly, I put a bullet in the heads of the two guys who come into sight first. Feeling someone come up behind me, I turn quickly to pull the trigger.

However, I'm not fast enough. The gun is knocked from my hand. I'm pushed back hard.

My back hits the cart and the momentum of the shove flips me over the top. I land on my feet and pull another gun from under the cloth over the cart. This time, I get two off into his chest before he can charge me.

I curse as the gun jams. Piece of shit. I toss it aside right as someone grabs my shoulder.

I don't take time to think. I throw my elbow back into his ribs. When he grunts but doesn't release me, I throw another elbow at the same spot and then the other at his face. I wiggle away before he can get a hold of me.

Spinning out, I plant a foot in his chest and pull a knife to toss into his throat. He drops to the floor, gurgling as he clutches his throat. I pull another gun and rush into the next room of the suite.

I find Aleksandr sitting in an accent chair in that room. I don't hesitate to put two in his chest and one in his head. A frown comes to my face. That was too easy.

My gut tells me something is off. Sound in the front of the suite causes me to snap out of it. I don't have time to think.

I can only react. I move quickly into the corner and squat down out of sight. As I glance around for my escape route, something catches my attention.

Hiding under the bed, trembling in fear, is a little kid. Now I understand why Aleksandr didn't put up a fight. I caught him off guard. The Krupins are known for trafficking, another reason why I think Ian should have cut his losses.

The kid's little blue eyes are locked on mine. I lift my gun to my lips to tell them to remain silent. I don't kill kids.

It's one of the rules. Kids are a hard no. Knowing I need to move this out of the kid's sight, not wanting them to witness any more than they already have, I quietly move toward the door.

Moving back into the other room, I make sure I can't be seen. I'm outnumbered and it's clear I'm going to have to shoot my way out. I tug at my bulletproof vest and smooth a hand over my belly. I need to get out of here and back to my baby.

I inhale and stay low as I run for the cart I left behind. Halfway there, I drop down to my knees and slide. I grab the rifle from beneath the cart and roll to my feet. In the next breath, I air the place out then grab my bag from the cart and take off for the door.

Once in the hall, I go to run to my right to head for the elevators. However, I spot more of Aleksandr's men heading in my direction. I turn and dash for the other corridor to race down the stairs.

When the door closes behind me, I snatch off the wig I'm wearing. Then I pull out the trench coat from my bag to toss on over the uniform I'm wearing and to conceal my rifle. Shouting comes from above as I race to the ground level.

I push a bit harder and make it to the exit. As I push through to the lobby, I take a calming breath. Calm as a cucumber, I walk through the lobby as if nothing is happening. I tug a hat from my pocket and pull it onto my head as I get outside.

"You can do this, love. One more block," I whisper to myself.

I keep moving, heading for the coffee shop I pinned for my getaway. The tension begins to ease as it comes up on my right. I jog across the street and push through the doors.

"Ach, excuse me. I'm sorry, love. Are ya all right?"

I look up into a pair of green-gray eyes, and my breath is taken away. He gives me a huge smile. I fall speechless and want to kick myself.

My baby's father did the same thing to me. I don't know what's going on with me. I've never been crazy about men like this.

"No, it's my fault. I'm sorry. Let me buy you another drink," I say as I snap out of it and look at his coffee-covered sweater.

"It's fine, but maybe I can buy ya one." He looks down at his watch. "I have some time. It's not every day an angel runs right into ya."

I look around. I need to go to the bathroom where I planned to stow away my things, but sitting with him will work.

"Sure, I just need to head to the ladies."

"Ach, no problem. I'll get our drinks and a table. Take yer time."

"Okay, thank you."

He gives me a wink, and I head to the restroom. As I'm changing into the clothes I left in the stall here, my phone rings. I wrinkle my brows as the number doesn't look familiar.

"Hello," I answer.

"*Da*, you and Lev have taken something from me. He allowed you to spill our blood. Now I will slaughter you and all you love. I will find you."

"Good luck with that," I snap and hang up.

I close my eyes and exhale. Ian isn't going to like this. I have no doubt that Lev Krupin is dead, and his brother got my number from his phone.

The Russians are definitely out. I knew they would be a problem. However, none of this is my business.

I finish up and head back out to the table where my coffee date is waiting. He looks up from his phone as I walk over. He gives me the most breathtaking smile.

"Please sit. I got ya some gingerbread cookies. The name is Angus."

"Helen, nice to meet you."

CHAPTER TWO

The Arrangement

McTavish

Fifteen years later ...

"Ach, ye don't listen. I told ya not to bring Jameson with ya. Lad, I need ya to stay right here in the car. Yer uncle and cousin will be with me."

"Okay, Granda," Jameson says like the good boy he is.

I turn my attention to the other two. Conor should know better. If I give an order, it's to be followed.

"Aye, now ye two, allow me to do the talking. Oland is a tricky oul bastard. He's not offering us anything out of the goodness of his own heart," I hiss at my son and grandson.

"But McDougal promised there would be a reward for whatever it is he wants," my son says.

"Ya think I trust Archie McDougal? His own da was seconds from putting a price on his head. What makes ya think he won't make me kill him? Ach, we trust no one here but our own," I say to Conor.

"I don't see why I'm here," my other grandson says, the spoiled brat.

"Yer presence was requested with ours, but I warn ya, lad, don't say a word. Not a single one."

"Aye, I hear ya. I have nothing to say. Let's get this over with. We want to head down to the field."

"Ach, I hope it's to practice and play. Not to watch the cailíní," Conor grumbles.

"The lads have an eye for the lasses, leave them be," I chuckle.

"Not the lasses. They have their eyes on one cailín in particular. They have a glad eye for the same lass."

"They're healthy young lads. Ya leave me grandsons alone. They're becoming big lads, they are."

"Spoiled brats yer making them."

I know he's talking about his own son. Jameson has always been a good lad, Boyle, not so much. I ignore my son and climb from the car to head into the manor, where Oland O'Brien and Archie McDougal are waiting for us. The O'Brien clan has been in power for centuries. There was a time when the McTavish name was connected to the clan.

Oland and I are somehow distant cousins, not that he would own up to it. He looks down his nose at almost everyone not of his own blood. People say the man would have married himself if he could.

"Here ye are. We've been waiting," Archie says as we're led into the study by one of the staff.

"McDougal." I nod.

"Och, why so formal? We're all friends here. At least I'm sure we will be once this meeting is over."

"Aye, whatever ya say. I've come and brought me son and grandson as ya asked. What's this all about?"

"It's been brought to my attention that yer young lad has a glad eye for McDougal's young niece. The softball player. The two are around the same age."

"Who?"

"They're talking about Deja Walsh," my grandson murmurs, earning a glare from me.

"Aye, he's a horny young lad. Why did ya need to drag me here to tell me this?"

"Ach, she's my great-niece. My da has decided to punish me for a misunderstanding and the little lassie will come into some of what should be mine," Archie explains.

"If I'm right, yer lad isn't the only one with a glad eye for the cailín. If she's engaged to yer lad, there isn't any way my grandson can have her. This will effectively teach him who runs everything here and in America.

"I will not be defied. Ya see, if ya do me this favor and agree to this arrangement, then the lass belongs to yer lad, and Archie will make sure some of those assets fall into the McTavish name and hands when the time comes. He will," Oland says dryly.

"Och, trust me, when this is all over, your lad will be the lord of the McDougal clan. I'll ensure it."

I don't like this. If this is the lass Conor referred to in the car, this is already a problem. Both of my grandsons like the cailín. Jameson is the quieter of the two. It would break his heart if I arranged this behind his back, and I would never do something like that to the lad. Especially not for Oland.

I snort. Besides, there is no way in hell Archie can pull off a promise like this. I have not lost my mind to go against Lennox McDougal, and as I said, Archie is a dead man walking.

"Ach, no—"

"He'll do it," Conor cuts off my refusal before I can finish it.

I turn to find him with stars in his eyes and my grandson nodding his head in agreement. I want to batter the two. They have just taken their own lives.

"Aye, it's settled. I'll give ya the heads-up when it's safe for ya to woo the lass and get her to fall for ya. Cole's absence will work in yer favor."

"But will she be okay with this?"

"I will make it so," Archie croons with an evil look in his eyes. "I want ya to do one more thing for me. Keep her away from me granddaughter. Make sure their friendship ends."

I grind my teeth to keep from growling as these two eejits nod. We have no business in the middle of this. The only reason Ian will forgive me for taking this meeting is because I told him first.

Two melters, the pair of them. Jesus, Mary, Joseph—what's so hard to understand about not saying a word?

CHAPTER THREE

Friends

Deja

Three years later …

"Jesus, Mary, Joseph, they're back. I swear, if Kate quits the team, I'm drowning her, I am. So it is," Aisling gasps.

"Ya don't tell a fib. How do they get hotter every year? Is it the water in America?"

"Quit yer drooling," I snicker and roll my eyes.

I already know they're talking about Logan and Cole O'Brien. They and their sister Connie attend school in the States while staying with their granda. However, most summers they return to Ireland to be with the rest of their family.

Their youngest sister Kate, is my best friend. I've grown up around the O'Briens nearly all my life. I'm immune to their looks. Do I know that they are handsome? Of course, no one can deny that, but they're more like my big brothers.

Besides, I'm six years younger than Logan and four years younger than Cole. Neither of them is worried about me. I'm sure the girls in America have secured their hearts already.

However, I do look forward to the summers when they return. It's been three years since they were last here. Granda Ian had been sick for a while before they lost him. For the last year, they have been busy with university and taking over the business in America for their granda.

I may not have set eyes on them in three years, but I do talk to Cole a lot by phone since I'm always with his sister. Although I've missed having them around for a good laugh. The O'Brien home is still lively, but not as lively as when the guys are home.

They have probably changed a lot since I last saw them. I know I look nothing like I did the summer I was fifteen. A lot has changed with me.

I turn around to set eyes on my friends. Kate has a huge smile on her face as she walks between her two older brothers with her arms looped through theirs. They are both looking down at her as they talk.

I smile. It looks like both brothers have gotten taller. They were over six feet tall the last time I saw them. I'll give each of them a few more inches in height.

Suddenly, the sun seems to begin to shine directly on Cole as he turns his head in my direction. My breath is stolen right from my lungs. He's even more handsome than I remember.

His green eyes seem to sparkle as they roll over me. The crooked smile he gives me makes my belly flip and do all types of things it shouldn't be doing at the sight of an O'Brien brother. I allow my gaze to roll over him to take him in.

He has on a white button-down shirt with the sleeves rolled up to the elbows. The black pants he's wearing cling to his thick thighs. His black shoes look too expensive for a day at the softball field with his little sister.

However, what has me captivated is the ease of his walk and his presence. He moves as if everything around him should answer to him and his whims.

My mouth runs dry. Quickly, I snap my eyes back to his face as my cheeks heat. My heart is racing like crazy, and I feel insane for reacting this way.

A glance at Logan tells me this is a Cole-related response. While Logan has gotten broader and is more handsome than ever, I'm still not blushing and ready to run into his arms the way I'm ready to jump into Cole's.

"Deja? Look at ya," Logan says with a smile. "I thought Kate looked all grown up. Looks like ya went and turned into a little woman on us too. Aye, Cole, we have been away for too long."

Logan pulls me into a bear hug and spins me around. I laugh and give him a tight hug. I'm relieved as his embrace feels like that of an older brother just come home.

He places me on my feet, and I look up at him with a smile. He reaches to tug at my ponytail and winks at me, still only the feeling of an older brother showing affection.

"Are you going to ignore me? Haven't you missed me too?" Cole croons, causing me to look at him.

He pulls me into the same type of hug as the one Logan gave me. However, his hug causes butterflies to fill my stomach and I can't help but take a deep breath. That's the wrong move.

My lungs fill with his delicious scent, and I want to moan into his neck. Instead, I bite down on my lip to stifle the response as he spins me in a circle. When he places me back on my feet, I can't force myself to look up at him.

"Ach, you haven't gotten much taller, but you're grown up all right," Cole says.

"Ew, it's more terrible in person. Ya sound like an American. That's worse than me height not showing up for me, it is," I tease. "What happened? Ya afraid ya wouldn't fit in?"

"Ach, ya think I've forgotten where I'm from?"

I shrug my shoulders. "Aye, sounds like ya have."

He tugs me into a headlock as he laughs. I wrap my arms around his waist and bask in his embrace. This shouldn't feel this good.

I pull away slowly and take a few steps back. "Welcome back."

"Ya can welcome me back by winning this game. Ya hit a home run and dinner is on me."

"What do I get for two or three?"

He winks at me. "Ya have to hit them to find out."

"Get yer pockets ready. I'm holding ya to that." I rub my hands together.

"Ye two live to taunt each other. It hasn't been five minutes," Kate says.

I laugh and shrug. Like I said, Cole and Logan have always been like older brothers to me. I spent a lot of time with Cole the last time they were here.

I think we became closer during that time. During that visit, I saw something I don't think many others did. Cole was struggling with something, and I wanted to help him out.

Kate had been focused on fourteen-year-old stuff. I don't think anyone else saw the stress on his face as they were concerned with Granda Ian's health. Kate's a year younger than me. Right now, we're both seventeen, but that's not going to be for long.

I turn eighteen soon. Cole is already twenty-two. To be honest, I look up to Logan, Connie, and Cole.

I plan to go to America just like them someday. That's where my mum and biological father are from. Mum keeps telling me she'll take me, but she hasn't yet.

Angus, my da who raised me, promised next year will be the year when he will take me himself. All I have to do is secure my spot on the softball team.

I guess I'll be in America next year. I'm going to play in the league here. I'm good enough. I'm ranked as one of the best hitters in Europe.

"Come on, DJ. Enough of everyone talking. Show me what ya got," Cole croons, pulling me from my thoughts.

I love his nickname for me. With a smile, I nod and turn back to my team to get my head into the game. I'll show him all right. Dinner is as good as mine.

Brooklyn

"Aye, she's still got it," Logan croons as DJ knocks another one out of the park.

I nod my head as I clap. She sure does. "Ach, I know they hate to see her coming," I chuckle.

"Your wallet is going to have the same feeling later," he taunts.

"I don't mind."

"Mm." He makes the sound, causing me to turn to look him in the face.

I try to dial it down, knowing I'm probably giving myself away. I should be ashamed of the crush I have on my little sister's best friend. I've always had a little thing for Deja.

She's a gorgeous girl inside and out. However, I wasn't expecting to see her like this. She's all grown up and so fucking pretty.

She's had those bangs for as long as I can remember, but they suit her face. They sit right above those pretty brown eyes, bringing a mystery of their own to her features.

Last time I saw Deja, she was flat as a board, front and back. Today, that softball uniform fits her curvy body in a way no man can ignore, but I must.

We're not here for our usual family visit. It's been best for Logan, Connie, and me to steer clear of Ireland. Our good-for-nothing granda Oland feels we betrayed him by living in America with our granda Ian.

Then I turned him down three years ago when he asked me to stay and work for him. Not under my da, but in my da's place. The bastard is an eejit if he thought I was going to go against my da and my brother.

Granda Oland knows Logan doesn't want to be my da's successor. Oland and Logan bump heads like bulls. However, Logan hasn't stepped away from doing what my da asks of him.

This has caused tension and problems for our da. We don't want to be a problem for Da, but Oland leaves a bad taste in the mouth of anyone he comes in contact with.

We've always preferred to spend time with Granda Ian over that bastard Oland. When the offer was made to follow Granda Ian to America and spend time in Scotland, we jumped all over it.

Logan and I thought it might ease things for Da. It did in some ways. However, it caused trouble in others.

This is why we're back. Not to see our family and have a good time. We're here because we've gotten wind of Oland being up to something.

Something that involves Kate and her best friend. It's a problem Da and Uncle Finlay thought we should look into. A problem that's going to get Oland hurt if there's any truth to it.

"Remember, we have to keep an eye out for McTavish. We probably should keep our distance as much as we can. I didn't mean to hug the lass. It's a habit," Logan whispers into my ear.

Deja will be eighteen next week. Her father plans to surprise her with a trip to New York at the end of the month. There's a chance she won't be coming back to Ireland. Not for a while.

My granda is up to something. Logan and I are here to confirm some things. Once Deja is in New York, I can finally tell her how I feel.

She'll be further out of Oland's reach. I'll be careful this time. What happened to Nakim will never happen again.

I grunt at Logan because I can't promise him anything. I find it hard enough to keep my feelings for Deja locked away. Whenever I'm around her, I need to be near her.

It's for her safety, Cole.

CHAPTER FOUR

Bonfire Whispers

Deja

A week later …

"Happy birthday, Deja," two newcomers call out.

I smile and wave. I wasn't expecting this party. Logan and Cole were called away last week after the game.

I had to take a rain check on the dinner Cole owes me. I was a little bummed, but I got over it. Then this morning, he called to tell me they were throwing me a bonfire party for my birthday.

I shouldn't have been so disappointed in the first place about the dinner. Cole isn't interested in me. It's not like we were going to dinner alone.

Besides, Boyle has been pursuing me for the last five months. I'm still not sure about him. I used to have a crush on him, but that was before he dated Ríona Gallagher.

She's a total bitch, and I do believe she only dated Boyle because I liked him. And I thought he liked me too, until they showed up at a party together. Knowing he kissed and probably shagged her fish-face arse is a total turnoff.

Everyone knows we can't stand each other. It kind of felt like a slap in the face when they got together. However, I had been ready to give in and let him take me out about a week ago.

Now I get this sick feeling in the pit of my stomach when he calls or asks me out. I keep telling myself it's not because of Cole. To be honest, it has more to do with the possessiveness Boyle has displayed over the last week.

I haven't agreed to be his girlfriend so it's not appealing to me at all. Even tonight, something has been off with him. I'm friends with his best friend's girlfriend, so he's a part of my friend group.

Actually, Boyle and his cousin Jameson are friends of mine. Jameson has never been super outgoing, but Boyle is just the opposite. Boyle has been acting an arse tonight.

I've tried to avoid him, but he hasn't gotten the hint. What's even more frustrating is the fact that Cole and Logan's old friends have joined the party, and Cole has been off with them most of the night.

"Who's in charge of the music?" Boyle grumbles.

"It's one of Deja's mixtapes," Kate replies.

"The ones she makes with the CDs yer brothers send ya?" Aisling says.

"Cole sends them for her. She just allows me to listen to them first," Kate corrects her.

"Gah, I would chew off me left arm for him to send me anything. A worn T-shirt, his sweaty jocks, a bottle of his bathwater. Ugh, the brush he uses for all that thick hair," Aisling drools.

"He's all right. Don't ya think yer going too far?" Boyle mutters.

I don't miss the frown on Jameson's face. To be honest, he's been acting out of character lately. Something is going on between him and Boyle. I shrug it off and mind my business.

"Don't be so jealous. The girl yer after isn't even interested in him," Croía says and rolls her eyes.

I bite my lip and look down at the beer bottle in my hand. I've had a few, but I'm not trying to get drunk and embarrass myself. Or better yet, blurt out to everyone that I am interested in Cole.

I don't know what's going on, but I can't seem to get him off my mind. I don't want to be that silly best friend Kate has to ask to stay away from her brother. I also don't want Cole to think I'm some sort of stook.

"Don't ya have anything slower? Something us lads can get ye ladies to dance with us to?" Flynn asks.

I laugh and take the escape he's offering. "Yeah, sure. I've got ya."

I turn and head over to the stereo. I pull the CD I'm looking for and pop it in. A smile comes to my lips as people get up and begin to dance together.

I'm grateful when I see Boyle heading my way, but Clodagh Murray stops him to dance with her. I move over to the fire and stare into the flames as I try to sort out my feelings. Nothing can ever happen between me and Cole.

He lives in America, and I live here in Ireland. I'm going into the league to play softball. I probably won't have time for guys at all. Cole, Boyle, it doesn't matter; I won't have time for either.

Suddenly, heat engulfs my back, and I'm locked in a one-arm headlock. If I didn't smell his cologne through the alcohol, I would still know it's Cole. I sigh and melt into him.

"Are ya having a good time?" he asks and kisses the top of my head.

"I guess so."

"It took me five stores to find this album for ya," he chuckles.

I tune into the music and listen to see which one he's talking about. Sisqó's "Addicted" is playing. Cole begins to sway and step from side to side as he keeps his hold on me.

I rock with him as my belly does a dance of its own. I can't help basking in the feel of his huge bicep and forearm cradling my head.

"Thanks for all the CDs."

"Anything for ya, DJ. Ya know I can't call ya that if yer not my personal disc jockey."

"Ya mean it doesn't stand for Dirty Jaw anymore?" I tease.

He bursts into laughter. "I felt bad for weeks after that, ya know? The prank wasn't meant for ya. Besides, I've always called ya DJ because of the music. Logan and Jamie started that Dirty Jaw shit."

One summer when his cousins were here, they had all been playing pranks on each other. I got ahold of a dirt cupcake that wasn't meant for me. I bit right into it before Cole could stop me.

Everyone had a good laugh at my expense. I was so mad. Kate helped me get them all back.

"That was one of the best summers ever," I laugh.

"Not for me. The last time I was here was the best summer I've had here."

"Really? Why is that?"

"There was this cute little fifteen-year-old. She saw me when no one else did. I was going through a ton of shit, and she gave me words I now live by."

My heart begins to race along with my mind. He's talking about me. Brothers call their little sisters cute all the time, right? No big deal.

"What could wee fifteen-year-old me have told a big nineteen-year-old lad like ya that would have stuck with ya?"

"Ya told me no matter what I decided, I needed to stick to my truth. Then ya told me to be who I wanted to be and give it my all," he says right next to my ear.

"Aye, sage advice. Sounds like me," I snicker.

"Ach, it was. Now it's time for me to return the favor. None of those melters is worth yer time. Yer too pretty, too smart, too mine to give them the time of day. I'll tell ya one of me secrets, DJ.

"I'm addicted to ya. Ya've always belonged to me," he breathes.

I snap my head up to look at him. He looks me right in the eyes, then moves his gaze to my lips. He drops his arm from around my neck to wrap around my waist.

It would only take a breath to bring our lips together. He leans a bit closer and our noses touch. I start to freak out because he's really going to kiss me.

"Cole," Logan growls as he comes and grabs Cole by the arm, pulling him away from me.

I let the breath I'm holding swoosh from my lips. I don't know whether to be frustrated or relieved that the kiss didn't happen. I'm a little confused.

Cole

"Have you lost your mind?" Logan hisses.

"No, we were just talking."

"With that bastard's spies right in your face. Bro, Granda was right. I mean, I've always known. *Fuck*," Logan growls and pushes a hand into the front of his hair.

"Known what?"

"You're drunk, Cole. You should call it a night."

"And leave her here with these eejits drooling over her?" I slur as I frown.

"That's better than it getting back to him that you can't stay away from her. You've been in love with Deja for years, Cole. You're not fooling anyone but yourself.

"I know it, Granda knew it, Uncle Finlay knows it, and it looks like Oland knows it as well. We have our answers. Everything McTavish says is true."

"They can't take her from me. Oland is fucking with the right one. We should just leave now and take her and Kate with us."

"And then what? You want her to end up like Nakim? That guilt is already eating you alive. Could you imagine if that were her?"

I stumble back a few steps. I would die before I allowed that. I would never forgive myself.

"This isn't fair to her. This will take softball from her. She'll have to walk onto a team in America."

"And she will do fine. She's more than good enough to earn a scholarship, but if she doesn't, Uncle Finlay will pay for any college she wants to go to. She can still play."

"Angus is willing to do this? He's really going to move them to America?"

"The plan is already in motion. Cole, it's going to be fine. She has a double target on her back because she's Kate's best friend. Allow us to do this the right way. We go home in the morning."

I nod as tears burn the backs of my eyes. This feels wrong. I know something is going to go wrong.

CHAPTER FIVE

Picture of Love

Deja

I stop outside the gate to our house and take my shoes off. These heels are killing me. I don't know why I dressed up for tonight.

It's only jeans, a nice jumper, and heels, but it's more effort than I normally put in. I'm still confused about what happened back at the bonfire. Cole and Logan left not too long after Logan pulled Cole away from me.

I have a million questions floating through my head. Surely Cole didn't mean what he said the way I took it. I'm crazy for thinking he did.

"Ya can ask him in the morning," I huff to myself.

The lights are on in the house. I had thought Mum and Da would be asleep by now. I hope they didn't wait up for me.

As I push into the house, music fills the air. I smile as Alicia Keys's "If I Ain't Got You" plays. This sounds like one of the CDs I made for them.

I move to the threshold of the living area and lean into the doorjamb. My smile grows wider. They are dancing in the middle of the room.

I love the way Da looks at her. Ever since I can remember, it's been the same. Angus Walsh has loved my mother with everything he is.

He has never made me feel like I'm not his daughter. He has loved me as much as he's loved Mum. If Mum never told me that Angus wasn't my biological father, I never would have known.

My thoughts go to Cole. How is it that I saw this same look in his eyes? I shake my head and cradle my shoes to my chest.

It has to be the drinking. What I do know is this is what love looks like. I don't want it if it's not like this.

Uncle Dougie looks at Auntie Kara the same way, even after six children. Uncle Donny looks at Auntie Iesha this way. It's all I've ever known. Someday the man I love will look at me the same.

Da looks up from Mum to find me watching them and his face lights up with his special smile for me. My heart swells. Someday the man I love will love me and our children this way. I know he will.

"Aye, there she is. Our birthday lass. How was yer party? Did ya have fun?"

"Aye, I did."

"Grand, the lads didn't let ya get too langered. I remember when I turned eighteen. I couldn't feel me face. I got pissed as a fart, me friends had to carry me home," he chuckles.

"Deja knows I would have grounded her until her twenty-first birthday if she came in here like that."

"I'm fine. Just ready for bed. I love ye, see ye in the morning."

Angus comes to pull me into a hug and kisses my forehead. I squeeze him tight. Yup, I'm a daddy's girl. Angus started me playing softball; he's taken me to every game.

Mum used to have to travel for work and he would take care of me. I've never been a burden to him. Just his little buddy.

He was the one to play Barbies with me when I was little. If I had a tea party, he would be my first guest. Where you found Angus, you found me.

"Love ya too, Deja. Happy birthday, love," he says as he releases me.

Mum tugs me into her embrace next. She kisses my cheek, then murmurs in my ear. "Good night, my precious girl. I love you more than you could ever know. You changed my life for the better."

"I love ya too, Mum."

CHAPTER SIX

Dark Lessons

The Shadows

"Aye, ya did right by coming to me, lad," Oland says to Boyle McTavish.

I sit and listen. That's all Oland ever wants from me. I've learned to blend in with the shadows.

That's where I've been all my life. Secrets always stay best hidden in the shadows.

I know right away this kid should have kept to the shadows and held his secrets there with him. Coming here was stupid. The fact that Oland allowed him in the same room with me says as much.

"I'll be in touch. Ya tell no one what ya told me," Oland continues.

"Aye, I'm still working on Deja. And I think I have an idea of how to come between her and Kate."

"Ach, ya don't worry about any of that, lad."

"Oh, okay, well, I'll be going now."

Oland waves him off dismissively. The kid gets up and looks at me, then licks his lips and rushes from the room. No matter how fast he moves, he can't get away from what he just started.

I shrug it off and turn to Oland. The evil gleam in his eyes says a million words. The wheels are turning and he's about to make someone's life miserable.

"Three years ago, this path was tolerable. Now that Ian is dead and I've made my new friends, I don't need to deal with that Scottish trash."

"McDougal?"

"Aye, since I don't know where the leak is coming from, it's time to wash me hands clean. So it is. He can go with the rest of them, he can.

"I have one last task for him. This one should get him killed for sure, it will. If it doesn't, ya will take care of him.

"It's time I erase the Walsh bloodline once and for all. The McDougals will get what's coming too. The Alliance will never see the light of day."

My mind races to understand his change in loyalty. If that's even what it can be called. I don't think this man is loyal to anything but himself.

"So you trust them?"

"Ach, I trust no one. At the end of the day, it will always come down to me Irish blood. Everyone else serves me purpose. Now go kill the boy. McTavish needs to learn a lesson, he does."

"Aye." I stand and leave.

CHAPTER SEVEN

Best Friends

Deja

The O'Brien home has always felt so welcoming to me. Even now, as Kate and I sit in the living room playing board games with Jamie and Dylan, I feel right at home.

I was excited when Kate asked me to come over for a sleepover. I was hoping I would get a chance to see Cole and talk to him about what happened the night of the bonfire.

I keep looking at the door, waiting for him and Logan to walk in. They haven't yet and it's almost time for bed. Kara has already told us we can play one more round before time to turn in.

I'm sure she meant that for Jamie and Dylan, but Kate and I usually call it a night when they do. Maybe I can get Kate to put in a movie.

I get lost in thought as my mum's voice from earlier comes back to me. She sounded off when I called to ask if it was okay for me to stay the night here.

She said yes, but there was something about the way she answered the line that tugged at my ear. I almost changed my mind. However, once I asked, she sort of had relief in her voice.

She and Da went to Dublin this morning. Da had to head there on business. I believe Mum just wanted to tag along.

"Oww, what's wrong with ya," Jamie groans.

"Yer a cheater," Dylan whines.

"So ya hit me?"

"Aye, I did. Stop trying to cheat." Dylan pouts.

He's so stinking cute. His blond hair has grown to fall in his face. He's been combing it out of his blue eyes all night.

Jamie grumbles under his breath as he rolls his eyes. It's the same thing every time. Jamie does cheat.

I think he only does it to taunt his little brother. The smirk on his lips says it all. Quickly, I take my turn before the two start to really fight.

The door opens and I perk up, only to sag my shoulders once again as I see it's only Uncle Dougie. Aunt Kara comes out to greet him with a kiss. I love Kate's parents.

Watching them always puts a smile on my face. I would never question their love for each other. It's clear to see by watching them.

Dougie turns to look into the living room where we are and a look crosses his face when he sees me. Something between sadness and pity. I'm not sure which as he clears his throat and comes to sit down on the couch.

"Ya kids wrap this. Ye should be getting to bed," he says.

"Aw, Da. Mum said we could finish one more game. Please," Dylan pleads.

"I will not tell ya again," he says.

"Ach, this week has sucked. First, Logan and Cole had to leave, now we can't even finish our game," Jamie mutters.

I whip my head in his direction and knit my brows. Cole and Logan left? I had no idea they had already left to return to America.

I sit here frustrated and confused. How am I to get answers now? What does this mean?

I have to fight against poking my lip out and pouting. Instead, I help Kate begin to put the games away. Sadness washes over me because I don't know when Cole will return.

"Ach, ye girls should head to bed. I'll drop ye to softball practice in the morning," Dougie says, breaking into my thoughts.

As I look at Dougie, I get this feeling there's something more he wants to say. He's watching me as closely as I'm watching him. I look away as I note the pity in his eyes.

Does he know that I have a thing for his son? Is he pitying me and my stupid crush? I shake my thoughts off and follow Kate to her room.

I'll have to wait until Cole calls, then maybe I'll have the courage to ask him all the questions I have floating in my head. I guess only time will tell.

Helen

"Finlay warned ye would come to my door," Ken McDougal says as I enter his study.

"Then you know what he has done?"

"Aye, I know what the bastard has done."

I couldn't go home without knowing if this happened because of me. Angus is dead. In the back of my mind, I have always known there was a chance that the Krupins would find me.

If this was them, I need to know now. I should have known the death of Ian Black was going to open up a can of worms. I disappeared for the most part when I met Angus.

Onyx died, and Helen was born. I fell in love with Angus that first day in that coffee shop; now he's gone.

It was a hit. That much I knew for sure before I arrived in Scotland. However, I've come to know Angus's family and I knew this could have come from them just the same.

That's why I came here to Scotland this morning. I watched as the man I love was taken from me. I felt so helpless as the woman I've become would have no need to carry weapons.

Angus died in my arms after I got him out of the wreck. People on the street yelled and screamed in confusion and concern. Yet the driver of the car that rammed Angus right outside our hotel got away.

I stared into my love's eyes as the life went out of them. However, not before I promised him I would find whoever did this and make them pay. I now have my answer and the name of the person who will die for this.

All I need now is permission. Archie McDougal is a dead man. That I will make sure of.

"I knew you were one of Ian's mercenaries from the time Angus showed up with you."

I turn to see Ewan McDougal has entered the room from a hidden entrance. I ready myself for a fight. I knew this was a chance I would take when I came here.

"Aren't you and I the same?" I scoff.

"Aye, love. Ye can relax. My quarrel is not with ye," he replies.

"I know what ye have come to ask," Ken says.

"He not only set in motion the events that took my husband's life, but he has also told the Russians how to find me. Pavel Krupin promised he would find and kill me. Archie has done half the work.

"All of this for a man who's sure to kill him next. Oland will always be out for himself. Archie is just a pawn, but he will pay for his actions." I seethe.

I am to be next, but not before Archie is wiped from the face of the earth.

"Och, we know this. Archie has been working outside the family for some time now with that auld bastard Oland," Ken says.

"He's our brother, but our da was right not to trust him. We never will again."

"Then you give your approval?"

"Aye, but with conditions."

"Name them," I bite out.

"We will watch."

I lift a brow in question.

"This must be completed without wind of who or how. We believe he was involved in Da's demise, but we haven't been able to prove it. Da was as fit as a fiddle.

"To drop dead of a heart attack. Rubbish. Now Angus.

"Our own nephew. Och, it's not right. The only reason I don't take his head off myself is because I don't want my own blood on my hands," Ewans says.

"All right." I shrug. "As long as you know I'm not going to show mercy."

"Aye, understood. Once it is done, you can never come back. We can't justify allowing our brother's murderer to walk Scotland. If anyone found out, it would end badly for all involved."

"Fine. Deja and I will leave and never return."

"Is that wise?" Ewan speaks up.

"What do you mean?"

"Ye said yerself Archie has revealed to the Russians yer whereabouts. Deja isn't our blood, but we love her like our own great-niece. Angus would want us to protect her.

"Mum would be devastated if something happened to her. She's already broken up about her grandson," he says.

"What are you suggesting?"

"Leave Deja with Mum. We will keep the lass safe. I can teach her just like Ian Black taught ye—"

"That's the problem. I never wanted this for her. I don't want her to become what I was," I say.

"Och, but do ye have that choice now?"

I ball my fists. Ian Black warned me I should have started training Deja years ago. I refused. I didn't want this for her.

"Once ye handle the Russians, ye can send for her. We will verify it's ye and hand her over," Ewan coaxes.

I swallow hard. I have no fear of the Krupin family. At least not when it concerns my life.

It is my daughter I fear for. Deja is in the path of danger every second she spends with me. I cannot return to her until I settle this.

This is why I came to ask permission first before my next move. I refuse to place another target on her back. Not killing everyone connected to the Krupin name before I retired was my mistake, not my daughter's.

They may be dangerous, but so am I. Once I handle Archie, they will still remain a danger I can no longer ignore.

"How do I know you won't take her life for Archie's? He is your blood after all. Deja and I are nothing to you."

"Och, that isn't true, lassie. Ye have become family."

"Yet you forbid my return."

"Ian taught ye a lot about this life. Ye know why ye can't return. We have no proof of the crimes he's committed to provide. If ever there is such, we will welcome ye home with open arms," Ken says.

"Deja is a bright lass. I only mean to make her stronger and capable of keeping herself alive. We have loved her as much as Angus has.

"I've known the lass from the time she was a wee bairn. The lassie has stolen our hearts. I'd be willing to lay down my own life for hers. Is she not safest with us?" Ewan says, lifting a brow.

"Dinnae fash yersel. We will take care of the lass. Ye are welcome to check in as often as ye like," Ken adds.

"If something happens to my daughter, your entire family will be next, and I won't come asking for permission. You have not seen hell as I will bring it over my child."

"Aye, we know," the brothers say in unison.

CHAPTER EIGHT

Here to Collect

Ken

"Da has to be rolling in his grave," Ewan grumbles from beside me as we sit in one of the rooms at the property we own next door to Archie's home, watching from the camera placed in his home just for this view.

I always knew this place would come in handy. It had become necessary to keep an eye on my older brother. Although it pains me that I haven't kept a closer eye.

As the second oldest, my father had always tasked me with protecting my brothers and sister. Archie's eejit arse included. The lad needs protecting from himself. It is with a heavy heart I sit here to watch this.

"Aye, no doubt he is. How did I allow this?"

"Och, this isn't on ye. It was all our mistake. Ian tried to warn us all a long time ago."

I release a heavy breath through my nose and purse my lips. Ian Black did indeed warn us of our brother's disloyalty. Our father knew … I have been the one in denial and now it has cost us all greatly.

"He's my older brother. I didn't want to believe it. I knew he could be an eejit, but I didn't ken he would harm his own kin."

"Dinnae fash yersel, ye have been the best brother ye can. Archie has been a bampot since he was a wee lad."

I grunt and shake my head. A crazy person is an understatement when speaking of the oldest of our siblings. As of late, I have wished that I had allowed him to fall into that well when we were young lads.

"He's on his way," I mutter as I get a message that our brother is not that far from home.

Ewan and I agreed we wanted to be here to make sure this is done and couldn't be traced back to us or Helen. The repercussions of what we are allowing could come back to haunt us someday.

Our people could turn their backs on us, and we'd lose the centuries of power we hold here in Scotland. We're good to our clan, but their loyalty to the McDougal name wouldn't allow them to understand what we have done without the evidence we are lacking.

Duncan is on board, but he wanted no part of this. As the second oldest, I couldn't leave this to rest on Ewan's shoulders alone. Archie brought this on himself, but it needs to happen.

None of us is safe as long as he remains breathing. He's power hungry and willing to go to great lengths to get to the power he seeks. At the moment, I'm probably next on his list.

With Da and O'Shea gone and the missing will, there's no one in his way, but I still challenge him when he gets out of line. It's only a matter of time. I know in my gut he's behind our da's death.

Finlay Black was able to confirm our brother's involvement. This was all Archie's doing. His own sister's child—our baby sister. Angus was a good lad. He did everything asked of him.

"This is it," Ewan says as he nods his head toward the screen.

I grunt and lock in on the feed. Archie appears, and Helen comes from the shadows. Our brother pulls his gun, but Helen is quick.

She disarms him in the blink of an eye. It happens so fast, I slide to the edge of my seat as if that will allow me to observe more closely.

Helen takes his gun, incapacitates our brother, then releases the clip and the one in the chamber, before tossing the useless weapon aside. Archie is on his knees, holding his throat as his chest heaves.

Our nephew's wife is a short but curvy woman. Our brother is six-three in height and a big lad at that. Helen has dropped the big Scot to her mercy in a single breath.

However, Archie does manage to get back to his feet. I tilt my head to the side and Helen stands there looking up at him through her lashes. She's swaying as if there is music playing, but there is none.

"This was a mistake," I breathe.

"Och, ye are wrong. Just watch," Ewan mutters.

Archie goes to throw a punch, but Helen reaches up in the slightest motion and guides his hand from the path of her face. It happens so fast. His arm floats right by her head and his momentum brings him into her reach.

She then reaches for his face and tosses him on his back. Archie hits the floor, and Helen puts her heavy black boot in his chest. Then another kick to his face.

I think she's going to go for the kill from there. However, she backs off and allows him to get back to his feet. This time, Archie makes sure to stay out of her reach, keeping a greater distance between them.

"Fuck," I growl when he lands a punch, and blood begins to pour from her nose.

I stand ready to head over there and end this myself. Archie has to die. Helen has been dormant for eighteen years; maybe this job isn't for her.

"Och, brother. She's toying with him. Take yer seat," Ewan says with a hint of amusement in his voice.

I note the grin on Helen's face and nod. Reclaiming my seat, I watch on. Helen runs her hand under her nose and shrugs her shoulders as if it's no big deal. The move is small and unassuming to the casual onlooker.

However, I know better. This is one of Ian's prizes. Archie begins to look more confident and closes some of the gap between them.

"Eejit," I bite out.

He doesn't see that she's just baited him. He moves in with his new confidence and Helen strikes. Reaching behind her back, she pulls two blades.

This time, when he throws a punch, she does as she did before. She uses his weight and momentum to move him around. Using her closed palm around the hilt of her blade, she grabs the back of his neck and drives her elbow into his face, busting his face wide open with the impact.

With the same arm she used to elbow him, she brings one of her blades across his face, causing more blood to flow while Arch tries to stumble back away from her. However, Helen doesn't allow his retreat this time.

She still has control of his head from behind. From the looks of it, she has him by the hair even though she's holding her knife. Bringing up the same arm she struck and slashed him with, she grasps his face while still holding the knife.

She then steps behind his legs and forces his body back until he drops back toward the ground, slicing his throat on his way down. I close my eyes and take the breath I didn't know I was holding.

My brother is gone. He has paid.

"That was for Da and Angus," Ewan says, causing me to open my eyes.

"Aye. She showed him mercy."

"Och, I dinnae ken that was for him. She showed mercy because we are watching."

"Aye, I ken ye are right."

CHAPTER NINE

All Falls Down

Deja

I'm lying here staring up at the ceiling. Since Connie is all grown and lives in the States with her brothers, I always sleep in her old bed in Kate's room when I spend the night.

I didn't sleep much last night. I was bummed out after finding out Logan and Cole have returned to the States. No goodbye, no we'll talk, nothing. Cole is just gone.

Now I don't know when I will get a chance to speak to him. I spent the night tossing and turning while asking myself if I had dreamt it all. Maybe I had more to drink than I thought I did.

Yet, I can still feel his breath against my skin and his words have been playing on repeat in my mind. I'm beginning to feel crazy and frustrated. Looking across the room, I see Kate is still knocked out with her hair in her mouth as it sits wide open.

No longer able to lie here, I punch at the bed and sit up. Maybe a shower will help. Climbing from the bed, I grab my things and head out to the bathroom.

I'm so sleepy as I stumble my way through the hall. Murmuring from the kitchen catches my ear, telling me I'm not the only one up. Most likely, Aunt Kara and Uncle Dougie are up getting breakfast ready for everyone.

I keep quiet and keep moving to the bathroom. Hopefully the shower will help to wake me or at least give me a chance to pull myself together. I never used to feel this way about Cole, so I'm not going to allow these feelings to consume me now.

I turn my thoughts to Mum. She said she wanted to go shopping this weekend when she and Da return. I'm excited about that. It's been a while since Mum and I have had one of our girls' days.

Maybe Kate will want to tag along. She did mention something about wanting a new dress for some party or something. Finally able to think of something other than Cole, I finish up and get out of the shower to get dressed.

I frown at my bangs in the mirror and poke my lip out. Mum is going to have to press my hair out for me again. I don't know what I would do without my mum. She's the greatest.

"Ya're going to have to learn to take care of yer own hair now. She can't come with ya to play ball, she can't?" I mutter to myself.

Once dressed in a pair of overalls and a T-shirt, I head back to Kate's room. I step inside quietly, but she's not here. I knit my brows and go to put my things in my bag.

Maybe she got up for breakfast or had to pee and went to use the guys' bathroom. I shrug it off and go to check my phone.

My mobile rings the moment I pick it up, pulling me out of my thoughts. I'm confused, as the name on the phone is Kate's. Getting this strange feeling in my stomach, I pick up the call.

"Hey, where are ya?" I say as I answer.

"Mum asked me to get up and run an errand with her. We'll be back soon. I'm calling because Aisling called."

"What happened now?" I snort. "Did she drop her curler in the toilet again?"

"No. It … It's more serious than that. Maybe I should wait until we get back."

"Yer not about to do that to me. Go on, tell me what's going on."

She sighs. My heart is racing as I think of Cole. Could something have happened to him? Was last week the last time I will ever see him?

"It's Jameson. They found his body down by the river. It looks like he hit his head and fell into the water. They think he drowned, not being able to lift his head from the blow to his noodle," she says.

"What?"

That sounds so crazy. I don't know what to say. I stumble to the bed and flop down on the edge and just stare ahead.

"But we were just with him," I whisper.

"They said he's been missing since the night of the bonfire. Maybe he had too much to drink and tripped or something. A man jogging found his body."

"I saw him leave with Boyle. He doesn't know what happened to his own cousin?"

"Ach, I hear he told the police that they separated. He went to see someone, and Jameson took off on his own."

"That's—"

I'm cut off as my other line beeps in. I realize that I've pulled my knees up to my chest and I'm slowly rocking. I don't understand what's going on. My friend was found dead.

"Kate, I need to call ya back. I have another call coming in. It might be Mum," I murmur. "I'll see ya when ya get back, yeah?"

"Aye, I'll see ya when we get back. I love you, Deja."

"I love you too."

I change over to the other call, feeling like I'm watching this all from outside my body. I'm still trying to process what all Kate has told me. Nothing makes sense right now.

"Hello."

"Deja, this is Finlay Black. I need ya to get dressed and come out to the kitchen, love?"

"Uncle Finlay?"

"Aye, love. I'm here at the house for ye. I need to get ye to Scotland," he says.

"Huh, I don't understand," I say and get to my feet.

"Come on out and we'll talk. I need to talk to ye face to face."

I'm numb. Something isn't right. I get the feeling Jameson is only the start of bad news today. I nod as if Uncle Finlay can see me, as my mind begins to spin.

Uncle Finlay Black isn't my real uncle. He's Kate and Cole's uncle. Their mum's brother.

I've known him since I was a little girl. My mum once told me that if anything happened to her, she would send Ian or Finlay Black to come protect me.

Ian Black is gone. However, if Finlay Black is here for me, something is wrong. I begin to shake, is that why Mum sounded off yesterday?

"What's going on? Where's Mum and Da?"

"Och, come to the kitchen, love. Not over the phone. I have something from her for ye. I'll give it to ye once we're on the road. Hold tight, love."

"Okay, I'm on my way out."

He hangs up and I'm left standing in the middle of Kate's room, scared and confused. Jameson is dead, something has happened to Mum, and Finlay Black is here to take me to Scotland.

My grandmother, great-grandmother, and great-uncles live in Scotland. Not my real grandmothers and great-uncles, but my grandmothers and great-uncles through Angus. They're the only family I've ever known.

In a daze, I turn to head out to the kitchen. My stomach twists into more knots with each step. Something about the house feels too still.

It no longer feels like the safe, warm place I've always known it to be. There is a chill in the air I can't seem to shake off.

There are no voices coming from the kitchen as there had been before my shower. However, the scent of coffee is in the air. When I enter the kitchen, I find Uncle Dougie sitting at the table with another man.

I know right away from the broad shoulders and the call that it's Uncle Finlay. He turns and gives me a warm smile. When he stands and opens his arms, I rush into his embrace, feeling like I'm going to need it after whatever he's going to say.

"What's going on?" I choke out.

"Yer mum asked me to come for ye. There has been an accident and ye can't return to the house."

"Where is she? Is she okay?"

"Yer mum is fine, but Angus is gone, love."

"What do you mean gone?" I ask as tears burn my eyes.

"Finlay, ye should go. It isn't safe here," Dougie grumbles.

"Aye, he's right. We need to go. My car is outside waiting."

I nod. "I need to get my things."

"Go on. I'll get yer bags and bring them out. Leave yer mobile on the table. Fin has a burner for ya," Dougie says and pulls me into a hug.

I try not to sob as I follow my best friend's uncle out of the house. As my mind spins with questions and disbelief, Finlay leads me to a black SUV with tinted windows. Nothing makes sense as I climb into the passenger seat.

Finlay climbs in behind the wheel as Dougie rushes out with my softball bag and my backpack, placing them into the back seat. My heart begins to ache.

My da is gone? What does that mean? I look to Finlay to ask for answers and freeze.

Finlay Black looks so much like his sister and brother, so of course, my mind goes right to Cole. I wish he were here with me to tell me everything is going to be okay.

If I'm going to Scotland, will I ever see him again? His grandfather is gone. It seems like America has become his home from now on.

I can't help but feel like I'm losing everyone I care about. I think I'm in shock because I still can't wrap my mind around the fact that my da is gone.

"Buckle up, love. We need to go," Finlay commands, pulling me from my thoughts.

I reach for my seat belt and click it into place. Dougie stands outside the vehicle, looking somber. I can't help but wonder if he knew all this last night when he sent us to bed. Dougie raps the bonnet of the SUV with his knuckles right before Finlay peels off as soon as I'm settled.

Looking out the windshield, I notice smoke rising in the distance. I knit my brows as I realize that's the direction of my home.

I blink a few times as the thick black smoke brings with it the heavy reality that I might never see my home again. My heart begins to race. I look to Finlay, but he's keeping his eyes straight ahead.

"Is that fire coming from my home?"

"Aye, I have a few of your things in the boot. Everything else is gone."

"What do you mean?"

"Ye won't be coming back here. Ireland isn't safe for ye."

"Can ya tell me what's going on?" I ask.

"There's a bag under yer seat. Yer mum left ye something. It should explain it all for now."

Tears prick my eyes. His words make everything seem so final. I can't hold the tears back as I reach under the seat and pull out the bag I know to be my mum's. For as long as I can remember, this bag has been in her office in our home.

My stomach drops with dread. This can't be good. Tears stream down my face.

My home is on fire, and my mum has sent someone to collect me and take me away. That has been my home since I was a little girl. I feel like I have stones in my stomach, as I know yesterday was the last time I will see my home.

Somewhere in the back of my mind, I know yesterday morning could have been the last time I'll see Mum or Da. I swipe at my tears and reach into the bag.

Inside, I find a recorder. I put the earbuds in my ears and press play as I inhale deeply and try to wrap my head around all of this. However, when I hear my mother's voice, I lose it.

I sob as her words are spoken to me, and reality begins to take root. Devastated isn't the word for what I'm feeling. I'm completely lost as I listen.

"Deja, if you're hearing this, Finlay should be with you. If he's not, I need you to be brave. The most important thing is for you to get to safety. I promise you, this will be made right, but I need you safe.

"From here on out, you trust no one. Your life depends on it. Do you understand?"

I nod as if she's here and whisper, "Yes."

Even though I don't. As we race away from everything I know, I have no idea what's going on. I remain silent as my mind fills with so many questions. What just happened?

"You need to get to your great-grandmother. You'll be safe with her. Your uncle Ken will look out for you until things are settled.

"Orla and Ken are family. They've always treated us as such. I am positive the two of them will help you.

"There's so much I want to say. I thought life with Angus would keep us out of this mess. Looks like I was wrong.

"I should have found a way to make everything right years ago. This is my fault," she says.

There is an awkward pause before she inhales deeply and begins again. "You're probably thinking you can trust the people I'm leaving you with. However, I meant what I said. Trust no one.

"If you're with Finlay. He's only going to get you to safety and then he has to part ways. He's doing me a solid.

"You will allow your great-grandmother and uncle to help you, but trust is something you can't afford to give your own shadow. I know you've always been close with Ken and Duncan. I don't think either of them would ever harm you, but I'm not taking any chances while you're without me.

"You know you don't have to worry about your uncle Ewan, as he always keeps to himself." She chuckles, causing me to laugh with her.

There's something about Uncle Ewan I've never put my finger on. Nothing bad. He's just odd in a soldier-in-waiting kind of way. I don't know how to explain it.

"However, I get the feeling he's going to be one of your greatest helps. I know you love your uncles, but you need to learn to follow your instincts. If something feels off, believe it.

"I won't be around to cover you. I've done things that might come back for me in the form of targeting you. I'm counting on the fear people have of the McDougal clan.

"Ian Black isn't here to protect you for me. So I'm going with my next option. You're smart, Deja. Protect yourself. Make everyone earn your trust.

"If you don't need them, don't bother giving them a chance to prove a thing. Everything I do is to protect you, my baby. All I've done has been for you. Remember, if I can't fix this and keep it away from you, I will be there when you need me most."

The recording ends and I'm left breathless. I still have so many questions. I lean my head against the window and sob.

CHAPTER TEN

New York

Logan

"No, you're right. She's safest with them," I say to my uncle as he updates me with what's happening in Ireland.

He arrived in time to collect Deja and get her to Scotland. With the McDougal clan is where she's safest for now. They can protect her from my granda and Helen's old enemies.

I may not have trusted Archie McDougal, but his brothers and mother will protect Deja like their own. Especially Orla.

"I don't want to get into what this all means," Da says on the other end.

I pulled him into the call before we got into things. Uncle Finlay picked Deja up from my parents' home. I was glad to hear she had spent the night there with Kate.

I look across the desk at LaSalle and see the wheels turning in his head. I'm pretty sure he's thinking what I am.

"I'll say it for ya. Oland has gotten bold because Da is gone. He's trying to stop what Da and Lennox set in motion," Uncle Finlay says.

"Are we sure Deja is safe with them?" LaSalle says. "Ken was in denial that his brother was involved in all of this. Who's to say Archie hasn't created a situation in Scotland we aren't aware of? Deja could be a sitting duck regardless of his demise."

"One, Ken, Ewan, and Duncan understand whose daughter they have in their care. They all know what this means. Two, Orla intends to keep Deja in the village with her.

"If and when she goes to the castle, it will most likely be under the watch of Ken. Oland and his remaining minions have to tread lightly now that Archie isn't his spy. We find those diaries and documents and things will change."

LaSalle grunts. "If this is what you want. However, I'd like to get those watchers in play. This is exactly the type of thing we'll need them for."

I nod. The watchers were a great idea. I actually think we'll be able to make that happen.

Oland has made moves as of late that have worked more in our favor than his. He just doesn't see it yet. I try not to grin as I think of how he has fucked up.

"Cole isn't going to take this well. How do ye plan to keep him from running in there to take her away with him?" Uncle Finlay says.

I sigh. I've been thinking about this. I know my brother. Going after Deja is the first thing he will do.

For her safety, I can't have that. Cole can't know the truth. I'm doing this for his own good.

"As far as he knows, Angus was in an accident and Deja is missing. This will remain need-to-know. Oland doesn't know we're onto him.

"The Walsh brothers' deaths were made to look like accidents. I don't want anyone outside of us to know where the girls are. Ken's request is reasonable.

"They shouldn't look like they're involved until we have a firm hold on this. Time, we need time."

"Och, I will continue to do my part," Uncle Finlay says.

"Thank you. If Oland knew Granda had already handed over the clan to me, he would force my hand. We're not ready for any of that," I reply.

"Where do we stand with McTavish?" my father asks.

"He's still willing to play ball. He knows Oland is behind his grandson's murder. He believes the target was his other grandson, but somehow there was a mix-up.

"He's out for blood. Oland has handed us another loyal ally," Uncle Finlay replies.

"Good, we'll keep that in mind. Let's do anything we can to ease his grief. Cover the funeral costs and anything else we can," I order.

"Already done. I took care of it," my da says.

"All right. Keep me posted on anything you guys hear. Let's not assume he's done making his moves."

"Aye, Logan. Talk to ye soon, lad," Uncle Finlay says before he hangs up.

Brooklyn

I roar with anger as I destroy Logan's office. I told him. I told him we shouldn't have left Deja behind.

My chest heaves as I place my hands on my hips and look over the mess I've made. I shake my head and run a hand through my hair. Stumbling to the nearest wall, I then press my forehead to it.

I don't want Logan to see the tears as they run down my face. Donald and Angus Walsh are dead. Wherever Deja is, she has to be destroyed.

I can only hope she's with her mum, safe and outside of Oland's reach. If I don't keep that hope, I'm going to lose it completely. I loathe that son of a bitch so much.

"I'm going to kill him." I seethe.

"Right now isn't the time. We take him off the board at the wrong time and it will all implode. For now, we leave this be."

"Leave it be. Leave it be? If he has hurt her or does because we've left him breathing. *Logan—*"

"I know, Cole."

I wipe the tears from my face and spin to face him. I don't understand how he can be so calm. Deja has been a part of our family for as long as I can remember.

I narrow my eyes at him. "Why aren't you angry?"

"I am angry, but emotions cause mistakes. I don't have room for mistakes. I have more than Deja counting on me to succeed.

"I promise you, Cole. Once the Alliance is in place, we will find her and bring her home. For now, I need you to remember the task at hand," he says.

"And how long is that going to take?"

"I don't know. Things are falling into place. LaSalle and I are on track," he says.

"Yeah, whatever. I need some air."

CHAPTER ELEVEN

Silent Takeoff

Brooklyn

Eleven years later …

I stare down at my phone as I sit on this plane, waiting for takeoff. I'm heading to Scotland myself. I still can't believe Felix found her.

I had hoped he would, but I didn't know it would happen this fast. My cousin is amazing at what he does. I knit my brows as I debate whether or not I should tell Logan where I'm heading.

"We'll be taking off momentarily, sir. Is there anything I can get you in the meantime?" the flight attendant says.

I look up at her and blink. "Aye, thanks. Let me get a whiskey."

"Coming right up," she says with a seductive smile.

I'm not interested. I barely see her in this moment. My mind is spinning with so many questions about what I will find when I get to Scotland.

I was in bed when I got the call from Felix. Once I got the location from the secure box, I grabbed a few things and took off. I didn't stop to think about anything else.

Eleven years. I've wondered for eleven years where she's been. If she's okay.

The Alliance didn't come together as fast as I would have wanted, but it's happening now. It's all within our reach.

That's the reason I was willing to ask Felix for his help. That, and the fact that I know in my gut Dylan is up to something. He has never forgotten or given up on Ciara.

I fear he's going to make a move to find her himself. I almost feel guilty that I have a lead on Deja, but nothing for Dylan to follow up on. I keep telling myself that's the reason I'm on this plane.

Once I get to Deja, I can see if she knows anything about Ciara's whereabouts. They are cousins after all. I keep telling myself this isn't because I want to lay eyes on her with my own.

This is because I want to get her to safety. I want to pull her in close so I can make sure myself that she's protected.

I thread my brows and tuck my phone away. Logan will only stop me if he knows where I'm going. I will talk to him when I get back.

Logan

"That was good. Yer getting better," I croon as I walk up behind Raven.

I bring her here to one of our private warehouses, which we sometimes use as a gun range at least once a week. Her aim is getting a whole lot better. I remember the first time I placed a piece of steel in her hands.

The fear in her eyes spoke volumes. However, once I knew I couldn't stay away from her, I had to teach her how to protect herself from my granda. I have too much responsibility to always be around.

Laki and his watchers have been doing their job, but you never know when things could change. I'm not willing to take that kind of risk.

She cranes her neck to look up at me. "How can I not? I have a great teacher."

"What do ya mean? Yer a natural."

"Ha, you and I know that's bullshit." She scoffs and laughs.

I peck her lips and tighten my hold around her waist. I've fallen in love with this woman in my arms. When I first met her, I didn't know I would fall like this.

I also didn't know I would spend eleven years keeping her hidden. I'm growing tired of all the hiding. Thank Christ that will all soon be over.

I can't wait to see the look on that smug bastard's face when we finalize our next step. I hope I've made my granda Ian proud. I wish he could be here for this.

"Hey, where did you go?"

I focus as she searches my eyes with her gaze. I love those beautiful brown eyes. They are always so expressive.

"I'm here. Just thinking," I reply.

"Are you coming home with me tonight?"

"Aye, I've missed ya. I plan to spend the entire night."

"Good, I've been needing some attention," she purrs.

I lift a brow and smile down at her. When she cups me over my jeans, I growl and dip my head to take her lips. Knowing just how I want to spend the rest of the night, I toss her over my shoulder and turn to head out of here.

I nod for Christan to clean this place up for us. He and Stuart can follow us back to the house once he's done. I think to call Brooklyn to tell him to handle all business for tonight so I can cut my phone off, but I remind myself I don't have that luxury.

I'll just have to pray we're not interrupted. For once, hopefully, things will go my way. I need this time with my woman.

"I love you," she whispers against my lips as I place her in the car and buckle her in.

"I love ya too. More than ya know."

CHAPTER TWELVE

The Arrival

Deja

"All I need is for ya to explain to me why yer brother believes he should be trying to arrange a marriage for me. I'm not going to meet any of the melters he's lining up," I say to Uncle Ewan and Uncle Ken then roll my eyes.

We're walking back to the castle after one of our weekly sessions. My mum said to let them help me. I've been doing so for the last eleven years.

My uncles are serious about my training. When I had to give up softball, I was devastated, but I didn't complain. The message my mum left for me gave me the feeling it wasn't wise for me to be on the world stage of softball, out in the open.

Training became an outlet for all my anger and rage. I lost my home, my parents, my friends, and my softball career all in the blink of an eye. I haven't spoken to Kate since that last call when she told me about Jameson.

"At some point, ye will learn we all humor Duncan. Not a one of us listens to him or takes his hairbrained ideas seriously," Uncle Ewan murmurs and snorts a laugh to himself.

"He does not tell a fib. Ignore our dear brother. Duncan has it in his head that since Mum is ill, we should help ye find a husband.

"Dinnae fash yersel. He'll find something else to go on about soon enough," Uncle Ken says.

"I'm twenty-nine years old. I can find my own husband, I can," I mutter. "Maybe I should just move to America and get out of all ye hair."

I don't miss that all the blood drains from Uncle Ken's face as it always does when I mention leaving and moving to America. I still don't know what that's about. I've been trying to head there since I turned twenty-one, but there's always an excuse from one of my uncles or my great-gran for me to stay.

If my instincts didn't tell me to listen to them all, I would be gone. However, I don't want to jump out of the pan into the fire. For now, I'll stay put.

Uncle Ken snaps out of it and begins to brush his hand over his hair as if trying to knock something from it. "Does it look like I have something in my hair?"

I laugh and bump him with my hip. He wraps his arm around me and gives a squeeze. I'm glad I still feel safe around these two.

"If ye take off, what will yer buddies do without ye?"

I smile as I think of Callum and Blair. They are brother and sister, twins. Ewan has been training them since they were thirteen.

They arrived around the time I did. I trusted them because they needed me and trusted me first.

They were afraid and skittish when they arrived. The two have since become my little buddies. I chuckle all the time because sometimes they behave as if they're my personal bodyguards even though I'm five years older than they are.

I still don't know how Ewan became their guardian. I learned to stop asking questions when it comes to Uncle Ewan. Uncle Ken and Uncle Duncan are the easiest to get along with.

Someone killed Uncle Archie just before I arrived here in Scotland, so I never had to deal with him while living here. I used to steer clear of him when I was younger.

However, Uncle Duncan is becoming a pain in the arse. My great-gran dying isn't going to change a damn thing. I'm not marrying anyone.

I haven't trusted anyone enough to even date. I don't need a man, so taking that risk is unnecessary. My great-uncles may not know why, but they all know I don't date. I don't know how my uncle thinks I'm miraculously going to marry someone I don't know.

"They're twenty-four now. Maybe it's time the three of us hit the road," I say with a cheeky smile.

"Ye will not be walking off with my assets. Ye can forget that idea right now, lassie," Uncle Ewan says.

I burst into laughter. To the outside world, my uncles might seem like three scary, grumpy old men. I know better.

All three have been fiercely protective and they show their love and humor in their own ways. I want to say they have earned my trust, but I'm always cautious with the lot. However, with these men, I don't play.

I will take your head off over all three of them. Even Uncle Duncan with his matchmaking arse. I know he's doing it out of love. My uncles are getting older, and they wish to see me taken care of.

I sigh as my laughter dies down, and we arrive at the castle. "I know he means well. Maybe the two of ye can make him understand I'm not interested in finding a husband."

"We love ye, Deja. Ye know ye could come out and tell us if ye seek a female's companionship instead," Uncle Ewan murmurs as he blushes.

I burst into more laughter. This time, I'm wiping at tears as I hold my stomach. I've never seen the brooding man look cuter.

"I assure ya I'm into the lads. I just … the one I had my heart set on when I finally did begin to think about boys … he disappointed me.

"Then I came here. After all this time, he's probably forgotten all about me. I'm sure he's married with bairns of his own.

"I'm not marrying anyone until I find that spark again. Maybe it is time I leave to see the world. My lad might not be here in Scotland," I say as I muse.

Since my uncle has been trying to set me up, I have been thinking a lot about what I plan to do once my grandmother is gone. It's not looking too good. I don't know how much more time she has.

It's been breaking my heart to see her like this. Eleven years ago, she was as fit and fierce as she was when I was little. In the last few years, I've been watching her health slowly decline with her age.

Orla McDougal is a fighter though. I know she will fight until the very end. However, I don't know what that end looks like for me.

I have no idea if it's safe to leave Scotland now after all these years. I haven't heard from my mum after that recording that day, eleven years ago. I've come to grips with the fact that my mother is never coming back for me.

I had held out hope for the first four or five years. I never asked for answers because I didn't think anyone around me had them. Even if they did, I didn't know who I could trust to ask.

"We would miss ye if ye left. I think Duncan is trying to find a way to keep ye here in his own way," Uncle Ken says.

"I would miss ye guys too. I think that's why, for now, ye be stuck with me."

I don't mention that once my great-grandmother is gone, I believe I will be too. I've been watching videos to learn fashion and to learn to hide my accent. This is nothing new.

I've been doing it since I was sixteen, when Kate and I used to talk about visiting her brothers in America. However, in the last eleven years, I've learned to style my own hair, and I've watched a ton of videos about New York City.

The dream is to one day see the place for myself. When Gran Orla is gone, I don't think I'll be able to live in that house in the village all by myself. I do get lonely sometimes.

"Well, ye don't have to make any decisions today. Ye be safe and take care of the auld dear," Uncle Ken says as he opens my car door for me.

"See ya," I sing as I hug him.

"See ye later, love."

"Come here," Uncle Ewan croons. He tugs me into his embrace then whispers into my ear. "Ye are welcome here in Scotland for as long as ye want. When Mum is gone, that doesn't mean ye have to leave."

"I know," I reply as I give him a squeeze.

Releasing him, I then turn and climb into my car to head home. I need a shower and something to eat. I'm sure Rhona is ready to get home to her family.

I appreciate that she comes to sit with Gran while I come to the castle to train. She's the daughter of Gran's old best friend. They were really close and now that her mother has passed, she comes by to help Gran whenever she can.

As I drive home, my mind goes to all the people here I would be leaving behind if I did take off for America. I will miss them all, but I want to go. It feels like there's something there waiting for me. I've given up on my daydreams of that being Cole.

I'm sure he's forgotten all about me. I can't help but wonder if Kate ever made her way there. I miss her often.

I'm lost in my rambling thoughts as I turn onto the road that leads to Gran's house. We don't live far from the village, but we're not in the center of it either.

No one comes out here much, so imagine my surprise as a fancy car comes into view in front of the cottage. A fancy car with a tall figure standing beside it.

I groan and roll my eyes. "This better not be one of Duncan's prospects," I mumble under my breath.

Then something about the guy's posture grabs my attention and throws me back in time. I'm back at that birthday bonfire. I pull up behind the vehicle and stop, blinking as I stare out of the windscreen.

The guy lifts his head from staring down at his mobile and turns toward me. My mouth falls open as the handsome lad stands up straighter. He's tall, big, and thick.

A fit one indeed. He looks like something out of a movie. The beard, the height, the stance—he was made for the screen.

He has on a gray newsboy hat with a gray waistcoat and slacks. The hat is low, but there's no mistaking his handsome looks. Beneath the fitted waistcoat that looks like a tailored piece to a three-piece suit, he has on a crisp white shirt that's rolled up to his elbows.

On his feet are a pair of suede-looking gray loafers. Everything about him screams he has a style of his own. With a smile on his lips, he removes his hat and runs a hand through his thick, dark locks of hair.

A gasp leaves my lips. No fucking way. It's him, this is him in the flesh. Cole O'Brien is standing in front of my home.

I sit frozen, wondering what in the world he's doing here. Shaking myself out of shock, I put the car in park and climb out almost in slow motion. My brain still hasn't registered that he's real. I feel like I'm in a dream.

"Hello, DJ."

"Cole?"

He opens his arms as the smile on his lips grows. My brows are furrowed as I stand staring at him. Cole has always been a fit lad, but my mouth is watering as I look him over.

His arms are stretching the fabric of his shirt, looking like they're about to burst through the sleeves. He seems so much taller and larger than he was the last time I saw him. For thirty-three, he looks damn good.

"Come here, love. Give me a hug. I've missed ya," he croons.

I snap out of it and rush into his arms. I'm overwhelmed with emotions as he crushes me in his embrace. His arms are so strong and comforting.

God, he smells good. He begins to sway with me in his arms and it's like the dam breaks. I burst into tears and squeeze my arms around him tighter.

"I'm here now, love. I'm here. I've got ya," he says into the top of my hair.

My brain kicks back into full operation, and it dawns on me he shouldn't be here. Why now? Can I trust him?

Slowly, I take a step away from him. He looks at me as if he's the one confused. I shake my head and wrap my arms around my middle.

"How are ya, love? Ya look good."

"What are ya doing here?"

I want to let my guard down and rush back into his arms, but my mother's voice keeps ringing in my ears. I need to get out of my emotions so I can think clearly.

Trust no one. Your life depends on it.

"I never break a promise. I've come to take ya to that dinner I owe ya," he says.

I snort. "Ya're eleven years too late."

"Ach, I never gave up on finding ya someday. I've come all this way after having to have someone track ya down. I know yer not going to make me go to dinner by myself."

"Why would ya have someone looking for me?"

He closes the small gap I've created between us and cups my face between his hands. I've missed those green eyes so much. I place my hands over his as if needing to, just to remain standing.

"I told ya before. Yer mine. No amount of time or distance will ever change that. When ya went missing, I thought I was going to go crazy," he says as he searches my face with his gaze.

"Missing?"

I look back at him in confusion. His uncle was the one who picked me up from his parents' home. Why would he say I've been missing? Better yet, why would he need to have someone search for me?

Couldn't Uncle Finlay have told him where to find me? My hackles begin to go up. Something isn't right.

"Aye, love. I was told ya were missing. If I had known where to find ya, I would have come for ya sooner.

"It's good to see ya. How are ya? Are ya okay?"

"I'm fine. Although I'm not sure ya should be here."

He makes a deep scoffing sound. "Who the fuck is going to keep me from ya?"

"Cole, I … maybe we need to back up a bit. I'm confused. Why are ya here now?"

"I told ya. I'm here to take ya to dinner. I want to eat and talk to ya."

"I can't. My gran is inside. I need to let her caregiver go home."

"Then we'll order in."

"Ya can't just show up here demanding I have dinner with ya, Cole. I don't know ya. I haven't seen ya in eleven years. How do I know yer the same person I once knew?"

"That's why we're going to have dinner. I want to know how ya've been and what's been going on in yer life. I've missed ya."

"No. No, no, no. This doesn't feel right. Yer here out of the blue.

"No one said anything about ya coming here and now here ya are. I can't afford to trust ya. I need ya to go," I say and turn to head into the cottage.

"DJ. Deja, wait."

I ignore him and continue heading for the front door. I still don't know why he left the day after the bonfire or why he didn't come to find me sooner. This could be a setup.

Nope. I'm not doing this. My gran has spent enough time without me today.

Brooklyn

I thought I was going to come out of my skin on the flight over here. It took way longer than it ever has to get from New York to Scotland. Not that the flight time changed in any way.

My mind has been telling me I need to be here. However, I was not expecting this when I arrived. Deja looks nothing like the eighteen-year-old I left behind in Ireland. Jesus, Mary, Joesph, all that ass. You can see it from the front.

She looks like the prototype for what women in America pay to look like. Small waist, big fat ass, and those thick thighs. Damn.

My mouth is watering as I watch her walk away from me. The leggings she has on leave nothing to the imagination. Her ass jiggles with each step. The zip-up sports jacket she has on hugs those huge tits like a loving friend.

A friend I want to be. I'm fixated on the globes of her ass as I try to figure out what's happening. Why is she walking away from me? I'm not leaving here without talking to her.

"Deja, I need to talk to ya. Will ya stop walking away?"

"Why are ya here, Cole?" she bites out as she turns to face me.

I move to stand in front of her. She looks up at me with tears in her eyes. I cup her pretty face once again.

She's still gorgeous as ever. Not a stitch of makeup on her face and her skin is still flawless. She still wears those bangs, which brings a smile to my face.

Her rich, deep, dark-brown complexion brings out the beauty of her face. Her lips, her nose, those long dark lashes and pretty brown eyes. I can't believe she's standing in front of me.

"I came to do this," I murmur before I can think better of what I'm about to do.

I dip my head and capture her lips. I didn't come here for this, but now that I have her in my hands, how can I not? Her lips are so enticing and having her in my arms is all I've ever wanted.

I start with a gentle press of our lips. It's more of a cherishing gesture. I've always cherished this woman, from the time she offered me her ice cream cone after my older brother knocked mine to the ground and everyone else laughed about it.

She hadn't licked it yet and her cone was the last one. It had been hot out and I was all sweaty. I wouldn't take it, but she had insisted, going as far as shoving it in my face and saying I had to take it because I licked it.

Which I hadn't. Not only did she keep me and Logan from getting into a fight, but she also brought a smile to my face. I had been so angry that day. Oland had made it known he didn't like that Deja had tagged along with us for the weekend.

That shit pissed me off. Deja was Kate's best friend and like a little sister to the rest of us. I became super overprotective of her after that day.

When she presses her soft lips back against mine, I begin to tease the seam of her mouth with my tongue. She releases a gasp, and I stick my tongue into her mouth.

I groan as she wraps her arms around my neck. Stepping in closer, I move my arms around her and pull her body into mine. Her soft body melts right into mine.

I deepen the kiss and palm her big ass. My heart swells with pride as I note that my woman isn't a twig I can snap. I'm a big guy and DJ has all the right curves to handle me.

"Wait," she pants as she turns her head to break the kiss.

"Don't ya think we've waited long enough? It was only supposed to be two weeks. Two weeks turned into eleven years."

"What?"

"Yer da had planned to bring ya to New York as a surprise. When I left, I thought I would see ya in two weeks. I planned to tell ya how I felt when ya arrived, but ya never made it."

She takes a step back, shaking her head as if to clear it. I watch her closely as she reaches to touch her lips. I tilt my head to the side and fold my arms across my chest.

"If we were going to New York, why didn't I know about it?"

"It was a surprise birthday gift from Angus. Ireland wasn't safe for yer family anymore, so he had planned to stay once ye all came over. What happened to yer mum?

"Where is she? She can confirm what I'm telling ya," I say.

"Ya should go," she bites out as the shutters come down. Her facial expression goes completely blank.

"DJ," I call as she storms away.

"I can't do this, Cole. Just leave. If ya care anything for me, go."

This time, I allow her to go. I can tell I've said something that has struck a chord. This isn't going to be as easy as I thought it would be.

CHAPTER THIRTEEN

Still Here

Deja

I'm lying in bed staring up at the ceiling. Normally, I would be getting ready for my shift at the pub in the village. The uncles own *Pints*. I've been working there since I was nineteen.

I practically run the place. Everyone knows my uncles own it and wouldn't dare step out of line. Anyone who doesn't know learns pretty fast—there isn't anyone in the village who would allow anyone to disrespect me.

However, I still keep a baseball bat behind the bar with me at all times. Guys still flirt, and when alcohol is involved, things tend to get out of hand. I can't help wondering if Cole is gone.

I bet if he were around all the time, I wouldn't need Patrick at all. Yes, I named my bat, and it's named after the man I haven't been able to get my mind off of.

Cole Patrick O'Brien has been on my mind all night long. I've spent the entire night thinking about that kiss. I've never kissed anyone before.

I didn't know a single kiss could awaken my entire body. Cole kissed me like I belonged to him, but isn't that what he said I am? *His*. I groan and pinch my eyes closed.

"Stop it, Deja. Ya're going to get yerself hurt," I mutter.

I sigh and sit up. For the millionth time, I think of taking the night off. Bevie will be here to spend the night with Gran soon.

If I'm going to take the night off, I should let her know before she makes the trip here. I glance at the clock. I have no real reason for not showing up at work.

None other than the fact that I can't stop thinking about Cole and that kiss. The way he grabbed my bum with his big hands … I bite my lip and moan. I knew one day my vow to a life of celibacy was going to catch up with me.

Cole is so fucking fit. I can only imagine what it would be like to have him … okay, no more of that. I squeeze my thighs together before getting my arse up to get dressed.

I'll be better off at work than sitting here staring at these walls thinking about something that will never happen. I don't know if I can trust Cole, so it's best that I keep my distance.

I mean, why doesn't he know anything about what happened? Does Uncle Finlay not trust him? If his uncle doesn't trust him, how can I?

"Get it together, D. He's just another guy. Before yer eighteenth birthday, ya didn't see him as anything but a brother. Let's go back to that, yeah?" I chide myself.

Still muttering to myself, I get dressed for work. With a cheeky grin on my face, I dress for a big-tip night. Donavon did mention a few parties coming in this evening.

Maybe it's time I find myself a fuck buddy. I'm not getting any younger. If a kiss can do all that … yup, I might be needing me a toy. The backless catsuit it is. I know just the shoes to pair with it.

***

I wipe my hands on a towel and count the drinks on my tray. We're down a waitress, so I've been working tables and the bar.

Gordon, Donovan's little brother, has been helping out, but he's terrible with carrying drinks.

Nodding to myself, I lift the tray and start for the two tables I have orders for. I drop off two pints to the couple who look to be tourists. I then move to a table of regulars.

"Deja, love, why is it ye never take me up on my offers to dinner?" Harold Wilson asks as I place the tray of beers on his table.

"Maybe because ya are a married man, Wilson. I would hate to have to bust Mrs. Wilson upside her head for coming in here trying to put her hands on me like she did Ailia," I sing and gave him a smile.

"Aye, she's got ye there," Odell Griffin croons and laughs.

Seonaid Wilson is crazy about her man. Ailia Campbell learned the hard way to stay away from her husband. Seonaid walked right into the coffee shop where Ailia works and gave a good show to the village.

"Och, she does," Travis McDonald adds.

I laugh and shake my head. I've known these guys for as long as I've worked here. Not only are they regulars, but they've become like friends and family. If I even look like something isn't right, they're the first to get up from their seats.

The big, scary-looking Scots have scared plenty of eejits away. They are also the jokesters of the pub. You can always count on them for a good laugh.

"Och, Ailia has a big mouth. Ye don't strike me as the type to play and tell," Harold says to me, ignoring his friends.

"Harold, do I strike ya as one to play at all?"

"The kind of playing I'm talking about … it would be a shame to let all that go to waste," he says as he looks me over. He pauses and gets serious, then looks around the pub. "I haven't seen ye dressed like this in a long time.

"Which one of these lads are ye giving ye heart to? I want to meet him. I have some questions for him," he says like a protective big brother.

"There isn't anyone. Can't a lass dress up for herself?"

He snorts. "Ye may have done it for yerself, but it sure does feel like a gift for the rest of us. Aye, the day the divorce comes through, I'll be at ye door like a proper gentleman," he says with a sage nod.

"She'll have that bat ready for ye too," Travis says.

"Depending on the mood, it might be a pistol. Don't bring yer arse to my door, Wilson. I don't want to have to kick it. Ye boys need anything else? I need to get behind the bar."

"We're good, love. I'll save ye the trip the next round and come for it myself," Odell says.

"Thanks."

I turn and go to head back behind the bar. Rolling my eyes at myself, I realize I could have passed on the heels tonight. My feet are starting to ache.

"DJ."

The name is growled behind me. I don't bother to turn; I already know it's him. No one else besides his family calls me by that name. If I didn't know it was him from the name, I would know from the possessive hold he has on me as he stands behind me with his hand splayed across my belly.

I look up at him and smile. "Hello, Cole. What can I get ya?"

Brooklyn

I walk into the pub I was told Deja works at and look around. It's a decent place. The word is it's owned by her uncles.

I'm still digging up information on them. I'm treading lightly so I don't trigger any unwanted attention; my whereabouts can't get back to my grandfather.

However, I need to know what's been going on around DJ. Like I said, I'm not leaving until we talk. I need to head back home soon, so I need to make that happen fast.

However, from the moment I walk in, I want to shut this motherfucker down. I don't know what DJ was thinking when she left the house this evening, but that shit is going to get someone hurt. There's no fucking way this is how she comes to work.

The clear stripper heels are one thing. Then there's the black bodysuit. Her back is on full display, showing off all that smooth, dark-brown skin. There is no denying that body with the fit of the fabric to her skin.

The tat down the center of her back is something I want to explore in more detail, but I hate that everyone else can see it as well. My slacks are so fucking tight right now.

"Hello, Cole. What can I get ya?"

I narrow my eyes at her. "Ya knew I was coming here, didn't ya? There's no way ya come to work like this every night."

"What would make ya say that?"

"Ya love to taunt me."

She turns to fully face me as I lift a brow at her. That little smile drives me crazy. It always tells me she is goading me, and she knows she has me.

"Taunting ya? Are ya implying I thought about ya as I got ready for work? Still cocky as ever.

"No, Cole. I didn't know ya were coming here. Would ya like something to drink?"

"What I want is to take my time and do this proper, but yer trying to make me bend ya over and fuck the shit out of ya right where ya stand."

Her eyes fill with lust as she looks me over. I'm dressed in all black, but I might as well be naked the way she takes me in. I grin and palm the side of her face. The deep waves framing her face and bangs are something new.

It looks good on her. Deja would be beautiful bundled in a potato sack. She smells amazing too.

"I'm not letting ya shag me so ya can go back to wherever ya come from. Do ya want a drink or not, Cole?"

I tug her to me and kiss her hard. Just as she did yesterday, she wraps her arms around my neck and allows me to devour her. I want to clear this place out and take her on the nearest surface.

The chemistry between us is insane. My skin is humming from being near her. If I ever doubted wanting to make her mine, the thought has gone out of the window.

"What are ya doing?" she pants as she breaks the kiss and looks up at me.

"Having a drink. Yer delicious, love. What time are ya done here?"

"Why?"

"We'll have a drink, and we can talk. I'm in Scotland just for ya. Nothing else. I want to understand what I'm missing. Why ya shut down on me yesterday."

"That's not going to happen. Ya might as well go back home."

I frown. "Those words just tasted like shit, didn't they? Ya don't want me gone any more than I want to leave ya."

"We have a problem here? Who is this, Deja?"

"I've got it, Harold. There isn't a problem."

"Aye, Harold. Be a good boy and go sit the fuck down," I bite out.

"Cole," Deja chides.

"Who the fuck do ye think ye are?"

"I'm her man. Not that I need to explain shit to you. Take your ass back to your table before I fold you and roll you back to it," I growl, allowing my New York accent to come forward.

"We'd like to see ye try," another asshole comes to help his friend as they stand here looking like they're trying to intimidate me.

I roll my shoulders and crack my neck to the side. I didn't get my workout in this morning. I have no problem doing it now.

I look them both over as a third joins them. I snort. They're not small men.

However, I'm making it out of here without a problem. I can promise that. I plant my feet and stand firm as if I own the place. I'm the last person they're going to intimidate.

"Guys, it's okay. Ye can go back to yer seats. I'll bring yer next round over in a bit, on me," DJ says.

"Are ye sure?"

"Aye, I'm sure. Thanks, guys."

I reach for her hand and lace my fingers with hers as we stand here waiting for these three to mind their own fucking business. There is an instant connection. My hand begins to warm and tingle as I hold hers.

Ignoring them, I look down at DJ, searching her face. She's glancing up at me. Giving her a wink, I then squeeze her hand. A mix of lust and confusion crosses her face.

I dip in to peck her lips, wanting to deepen the kiss, but using restraint instead. She tugs her hand from mine and nods for me to follow her. I move closely behind her to block the view from anyone else other than me.

She laughs. "Really, Cole?"

"Brooklyn."

"Huh?"

"Ya should get used to calling me Brooklyn. That's what I answer to in America."

"Are ya shitting me?"

"Ach, not at all. There's a lot ya need to know before I take ya home."

She stops in her tracks and turns to me. So many emotions are running across her face. I place a hand on her waist and search her eyes.

"Okay, ya can stay. I'll listen to ya."

"That's my girl."

CHAPTER FOURTEEN

I Didn't Know

Deja

We're sitting in the pub after the place has closed, and everyone has gone home. Cole has helped me to clean up and set up for tomorrow—or should I say Brooklyn?

I was a little thrown when he asked me to call him that. I knew it was a nickname of his, but Kate told me he used it for business, not family.

I couldn't help but feel like he was establishing the difference earlier. I'm no longer family, I'm an outsider. Or his presence here is strictly business.

"I didn't know any of that," I say as we sit in one of the booths in the back while he tells me that my uncle Donny was murdered around the same time as my da.

I had no idea, and I have no clue where Ciara has been. If I had known, I would have wanted her here with me. Ciara was such a wee little thing. She was only about eight the last time I saw her.

At the time that Finlay came for me, Uncle Donny and his family were all in America already. I don't know much about what happened, but what little I do know, I'm not about to share with Cole.

I'm still uncertain about him. This connection is one thing; my life and ability to trust are another. I chew on my lip as I think over everything he's told me.

"You're sure you don't know why you were brought here?"

"Ach, there ya go sounding like an American again," I say to deflect.

"You'll get used to it. Dylan has lost his accent altogether unless he's pissed. Kate and Jamie tend to have theirs around family the most. You might get lucky and keep yours," he says with a smile.

I inhale deeply. I want to go to America, but I'm not sure going with Cole is the right thing to do. I need more time to think about it—time when he's not so close.

Right now, his entire presence is consuming me. His cologne has filled my head and his big thigh is pressed close to mine. Every time I slide away, he moves closer.

I reach for the bottle of whiskey sitting between us and pour myself another. I'm doing my best to keep my hand from shaking. He hasn't tried to kiss me since we started this conversation and that's sort of freaking me out.

"Why do you take a drink every time I mention New York? You do know Kate and the rest of the family are there. It will feel like home after a while."

"What if I don't want to go?"

He covers my glass with his palm and slides it away from me. That intense look fills his green eyes, sucking me in. I'm holding my breath as I await his reply.

I don't want to kick his ass, but I've mapped all my options since he placed me in this corner. If I can't trust him and he's here to harm me, I'm going to fight until one of us isn't breathing. Preferably him.

"What aren't you telling me, DJ? Why wouldn't you want to come with me?"

"I told ya before, I don't know ya anymore. I may not know why I was brought to Scotland or what happened, but I know it was for my own safety. I can't go with ya without knowing I can trust ya."

"You can always trust me," he says, sounding as if he's hurt. "I would never do anything to hurt you. My life's mission is to make your life as safe as I can."

"Yet ya keep hurting me ears, Brooklyn," I taunt.

"Ach, on second thought." He pauses to lean into me. He's a breath away when he begins to speak again. "I don't want to hear that name on yer lips unless we're back home and around business. I'm yer Cole. That's what I want to hear fall from yer lips."

With that, he takes my lips in a searing kiss. The booth isn't giving him enough room to maneuver as he devours me. He breaks the kiss and bites out a curse.

The next thing I know, he plucks me up from the bench seat and places me on the tabletop. Hovering over me, he takes my lips once again. I moan when he grabs my thighs and wraps my legs around his waist as he kisses his way down my neck.

A voice in the back of my head is screaming for me to stop this. However, I'm a twenty-nine-year-old virgin and this man is the only man who has ever made me want to change that status.

"Cole," I whimper as he covers my nipple over the fabric of my catsuit with his warm mouth.

My belly flips and drops as my core floods with my juices. The way he's sucking on my peak has me wanting to strip bare to allow him to fuck me right here.

"I want ya so bad, DJ. Yer so fucking sexy. Everything is going to be fine when I get ya home."

His words are like a bucket of ice water. Why does he keep insisting I go to America? Does he need to get me away from the uncles?

"Please stop. I can't do this," I say and begin to push him away.

"What? Am I moving too fast, baby?" he asks as he searches my eyes with concern.

"Aye. This isn't how I want my first time to be," I mutter.

"Excuse me. Yer what?"

"My first time, Cole. I've never had sex before. It hasn't been at the top of my priority list."

"Aye," he says and pulls a hand down his face, bringing attention to that sexy beard. "Right, ya live with yer great-gran and spend most of yer time with yer great-uncles, it makes sense."

"Does that turn ya off? Have ya changed yer mind?"

He cups my face as I sit here on the table, feeling embarrassed. I should have kept my mouth shut. If not for the warning bells ringing in my head, I wouldn't have stopped him.

I want sex. I want sex with him awfully bad. If he kisses like that, I know sex with him will be amazing. At least I hope so.

"Ya, DJ, are mine. I don't care if yer a virgin or not. When I take ya no one else before me will matter. There will be no one after.

"Am I proud of ya for not giving away what's mine? Aye. That means I get to fully corrupt ya. There is nothing ya could do that would turn me off."

He finishes his words with a kiss that has my head buzzing. I run my hands through his hair and hold him close as he drinks from my mouth. Shite, I shouldn't have stopped him.

He breaks the kiss and moves his lips to my ear. "Don't worry, I'm a good listener. I've heard everything you've said and all that you haven't.

"I'm going to show you you can trust me and I'm going to give you a first time you'll never forget. I'm not here to hurt you, DJ. I'm here because I care about you."

"If ya care about me and don't want to hurt me, stop with the accent." He finishes the end of my sentence with me and we both laugh.

"Come, let's talk some more. I'll try my best to stick to Gaelic just for ya," he says with a grin and proceeds to spend the rest of the night speaking to me in Gaelic.

Brooklyn

I'm in my car following behind DJ. I want to make sure for myself that she reaches home safely. I probably should have let her go home hours ago.

However, sitting and talking with her in Gaelic felt so familiar. It felt like home. My family doesn't use the language as much as we used to.

For the most part, we've all become Americanized. I'm going to enjoy having DJ in New York with me. She's even picked up a few Scottish nuances I'm able to appreciate as they remind me of my mom.

"Aye, she's perfect," I murmur to myself.

My thoughts go to her earlier words. She doesn't think she can trust me. Something has changed with her. Deja was never this cautious. She took to new friends easily.

In fact, as I remember, she was the first to welcome the new person in. Deja has a big heart and an old soul. She has been a listening ear for as long as I can remember.

She's smart as a whip and witty. I can't imagine what has made her so cautious. I tighten my hands on the wheel as I think of all the things I could be missing. I need answers.

DJ pulls up in front of the cottage and parks. I place my car in park and step out. When I get to her car, I open the door for her, and she steps out.

A smile comes to my lips as she's wearing my vest that's swallowing her. I gave it to her when we stepped out of the pub. It's a bit nippy this time of morning with the frosty bite in the air.

I didn't want her to catch a cold with her back bare. As great as she looks in the sexy outfit, that's a lot of bare skin to have out. I tug the vest around her to keep her warm, then reach for her hand to walk her to the door.

"Ya don't have to walk me. Ya should head to yer … hotel?"

"Ach, no hotel. I'm staying with family. Uncle Finlay keeps the doors open to us even when he's not in town."

"So you're staying at Uncle Finlay's, but he's not here?"

"Aye."

"Well, thanks. Ya didn't have to follow me home. I would have been fine on my own," she says as we stand outside the front door of the cottage she lives in with her great-gran.

"I feel better knowing I've seen ya to yer door," I say as I wrap my arms around her.

"I had a good time. It was nice to feel like I was back home."

"Aye, it was."

I dip my head and peck her lips. The gentle kiss quickly turns into a heated one. It's nearly impossible for us to keep the passion out of our kisses.

I can feel she wants me as much as I want her. I was blown away when she said she's still a virgin. I want nothing more than to make her first time special for her.

I pull away and look down at her when I feel we're about to get carried away. She sucks in a sharp breath and begins to squirm in my embrace. I grin and plant a kiss against her temple.

She smells like alcohol and something sweet. My mind goes to what her skin will taste like when she's beneath me, screaming my name. I intend to make Deja mine in every way there is. No one and nothing is going to stop me from that now.

"I'll see ya tomorrow," I murmur.

"Okay, seven?"

"Aye, wear something that's not going to get anyone killed."

She laughs and gives my waist a squeeze. I lift a brow as she looks up at me while biting her lip. That little smile touches the corner of her mouth.

"Wear something that will get my knickers wet. Ya have been doing fine since ya arrived, by the way."

I growl and bury my face in her neck. "Ya drive me crazy. I don't want to leave ya."

"Give me yer mobile. I'll give ya my number and we can chat like we used to."

I reach for my phone and hand it over to her. "Ya have no idea how much I miss those talks. Kate would be pissed if she knew how many times I called, hoping ya were around for me to clear my head."

"Now ya don't have to go through yer sister to chat with me. Call me anytime ya need."

I lean in to take her lips once more. As our tongues dance together, I'm growing hard as a rock. When DJ reaches to palm my balls between my legs, I know I need to leave.

"Don't be naughty, baby. I made ya a promise."

"I just wanted to feel the wares. Ya have a good night, Mr. O'Brien. I hope ya dream of me."

"I know I will, love. I know I will."

I kiss her on the forehead and turn to leave. My mind goes to home and the calls I need to make. Logan should know where I am. I can't keep putting this off.

I look down at the time on my phone and whistle. I won't be making that call now. My brother would bite my head off.

I'll call him later.

CHAPTER FIFTEEN

Trust Me

Deja

"Ya could have told me the date would be here. I could have saved ya the trip to come get me and driven myself," I say as Cole opens my door for me.

He holds his hand out for mine, giving me a pointed look as he purses those sexy lips. Taking his hand, I step from the car while biting my lip. I can't help looking him over.

"There was no way I was going to allow ya on the road without me now or later."

"I'm a big girl, Cole. I know how to take care of myself."

"Aye, but as long as I'm around, ya don't have to."

He gives me a smile and my breath hitches. Cole is already a gorgeous man, but that beard is enough to make a woman drool and swoon. I asked him to dress to make me wet and he has. He's in white slacks and a light-green shirt this evening. No waistcoat this time.

It's his tight ass, broad back, and thick thighs for me. Then there's the way his arms stretch against his shirt. He's absolutely mouthwatering.

He places my hand in the crook of his arm and flexes his muscle. I look up at him and smile. He knows exactly what he's doing.

"Speaking of ya being around. When do ya plan to head back to America?"

"When you're ready."

"Cole, my gran is ill. I can't up and leave now."

He looks down at me as the wheels turn. I've thought about this all night. I want to leave with him.

I miss Kate and the others. I could start a new life in New York City. Having Cole in my life would be a bonus.

If things don't work out, I'm resourceful. I'm not the same girl who was whisked away to Scotland. I can protect myself now.

I don't have to be as fearful as I was back then. I actually don't have to be fearful at all.

"I don't mean to pry, but I heard she's not doing well. I wouldn't be able to wait with ya, but I can come back for ya. Ya know, when ya don't have to be here to care for her, I can come to get ya.

"I'll come to visit as often as I can. Logan has some dealings I'll be needed around for, but that shouldn't stop me from coming to see ya as much as I want. I'm not going to rush ya, love," he says.

I sigh in relief. More time to figure things out without him around will be grand. I'm not going to flush everything my mother said to me down the drain.

"So there's no girlfriend back in New York who's waiting for ya?"

He stops in his tracks and turns to glare at me. I start to snicker when he pulls me to him and puts me into a one-arm headlock, the way he used to do when we were younger. He kisses the top of my head as he sways me in his arms.

"Shut the fuck up." He snorts. I'm not offended. I know it's a New York thing.

I actually smile. This is the Cole I remember. He kisses the top of my head once again before he continues.

"I traveled over three thousand miles to come see ya. Do ya really think there's anyone else?"

"I don't know. That's why I'm asking."

"I haven't been in a steady relationship in years. I can't stand airheads, but they seem to love to chase me. I'm too busy for that shit. I stopped fucking around the moment I asked Felix to look for ya."

"Felix Black?"

"Aye. Wait until everyone sees ya."

"The Blacks live in New York?"

"No, they're still in California, but I travel there for business enough. Yer bound to see them all sooner or later."

"How are they? Yer cousins and Uncle Joe and Aunt Cass?"

"Ach, they're all doing grand. Keeping busy with the PI and bounty business, as far as I know. We see more of Felix because we're doing him a favor with a friend."

"Oh, now that sounds interesting. Is this friend a lass?"

"Aye, they are. Enough about them. Come, I want ya to see what I've set up for our date."

He releases his hold around my head and laces his fingers with mine. I'm a wee bit bereft of his arm around me. It's such an intimate embrace that says so much about us.

I'm having trouble preventing myself from falling into old comforts around him. With my hand in his, he leads me through the castle. I've been here quite a few times when I was younger, before my mum disappeared.

I would come to play with Kate when she was here, and I was with my family for a visit. Mum would bring me and stick around for a bit with Ian and Finlay Black. I can remember a few times when Wyatt, Noah, and John were here visiting too.

The place is still as magical as I remember. There's something special about the Black Castle. It has an aura of its own.

As Cole leads me down the stairs to the lower level of the castle, my words are only proven to be true. There have been renovations since I last was here. The winding staircase now has new sconces mounted on the walls. Not the old ones that needed to be manually lit.

These have a vintage yet modern vibe about them. They are definitely brighter than they used to be. As we get to the bottom of the stairs, I smile.

I know exactly where he's taking me. The Black Castle has its own underground indoor pool area. It's huge. Ian Black once told me that the space had once been a bathhouse. He was the one to turn it into an indoor pool instead.

"I used to love it down here. Kate would get so spooked out, but it has always made me feel … I don't know," I say as I lift my shoulders to my ears.

"Like ya were stepping into a whole new world? Isn't that the song ya would sing every time ya came here?"

I look up at him in shock. "Ya remember that?"

"Aye, ya were cute. The way yer face would light up. I think ya were one of the only ones who got what Granda was doing," he says.

He was getting us to use our imagination to get out of situations. The pool never once looked the same. One time, there was a dragon whose mouth opened up as a waterslide.

That one was one of my favorites. You had to find your way around the dragon's body to get to the steps to slide back down. I was one of the first to find the stairs.

"Do you remember that time he had the pool frozen over and we all became human chess pieces?"

"Aye, we all had to work together to play the game. I remember because that was the year Sam came with Logan."

"Sam?"

"Aye, Logan's best friend. The Italian."

"Oh, with the gray eyes. Ach, I do remember him. That was fun.

"All his ideas were fun and made ya think on yer toes."

"It was all fun and games back then, but now I have to wonder what he was getting us all ready for. I mean, his quests have helped me in training, but—"

"Training?"

Shite. I've said too much. The pool area comes into view right in that moment. My eyes widen and I gasp.

"Oh my God, Cole. It's beautiful. Did ya do this for me?"

He tugs me into his chest and wraps his arms around me. "Aye, I remembered what ya told me ya would want this place to look like if ya could choose the theme. Did I get it right?"

I look around and take it all in. Did he get it right? He did.

It's better than I imagined in my head. The pool is lit from within with what looks like candles. The light-bluish-green water itself is sparkling as if sprinkled with glitter.

More candles surround the poolside along with teal and pink flowers. There are bright pinks and rich teal colors everywhere, taking the space from dark and dim to bright and breathtaking. Then there's the table set for two with candles on a holder that has three tiers, a candle on each.

I look back to the pool and squint. It looks like pages are floating on top of the surface. I knit my brows until I remember what I told him so long ago.

"The prince's letters to the princess?"

"Aye, took forever to figure out how to get candles underwater. Felt a bit stupid when I figured it out," he chuckles as he rubs the back of his neck.

"LED lights. Yeah?"

"Aye, I had the LED lights epoxied into old candle glasses."

"How are the pages floating without getting ruined?"

"Take yer shoes off, I'll show ya."

Excitedly, I take off my shoes. Cole kicks his off too and begins to roll his pant legs up. He then takes my hand and leads me to the edge of the pool where the invisible steps are.

They make the pool seem seamless, like there's no place to enter, but I know they are there. We glide down the steps into the pool. The skirt of my dress is getting wet, but I really don't care.

I reach for one of the letters and can't help but smile. He had them laminated. I begin to read the letter and tear up as I see it's actually one of the originals.

"I found them here in storage. Granda must have kept them," he murmurs into my ear as if he has read my mind as he holds me from behind.

I'm choked up. Kate and I came up with this elaborate story about the prince and princess who met and fell in love in this castle. When we were teens, Kate and I decided the two had a love correspondence. I then wrote a bunch of letters to the prince and Kate talked Cole into helping her write a bunch back to the princess in response to mine.

"Ya do know I meant every word? Ya were writing to some fictitious character, but each time I replied to the mischievous, brilliant writer of those letters. I didn't realize how far gone I had been even back then."

I turn in his embrace and look up at him. As I think of the letters, I remember how the prince and princess started as friends and developed a deep, passionate connection over time.

I loved Princess Skye and Prince Pádraig. Their friendship was awe-inspiring. However, I don't think I ever thought of it as ours until right now.

I was seventeen the last time we exchanged letters. I stopped writing because he had so much going on with his granda and all. I thought the letters had been childish even though he replied to every one.

I begin to laugh. "Is that why ya changed his name from Clyde to Pádraig? Kate was so mad at ya for that."

"Aye, if I was going to speak for him, he had to have my name." He winks at me.

"I knew it. Pádraig, Patrick. Ya always had to have yer way. Clyde was a grand name."

He cups my face and dips his head to peck my lips. "Aye, but it wasn't my name."

"My name isn't—"

He lifts a brow, cutting my words off. I feel my cheeks heat. Cole gives me a crooked grin.

"Oh, ya know my middle name?" I say in awe.

"Aye, as ya know mine. Come, let me get ya dried off so I can feed ya."

If I had driven myself, this would be the point when I would have bolted and gotten my butt out of here. I'm fully in my feelings. If Cole is trying to take my life, I'm a goner.

He already has my heart. This is a date I will never forget. There is something majestic in every corner I look in. Details even I had forgotten I shared with him.

Wow. Cole steps out of the water and holds his hand out to me. This is so unfair.

He's covered in glitter and dripping wet. The print running down his leg looks more like a glittering sign. I bite my lip and look away quickly.

"I should've thought that one through better," he chuckles as he looks me over.

I look down at my soaked, glittering skirt and feet and laugh with him. I don't mind. This moment has meant so much to me.

Brooklyn

"Are ya still making yer mix tapes?" I ask over the rim of my glass as I run my gaze over DJ.

We've had dinner after I found us something to change into. I have to admit, although it's swallowing her, I love seeing her in one of my dress shirts. Having an unobstructed view of her thick, silky-looking brown thighs has me hard and wanting.

Now that dinner is over, we're sitting by the side of the pool on the satin pillows I had arranged for a moment just like this. DJ is sitting with her legs stretched out as I face her with one knee bent.

She shrugs. "Not so much. My supplier kind of disappeared. I didn't have anyone to keep me up with the latest trends on American radio."

"Fair point. We'll have to get ya up to speed. I miss having my own personal DJ."

She tilts her head to the side as she smiles at me. I reach for her thigh and place my hand on it. DJ bites her lip as she stares down at my hand on her soft skin.

I smile and reach for my phone with the other hand. Keeping my eyes on her, I hand her my phone. She takes it but lifts a brow.

"I have all yer mixes on my phone. Pick one," I say.

"O … kay. It's locked," she says and goes to hand it back.

I call out my passcode for her to unlock it. A smirk comes to her lips. I inch my hand up her thigh as I lean in and kiss her lips.

"I trust ya, love. Besides, I have nothing to hide," I say against her lips.

"Um," she murmurs as she unlocks the phone and begins to scroll through my playlists.

I sit watching her as she looks through all the playlists I have on my phone that she's made for me. A naughty grin comes to her lips as she taps at her selection, and it begins to flow through the sound system down here.

Janet Jackson's "Any Time, Any Place" fills the air and a smile of my own takes over my face. I had planned to dance with her. This isn't the type of song I thought she would pick.

Shaking my head, I stand and hold my hand out to her. I catch her staring at my tented sweats as she bites that sexy lip. I roll my eyes at her.

Pulling her up to her feet, I then tug her into my embrace and begin to sway with her. We lock eyes and that energy that's been flowing through us seems to take on a new life.

"Is that—?"

I roll my eyes again. "Aye."

Yes, I'm stabbing her in the belly, but I'm trying to ignore that fact. However, she's not about to let me. She reaches into my sweats and wraps her warm, soft hand around me.

I lift my gaze to the ceiling and swallow hard. I'm so hard as she begins to stroke me lightly, almost tentatively. She snickers a bit as I twitch in her palm.

"Cole, look at me," she says softly.

I drop my eyes to her face and bounce my gaze across her features. Lust has filled her eyes as she looks back at me. She's so fucking beautiful.

Just looking at her is making it hard for me to resist her. Thoughts of those lush lips wrapped around me fill my head. I can't wait to make those bangs all sweaty, so they stick to her face.

I groan at the thought as she runs her thumb across the precum leaking from my tip. She parts her lips and sticks her tongue out the side of her mouth. I get the feeling my girl is going to turn out to be naughty in bed. I like that.

"DJ, I'm warning ya, love. Ya want to get yer hand out of my pants. I have but so much restraint," I say tightly.

"And if I don't?"

I pinch her chin and lift her face before taking her lips in a searing kiss. I nearly eat her face. She whimpers as I reach between her legs and find her seam. I growl as I find her bare, wet pussy.

"Cole." She drops her head back and moans.

"Yer so wet. Do ya want to come, baby?"

"Aye, I do. I really do," she sings.

"If I let ya come, will ya be a good girl for me?"

"I don't know. Will ya fuck me?"

"No."

"Why not?" she almost whines.

"I don't have any condoms with me and it's too soon for me to saddle ya with my bairn. I think we should be married first," I say as I continue to finger her.

"Please," she begs.

It's music to my ears. I want nothing more than to lay her down and take her, but I know I'm not going to want to pull out. This is the right thing to do.

I promised her a first time we would remember. I don't want that to be because I knock her up like an asshole. We still have so much to work out. There's no way I'd leave her behind to wait for her gran to die if she's carrying my baby.

She grabs my wrist and lifts onto her toes. I watch as her eyes roll back, and a look of bliss comes over her face. She falls forward into me as she shakes from her climax.

"That's my girl. Felt good, didn't it?" I croon as I pull my fingers from her pussy and bring them to my lips.

She lifts her head to look up at me drunkenly as I hum around my soaked fingers. Her juices taste amazing on my digits. It's going to kill me, but I'm going to wait.

I wink at her and then peck her lips. My smile grows as she sticks her hands underneath my T-shirt and runs her hands up my sides. Moving my hands to her ass, I begin to sway us to the music once again.

I dip my head for another kiss. This time biting and nipping at her lips. She moans loudly.

"Ya really should keep condoms with ya," she says sleepily.

I scoff and squeeze her ass. "Yer right. I'll keep that in mind."

CHAPTER SIXTEEN

Summoned

Logan

"Where the fuck is Brooklyn?" I growl as I sit behind my desk in my office at the warehouse.

"He called looking for you earlier. He said something about not being able to reach you on your cell," Kaye says as she pops her head into my office.

Kaye has been doing a great job, but I get the feeling Felix wants her back home with him. I would feel the same way. However, as long as she's here in New York, we're going to keep her safe.

I frown and give her a nod. I have this feeling in my gut: Cole is somewhere doing something he shouldn't. We're so close to bringing the Alliance to life.

I can only hope he's not off doing something that's going to make me need to kick his ass. My mind goes to Deja. I didn't think I would have to keep him away from her for so long.

I couldn't imagine having to be away from Raven for eleven years. It had to be done. I know Cole and his temper.

If Cole knew why we're keeping the locations for the cousins' secret, he'd lose his shit, and Oland would be dead before we could accomplish our goals. As guilt begins to settle in, my cell rings on my desk. When I see it's my granda Oland, I get a sour feeling in the pit of my stomach.

"Cole," I groan before even answering the call.

"Hello."

"Aye, Logan. It's yer granda. What about ye, lad?"

"Hello, Oland. How can I help ya?"

"It's been too long since ya have been home. I have some things I'd like to discuss with ya. I need ya here in Ireland," he replies.

I bare my teeth, knowing for sure Brooklyn has caught his attention. *Fuck.* If I don't go, there's no telling what he'll do to my brother.

"When did ya want to see me?" I bite out in frustration.

"I expect to see ya here tomorrow. I'll be waiting, lad."

Without another word, he hangs up. I restrain myself from throwing the phone across the room. Instead, I dial Cole's ass to find out where the fuck he is.

It goes to voicemail, sending my blood pressure through the roof. I hang up without leaving a message and call LaSalle instead. I need to talk to him and give instructions for what to do just in case my granda has something up his sleeve.

"Fuck, Cole. Fuck. What have ya done?" I fume.

Brooklyn

I didn't want to leave, but I needed to get back to New York. For some reason, I just haven't been able to bring myself to call Logan and tell him what's going on. I feel like Deja is a secret I need to keep to myself.

"Can I get you another drink, sir?" The flight attendant asks.

"No, I'm fine," I grumble.

I've been in a foul mood since I left DJ to catch my flight. Something felt off when I said goodbye. Not between us, but with the situation overall.

Almost as if someone were watching us. I almost didn't leave at all, but I knew I had to. Logan will already have questions when I get back home that I don't know how I'm going to answer.

"This is going to fucking gut me," I mutter to myself. "Shit."

CHAPTER SEVENTEEN

Meet the Uncles

Brooklyn

Two months later …

I haven't been back here since my first visit. Logan has been missing. All my focus has been on finding my brother.

I get the feeling all of this is happening because of me. Now that we know for sure that Logan is lost in some prison in Ireland, I know it has something to do with my grandfather. I almost didn't come here, but the McDougal name has come up, and I didn't like my father's response when it did.

I hopped on a flight to check in on DJ, and because I now have more questions about her uncles. My da was adamant that he deal with the McDougal clan himself in place of Logan.

Something was off about it. I've taken over everything else in Logan's absence. Why the fuck did Da freak out when I mentioned Scotland and this family?

"We're about to find out," I mutter, pulling into the courtyard of the McDougal Castle.

It reminds me of the Black Castle. I'm not surprised, as both families go way back. Old money, older roots.

I pull to a stop in the courtyard and park. A smile comes to my face as DJ appears with two large older men. I wasn't expecting to find her here.

I swallow hard as I take her in. She's in a pair of those tight leggings again. However, this time she has on a bra top.

I groan and pull a hand down my face. I've come for answers, not to claim my woman. I'll be chanting those words in my head this entire visit.

Stepping from the car, I move to the front of it and rest my ass against the hood. I note the moment DJ sees me and her eyes light up. I open my arms for her, and she comes rushing forward.

I stand up straight and step away from the car. I chuckle when she yelps in surprise as I lift her thick ass onto my waist. As she wraps her legs around me, I take her lips in a kiss.

She cups my face and gives back the passion I'm giving to her. I groan into the kiss, missing her sweet mouth. Before we get carried away, I allow her body to slide down my front.

"Aye, love, I missed ya too, baby," I say against her lips before pecking them once more.

"Why didn't ya tell me ya were coming?"

"I wanted to surprise ya."

"What are ya doing here though? Why didn't ya go to the cottage? How did ya know I was here?"

"I didn't know ya would be here. I came to see yer uncles," I reply.

Her smile falls and she takes a few steps back from me. That distrustful look fills her eyes. I thought we had worked past that.

"Cole, why would ya be here to see me uncles?" Her accent comes out thicker than ever.

The last thing I want to do is argue with her. I had hoped I could come here and have a conversation with the McDougal brothers and after I planned to stop in to see her at her gran's.

"You're Cole O'Brien. Aren't ya?" One of the two men says.

"Aye, that's me."

"Come, ye shouldn't be out here in plain sight. If ye want to talk, we should do so inside. Ye don't belong here."

My hackles go up. I'm not fond of anyone telling me where I should and shouldn't be. The guy who spoke frowns.

"Dinna fash yersel. What he means is ye shouldn't be seen with our niece. If it gets back to the wrong ears, that could be a problem," the other guy says.

"Deja has been safe because we keep her that way and she hasn't been a threat to Oland since she's been here. He's left her alone. Come, come inside before someone sees ye," the first one who spoke says.

"Uncle Ken, what the hell are ye two talking about? Oland? As in Oland O'Brien? What does he have to do with anything?" Deja says, sounding confused.

"Inside," the one she called Uncle Ken snaps.

I reach for her hand and lace my fingers with hers as we both follow the two men into the house. That ever-present connection is still there, no matter how much I can feel her trying to fight it.

Pulling my key for the car, I push the button to lock it. Then I look down at DJ, searching her face. She glances up at me, anger clearly written on her face. Giving her a wink, I then squeeze her hand. A mix of lust and confusion crosses her face.

Once we're fully inside the house, she shakes her head as if to clear it. I take in the house and note some of the similarities to the Black Castle. The house where she lives with her great-grandmother is way more modest from what I could tell.

I can't help wondering why they don't stay here. I shrug the thought off as everyone takes a seat in the drawing room. Deja tries to pull away to take one of the seats across from me, but I tug her into the seat beside me.

Then I wrap my arm around her shoulders and lean into her ear. "It's been two months since I last saw ya. Stop trying to run from me. I've missed ya. I want ya close."

She blows out a frustrated breath, but begins to squirm a little beside me. I grin and plant a kiss against her temple. She smells like sweat and that delicious scent of hers.

Something like peaches and champagne. It's so intoxicating. If beauty has a scent, it would be named Deja and I would clear every store out of it.

I want to bask in her body, her flavor, her scent, and the sight of her. I didn't know how much I had been missing her until now. I don't wish her grandmother any harm, but there has to be something I can do to get Deja back home with me.

"We need to be quick. The longer ye are here, the greater the risk we're taking," Ken says.

"What brings ye here now? Last I heard, Oland was still up to his old tricks. Deja will for sure be on his radar if he finds out ye've been here.

"Your granda isn't eejit enough to step foot on this land for a hunch or rumors he can't trust. However, mention of ye could change everything he's willing to risk. Our conditions remain the same."

"Uncle Ewan, what are ya talking about?"

"Dinna fash yersel. We mean to keep to our word more than ever. Ye are safe here with us," the one she called Ewan says.

"Ewan, we've said enough," Ken says.

"Ye have said nothing," Deja bites out.

"That is for ye own good. Trust us."

Deja jumps to her feet. "I trust no one but myself. This is starting to feel like a problem. Ye guys have never kept secrets from me. Why now?

"And ya, ya show up and bring trouble with ya. Go back to where ya came from. I don't need ya or want ya here."

I stand and tower over her. She takes a step back and glares up at me. I smile back at her.

"I doubt ya don't want me here. As for needing me, I'm sure ya're wrong about that too. I have a few questions I want to ask yer uncles alone—"

"Fine, ya go on and have at it. I'm leaving," she hisses and shoves by me to leave.

I stumble back a bit, to my surprise. Moving quickly, I grab ahold of her arm and halt her. She turns to glare down at my hand wrapped around her wrist.

"If ya want to remain the owner of that hand, ya will get it off me. I mean it, Cole," she growls.

I hold my hands up in the air, still grinning down at her. I love the fire in her eyes. If I didn't have questions for her uncles, I would follow after her so we can sort this all out.

However, the mention of my granda and Deja's confusion has a number of questions running through my mind. I have no idea what I just walked into, but it's starting to smell and sound like the Alliance.

I grit and bare my teeth as I turn to reclaim my seat. Both uncles are watching me closely. I sit back in my seat as if I own the place.

"What am I missing here?" I ask.

"If ye don't know, it's not our place to tell ye. Where's yer brother? We'll talk to him or the Italian. Preferably yer brother," Ken says.

"Aye, Deja will remain with us until our terms are met or when those who sent her here come for her," Ewan adds.

"We've just learned my brother is being held in an Irish prison thanks to dear oul Oland. The Italian. You're speaking of LaSalle, I take it."

"Aye, that's all we're willing to say to ye," Ewan says.

"Ye should go. Don't come back here. It isn't safe for ye or Deja."

"Ach, I'd like to see who plans to make it unsafe for me. I'll respect your request because of her and only because of her."

"Och, yer not going to listen to a word we say. I can see it in yer eyes. Yer as hotheaded and stubborn as Ian was.

"I hope ye have his heart too. Yer going to need it. Ye've walked right into the lion's den," Ken scoffs.

"Remember, lad. Don't be fooled by Oland when he says he'll never work with anyone who's not Irish. He's not so much against Deja because of what she is. It has more to do with who she is and what that means to all the things he's trying to prevent—"

"*Ewan*," Ken bites out.

"Aye." Ewan nods.

I grind my teeth in frustration. These two seem to have all the answers I need, but they're not willing to share. I have a problem with that, but for now I'll have to suck it up.

Ken looks me over then locks eyes with me as I guess he finds whatever he's looking for. "I will give ye one final warning. Oland has eyes and ears everywhere.

"We McDougals want to keep the peace on our land. Tread lightly when yer around Deja. She's important to this family and Oland will use that in any way he can."

"What does my brother have to do with all of this?" I ask tightly.

"Ye need to wait for him to tell ye. Until our terms are met, none of this is our business. We promised to keep her safe; that's our only task in this until we get answers. Ye should head back to the states," Ken says.

"Och, as if he's going to follow that advice. Look at him," Ewan snorts. "I feel like I'm looking at Ian Black in the flesh. He aims to rock the boat. I have a mind to send the lass away."

"You do that, I will find her," I bite out.

"Aye, we know. Ye should take a step back and think about what yer doing. What happens when ye cause Oland to raise his head?" Ken says, narrowing his eyes at me.

"You sound like you're afraid of the oul bastard. I did some digging. I know who you are. Why not just kill the oul piece of shit and be done with it?"

Ewan snorts. "Ye think we've been who we are by charging into every battle headfirst. Yer a young lad, so I'll give ye a pass.

"I know Ian taught ye better. Every cause has an effect. Removing O'Brien comes with consequences. Ireland remains balanced with him where he is.

"He is feared and with good reason. His replacement has to be as feared and steadfast as he is. Not someone who's all talk, but someone who's going to get the job done.

"Yer da has already expressed he doesn't want to return to handle the job. Yer brother has plans of his own, and from yer words, he's not currently available. Who does that leave?

"Ye? Every family in Ireland and Scotland who's ever wanted to be at the top will become volatile. That's a war many aren't in a position to fight right now, but will find irresistible to deny.

"It's not worth the blood of our people. We chop off his head, all the bullshit that follows rolls downhill. That becomes our problem.

"That affects more than our clan or his. Some things have a bigger answer and solution. Our solution has been discussed. We're doing our part for now."

"You're talking in circles. I see a problem, I handle it. My da is the only reason I haven't handled my granda. He owes me," I snare.

Ewan throws his hands up. "Ye don't understand a thing. Why am I wasting my time? Ye need to go."

"Not before ya tell me where I can find yer nephew's daughter."

Ken narrows his eyes at me. "Aye, ye don't understand what ye have stepped into. Stop asking questions and leave.

"We shouldn't have said this much. We don't know if we can trust ye. Weren't ye the grandson Oland wanted to leave things to?"

I snarl and get to my feet. "You know nothing about me. I would kill that bastard sooner than I would join him. I will not return here if that means Deja remains safe, but I'm not leaving Scotland until she and I have an understanding."

"Then ye be making a mistake. Don't say we didn't warn ye and when ye get her hurt, we'll be the ones ye have to answer to," Ewan snarls.

"So be it."

I storm out, pissed off. I now have more questions than answers. The one thing I do know is that I won't put Deja in danger.

However, it's not an option for me to leave her alone. I need to think through my options and how to move forward with all of this.

The one thing that's been loud and clear is that Deja has been here for her own safety. What that has to do with my brother, I have no idea. It's not like I can get answers with him lost in a prison where we can't contact him.

It's time to do things the Brooklyn way.

Deja

I'm so mad fire could come out of my ears. This is the first time my mother's words about not trusting my uncles have rung true for me. I'm both confused and lost about what I should do next.

I had to come home to clear my head. I begin to play what was said today over in my head and then my mind begins to replay what happened all those years ago to bring me here.

It's been eleven years, but I still have no clear idea of what happened. I'm angry with Cole for showing up and opening all those wounds. I take a breath and begin to play over the things Cole said when he first came here.

Missing?

Why the hell did he think I was missing? Finlay had always known where to find me. As I push into the house where I stay with my great-grandmother, my head hurts from trying to put it all together.

"Deja." *Cough, cough.* "Come here, love. I've missed ye today," my great-gran says between a coughing fit.

I move into the sitting room where she is sitting on the sofa under her favorite blanket. I smile as she looks a bit better today. There is color to her cheeks.

I guess it's best that I now know I can't trust Cole. It doesn't look like I'll be taking off anytime soon. At least not with him.

I enter the room and take a seat on the sofa with her. Gran lifts the blanket and covers me with it as I settle in beside her. I smile and move into her side.

"How are ya, Gran?"

"I've been better. How are ye, Deja?" She cups the side of my face and turns her head to kiss my forehead.

"I'm grand. No need to worry about me."

"Och, but I do. I worry about ye a lot. Especially when yer name comes up from auld friends," she says as she looks at me.

I lift my head and sit up a little. She's looking back at me searchingly. I have no idea who she's talking about.

"Auld friends?" I lift a questioning brow.

"Aye, there's an auld gypsy named Phoebe Romaine. She lives in America now. Years ago, she told me some things I had a hard time believing.

"I wish I would have listened back then. Your da' would still be here and ye would have had the life ye wanted instead of being stuck here with an auld dying woman." Her words are cut off by another coughing fit.

"I'm not stuck here. I love it here with ya."

"That's a load o' mince. Blaeflummery ye speak. Yer a young lass, ye don't date, ye work in that crumby auld pub when ye are smarter than most the people in this village and ye never bring friends around.

"What type of life is this? Ye should be off with a young lad of ye own. I feel like I'm robbing ye of yer life."

"Now that's rubbish. I could date if I wanted to. I just don't want to. Friends are overrated. I love being here to look after ya and soak in yer wisdom," I say with a smile.

"Wisdom," she snorts. "Wisdom would have been holding Archie's head under water until he stopped breathing or telling Lennox to take him out back to put a bullet in his head before the blood of the innocent rained down on our heads."

"Huh?"

"Those were Phoebe's words: '*The blood of the innocent will rain down on your heads*'. Archie was a bad egg. She warned me, but what mother wants to be responsible for taking her own son's life?

"Instead, I'm responsible for the deaths of my two grandsons and the love of my life. I will take that pain to the grave, but I'll tell ye what guilt I can't bear.

"I will not hold ye here with me until my death. Ye will leave me soon and I want ye to know yer supposed to. It will be fine."

"Gran, I'm confused. What are ya talking about?"

"Phoebe has sent a letter. In it, she has told me ye don't belong here anymore. Ah dinnae ken everything she has said, but the one thing that's clear is that ye will be leaving and greater things await ye."

My mind is racing as I try to follow what she's saying. This day is only getting stranger by the second. I think everyone has lost their noodles.

I lick my lips as I think to ask my gran what in the world my uncles were talking about. I have no idea what this old woman could gain from lying to me. I've been good to her.

"Gran, I have a question. Why did my mum send me here? What am I hiding from?"

She smiles and her eyes mist up. "Aye, Phoebe said this would be the beginning. Once ye asked after ye mum, it would all fall into place. The lad who loves ye is already here, isn't he?"

I jerk my head back. My mouth is flapping open and closed. I feel like I've stepped out of my body as an observer at this point.

"I'm not sure I know what yer talking about."

"Aye, ye do. Ye will see. Phoebe says ye have to unlearn a thing or two, but ye will. Ye will have friends and comfort and family.

"Just not here with me. Deja yer journey is coming. Ye have the gift the old man wanted ye to have, now it's time ye use it. *'A mother will be scorned, but the child of the lions will rise to roar.'*"

"What are ya talking about, Gran?"

"Those were her words. Yer mum and da ..." She begins to cough again.

I'm on the edge of my seat to hear what she is about to say. However, after a few moments pass and her coughing spell doesn't, I snap out of it and get her a glass of water. Gran finishes the water and waves me off as she closes her eyes.

I sit beside her once again, staring into space as I replay her words. When her snores begin to fill the room, I sigh. I don't know how to feel about any of this, and I still don't have any answers.

CHAPTER EIGHTEEN

Take His Place

Brooklyn

"Now that I know where Logan is, I'm doing everything I can to get him home. However, that's not being made easy, and I have to be careful," Sam says as we sit in a private room at Club Desire.

"What do ya mean careful?"

"He's in their prison system, lost under someone else's name. How hard do you think it would be to make him disappear for good?"

I ball my fists and grind my teeth. The bullshit seems like it's never-ending. My visit to Scotland yielded me nothing but more hatred for my grandfather.

The digging I did only brought on more questions. Reading between the lines and given the little information I was able to find, I only know that my siblings and our relationships with Deja and Ciara somehow threatened Oland. It's this fucking alliance.

I know it is. If it weren't so important to my granda Ian, I would burn it to the ground myself. However, I do know how important it was to the old man.

"How do we know he's safe in there while ya work to get him out?"

"This is Logan. He'll survive. Besides, I'm working to get my own eyes and ears in there."

I grunt and nod. He's right, Logan isn't going down without a fight. Nine times out of ten, he's walking away while the other party isn't.

"I want to know something, and I want ya to be honest with me, Sam. Oland has something to do with all of this, doesn't he?"

"Did you really need to ask?"

"Ach, not at all."

"Listen, Brooklyn. There are reasons we haven't taken him out. Right now, I need your help. You and I will have to cover for your brother until he's home."

"Aye, I'm already covering for him. I've got ya."

"No, you're taking care of O'Brien business for him. I need you to learn the Alliance business now. You will sit for your brother until his return.

"We can't show weakness at the moment. I know you're up for the task. Can I count on you?"

"Aye."

"Are you sure? Logan's role is a heavy one to bear. Once you see the Alliance from his seat, everything will change. You will have a greater understanding of why this is necessary. Why we are risking everything to make it happen."

"I said I'm ready. I already know enough to want to see this through."

"Good, the first thing you will need to know is the structure. In the Alliance power will run from the head down, but it will cycle in a way that will never topple the infrastructure. To implode the middle is to swell the top," he begins.

I listen closely so that I can represent not only Logan but our granda's memory.

Deja

"What are ya up to?" Blair asks as she peeks over my shoulder.

"Deciding where I would go if I went to America," I mutter.

"So it's true. Yer thinking about leaving us."

I look up from my tablet and search her face. The glum look on her face and sadness in her eyes tugs at my heart. I've known her for as long as I've been here.

She's become a big part of my life. I can only imagine what my presence must mean to her. If not for me, she'd be the only female.

Ewan doesn't go easy on us because we are women, but it can be rough some days to be the female trainees. We've leaned on each other over the years.

I think it has made us both tougher. I know I try to lead by example. On days when I want to give up, I always think of her and keep pushing.

"I'm not leaving ya. Wherever I land, my door is always open to ya. Ewan would kill me for saying this, but ye guys could think about coming with me," I say and wink.

She throws her arms around my neck. "I'm going to miss ye. I've always known things would change. It's just hard knowing that time is actually coming."

I turn to fully face her and wrap my arms around her. I really do wish she and Callum would consider coming along. I would love to have my little family with me. I think we would be great out there together.

"I'm about to head out to the range. Ya want to come?"

"Aye, Ewan's been complaining about my target time." She rolls her eyes.

Blair could pick a room off with her eyes closed. Ewan is just a stickler for perfection. If he had it his way, we would train day and night. In the beginning, we used to. It drove us all crazy.

I go to get up to head out with her, but my phone rings. It's Cole. I've been ignoring his calls since I walked out on him and my uncles.

I bite my lip as my gran's words come back to me. *The lad who loves ye is already here, isn't he?* I don't think I can say Cole loves me, but who else would Gran have been talking about?

I want to trust him, but my mum's warning is ever present in the back of my mind. Releasing a sigh, I hold a finger up.

"Give me a minute, I'll be right out. I need to take this," I say.

"I'll set us up."

"Thanks."

Blair nods and bounces out of the room. I can't help smiling after her. She's always in such a good mood. Ya would never expect how lethal she is.

"Hello," I say as I answer the call.

"Hey, baby. I've been trying to call you for days now."

"Ew, I can hang up, and ya can try again," I tease.

"I'm not in Ireland, so no, I don't sound like I am," he grumbles.

"What's eating yer arse?"

I'm only teasing and he knows that. There's no need for him to sound so frustrated with me. I get up and walk over to the window to look out while I wait for him to speak.

"Ach, yer right. I'm sorry. I just have a lot on my mind, and I miss ya. How are ya, DJ? How's yer gran?"

"She's still alive and kicking if that's what ya want to know."

"I didn't mean it like that. I told ya, I'm not going to rush ya. If there's anything I can do to make her more comfortable or to relieve yer stress, let me know. I'm here for ya."

"Um, there is something ya can do for me."

"Aye. What's that, love?"

"Tell me what me uncles were talking about?"

"Ach, I wish I could, but I still don't understand everything that's going on."

"Someone is lying. I don't know if it's ya or them, but it's a fib I hear, I do."

"Why would I lie to ya? What would be the point in coming to find ya just to lie?"

"I don't know, Cole. That's what I'm trying to figure out. Along with why ya came here for me in the first place."

He scoffs hard. "Un-fucking-believable."

"Excuse me?"

"I came for ya because I'm in love with ya. I love ya, DJ. I'm absolutely crazy about ya.

"If something happened to ya, I would torch the fucking earth because of ya. I came for ya because I wanted to tell ya my feelings years ago, and against my better judgment, I came running to tell ya now," he growls into the phone.

"Against yer better judgment. What's that supposed to mean?"

"I'm getting this sick feeling that I fucked up. First, Logan comes up missing, then yer uncles said what they said and got me to thinking I never should have been there in the first place. I don't think straight when it comes to ya. I never have."

"Where is Logan now? Is he still missing?"

"Ach, we know where he is, but we're having trouble getting him back home."

"What can I do?"

"Yer doing it. I needed to hear yer voice. I'm sorry I started this shit. I … ya belong with me.

"I don't know how to explain it, but I know ya belong with me. I'm going to keep ya safe, I promise," he says.

"I can take care of myself, Cole. Ya would be surprised."

"I can't lose ya again." He pauses as it seems someone else is talking in the background. "Fuck, I have to go. If ya need me, call me."

"Aye, ya do the same. Be safe, Cole."

"Aye, I always am."

"Cole?"

"Aye, love."

"I … I … I love ya too."

"As if ya had a choice. Prince Pádraig had mad game," he teases. "Talk to ya later, baby."

I hang up with a smile on my face. Maybe Gran's friend does know what she's talking about. It looks like New York is where I'll be calling home. Maybe.

CHAPTER NINETEEN

Through the Water

Ken

Two months later …

"It's our best option. Oland is coming for her. He knows O'Brien was here," I bite out in frustration.

I don't like this either, but it's been confirmed. Oland is making moves. His men are probably heading here now.

"Why am I just hearing about this?" Duncan bites out.

"Och, I had a ton of other things going on. It slipped my mind to tell ye."

"Slipped yer mind?" Duncan growls.

"Let him come, I grow tired of him. I think it's time we take a stand," Ewan bites out, ignoring our brother.

"Ye know that's not the way this goes."

"Ye and Mum want to listen to an old gypsy, ye go right ahead."

"Yet ye have been training the twins on her word," I snap. I take a moment to inhale deeply. "It will be better to send her away."

"She's my niece, my prodigy. I know what she's capable of; she doesn't need to run."

"Aye, he's right, Ken. I ken what she can do. I don't think she needs to run. Besides, we're here to cover her," Duncan chimes in.

"Och, and what do ye think she means to me? I ken what the lass is capable of. I ken what ye have done to prepare her, but I also ken Phoebe has never missed in her words. This isn't our fight, not yet. She needs to go with the lad."

"Have ye lost yer mind? Ye met him. He's a hothead."

"So was Ian."

"No, Ian was a calculated savage. That lad showing up here shows he's not like his granda. He doesn't think first."

I open my mouth, but the alarm system goes off. I pop my head up and look at the monitors on the wall that reveal the training grounds.

The screen is flashing red with views of the intruders moving onto our property. My head is ready to explode. Deja and the twins are out there. There isn't enough time for us or anyone else to get out to them.

"Ye have company," Ewan growls.

I know right away he's talking to the kids. They keep comms in during training. I grab the controls for the monitors and pull up a view where we can see Deja and the others on one screen and the intruders on the other.

I then grab a comm to listen in and text for backup. We're of more use here than trying to get to them to help.

"Aye, yer outnumbered," Ewan snarls.

"I can get up top and draw them away. Ye guys can get back to the castle," Callum says.

"And leave ye here alone? Over my dead body," Blair says to her brother.

"We're not leaving. Ya head up top to draw their attention and pick off as many as ya can. Blair, ya take cover and take down anyone who gets by him. The two of ye can push them to me. I'm going for a swim," Deja says, bringing a smile to my face.

"Good thinking," Ewan coaches. "Duncan and a team are en route."

I watch the screen as Callum nods, places his rifle on his back, and turns to climb the tree on his right. Once up in the tree, he settles into place. Deja and Blair move toward the pond a few paces ahead.

"Ugh, my hair, this isn't a wash day. This is going to suck. I'm going to make them pay for this," Deja mutters, causing me to laugh.

Aye, she's going to make them pay and when she's done, I'm going to bring this war right to Oland's door. The balls on him, he sent men here. He has lost his mind.

I lock in on the screen as shots are fired. Oland's men look confused and scatter as Callum begins to pick them off from the treetop with his semi-auto rifle.

Bodies are dropping and they can't move out of the line of fire fast enough. They're not sure where the fire is coming from, so they don't know where to aim or dodge. Their numbers are falling quickly.

A few get by Callum, running away in the direction Blair and Deja went. I know the moment they come into Blair's line of sight. The first one drops to the ground with his head blown open, then the next.

The lass takes out another ten or so. Like a proud papa, Ewan stands with a grin on his face and his arms folded across his chest. Their numbers are almost manageable until help can arrive on the grounds.

A few head to the pond. I assume they aim to cross over to the other side out of the line of fire. I watch with a smirk on my face as the first one tries to carefully wade across to the other side. Another steps in after him, then another.

The first one disappears into the water, causing the other two to freeze and look around frantically. The second one goes under, and I nearly laugh. The third one has no option but to remain in the water as Callum and Blair are boxing them all in on land.

That's when Deja rises out of the water like a phoenix with the look of a warrior on her face as she aims her rifle. My heart nearly bursts with pride as she fills the bastard with holes while she moves through the water to get back to land, where Blair and Callum are still herding the others to their deaths.

"That's my girl. Ye be ready," Ewan croons. He then turns to me. "Tell the lad to come get her."

"Aye." I nod.

I don't mention that I don't need to call the lad myself. Deja will make sure the lad comes running. I have an auld Irish bastard to see.

Brooklyn

"Fuck ya, ya big-headed bastard," I laugh out as I walk through one of the warehouses with my guys.

We're making the rounds today. Last night I went out with them to the club since it was Nakim's birthday. Nakim might not be able to be out here with us, but we're always there for him.

I wouldn't have missed his birthday for the world. Taking him to Club Desire made his night. I think the rest of the guys had a good time too. Even though we're all feeling it today.

We're just getting to the warehouse because we've been dragging our asses. There's no way we should just be here at one in the afternoon.

I'll probably head home after I get things settled around here. There are some shipments I need to check on, and I want to make sure inventory has been done.

"Don't be mad at me for bagging the baddest chick in the place," Emory croons. "I'm going to give her a call when I get home."

I look at him pointedly. One, she wasn't the baddest chick there. Two, I could have bagged her if I wanted.

I wasn't interested. She couldn't hold a candle to DJ. My girl has been on my mind all day. We speak almost every day now since she finally answered my call that day.

I love our talks. It's getting harder to say goodbye. I want to bring her home more than ever.

I haven't missed her questions about life in New York. It's good to know she's getting used to the idea of being here with me. I'll be making that happen as soon as I can.

Things have just been awkward around here with me stepping in for Logan. I don't have the time or the focus to have DJ here. Not like I want.

"Aye, ya have at it," I snort.

"What's been up with you? I haven't seen you with the shorties in months now. You batting for a new team?" Arnez asks, causing Emory to laugh.

"Aye, I've been batting at your mother's tonsils. Team gums and guzzle."

"Oh," Emory croons. "That's foul, killer."

"Not as foul as your breath," I shoot back.

"Ach, I swear ye two walk into it every time," Seán chuckles.

These are my guys. Other than Nakim, they have been my oldest friends. Next to my brothers, I know these three will always have my back.

"Nah, he has a shorty somewhere in hiding. She's either fine as fuck or ugly as a motherfucker."

"When have ya known me to fuck with anything less than a ten?" I scoff.

"You know what? I think Emory is right. He has to have some chick. Anyone else notice the accent standing out in the last four or five months?"

"Aye, Jesus, Mary, Joseph. Yeah, man, I have. Is she back home or something? Is that why we don't know about her?" Seán asks, sounding like he's stumbled onto the answers to some great mystery.

"She's none of your business. Get to work so we can get the fuck out of here," I bark and walk off.

My phone rings as I jog up the stairs to the office. I smile when I see its DJ. A glance at the time makes me furrow my brows.

She should be heading to the pub. The last time we spoke, she said she had to stop at the castle for something and then she would be at the pub. Something must be wrong.

"Hey, baby. Are ya okay?"

"Aye, but no."

"*DJ*, tell me what's going on," I say.

"I don't know why I called ya. Yer there and I'm here. I have it under control."

"Have what under control?" I ask as I turn around and head back down the stairs.

"There were men here at the castle today while we were out training. There were so many of them. I think they were here to kill me," she begins to ramble.

"After what ya told me that day about not coming here, ya were the first person I thought to call. I shouldn't have. I need to get out of here. If they were after me, then I need to go so no one else gets hurt."

"DJ, baby, slow down. Men were there to do what? What happened to them?"

"I took them out. I mean, Blair, Callum, and I took care of most of them before help could come. There were so many of them. If I had been home with Gran … I don't know what I would have done. She could have been hurt."

"*Fuck*," I roar.

The guys come running to see what's going on. I wave them off as I rush out to my car. I need to get to Raven. If this is Oland, like I think it is, I need to make sure my brother's girl is safe.

"DJ, can ya get somewhere safe until I come for ya?"

"I don't know where to go."

"Go to Castle Black. Stay there until I come for ya. Oland is a lot of things, but he's never been crazy enough to step foot on Black ground.

"I'll call Uncle Finlay and tell him yer on the way. I love ya. I'm coming, baby. I promise."

"Okay, be safe, Cole. Don't do anything crazy."

I snort. "That I can't promise."

I hang up and peel out of the lot. I need to get to Long Island, but first I need to pick up some backup. I can only count on family for this.

I get the feeling I should have made this trip weeks ago. There were so many reasons to stay away from Raven. However, now my gut is telling me I need to at least lay eyes on her.

"*Fuck*," I roar.

CHAPTER TWENTY

Pay in Blood

Brooklyn

"I'm going to make this right, Logan," I whisper to the brisk morning air.

My brother has a newborn daughter. Her mother has been killed. However, above all of that is the fact that my so-called grandfather sent a fucking army after my woman.

I had already left the hospital after getting the baby checked out when Ken McDougal called to tell me he wanted me to come for DJ. They don't believe she's safe there anymore.

Why isn't she safe? Oland "Deadman Walking" O'Brien. As long as he's breathing, he's a problem for me. Little did her uncle know, I had already been on my way to my flight to Scotland.

Once he told me that Oland sent over forty men after DJ, I made a course correction. Ireland is where I'm needed. Nothing is going to happen to DJ while she's with my uncle.

However, Oland needs to see me now. I told that bastard no and he's been fucking with me since. First, he had my best friend in America shot, placing him in a wheelchair for the rest of his life, then he made sure Deja was taken away from me, and now this.

Oland must die. If he could send those bastards after a woman and a child, he can answer for his crimes. I won't bother to ask for forgiveness for this. I have no remorse for what I'm about to do.

I'm not asking for permission. I'm not waiting for anyone to tell me it's okay. This motherfucker dies today.

For all the time Deja and I have lost, for my best friend's ability to walk, for my brother's girl, for my niece and the life she almost lost. This morning, I'm the grim reaper and that bastard is at the top of my list. I've come here alone.

The fury running through me wouldn't allow me to call for help. Dylan and the others are with my wee niece, who needs them. My friends never should have been dragged into the middle of this, so here I stand in Dublin, at two a.m. in the morning, across from the gates of the O'Brien manor.

A one-man killing machine, here to collect in blood. My mind keeps going to Raven taking her last breath in my arms. How am I to tell my brother any of this?

"Time's up, ya oul bastard," I mutter before I pull the two pistols with the automatic switches, suppressors, and hundred-round drums.

Oland has done enough shit to keep this place surrounded by men at all times. There are always at least a hundred men on the grounds. If any of them get in my way, they're as good as dead right along with the oul bastard.

I come out of the trees and jog across the road, taking out the two guards at the front gate. Then I shoot the lock panel for the gate and kick the entry open. I move swiftly up the driveway, hugging the shadows of the trees. It's early, so no one is moving this way.

I get to the courtyard before I see anyone else. The front of the house is heavily guarded as if the oul bastard knows I'm coming. It doesn't matter.

I air them all out before they can get off a shot. It's not until I get into the front door of the house that someone other than me fires off a round that could announce my presence.

I don't miss that the inside of the house is more lively than it should be. Men come running out ready to take me out, but I lay them down like a man on a mission.

I move forward to the oul man's study as that seems to be where the action is coming from. Like I said, you would think he knew.

Once to the study, I step through the doors, aiming right for my dear oul granda. One of his guys in the corner of the room pulls his trigger, but misses me. I put a bullet right through his skull.

Jimmy, his counsel, stands beside him with wide eyes. Jimmy isn't muscle so he's unarmed, but I don't underestimate the two. I train a gun on each of them.

"Cole, it doesn't have to come to this. Think about what yer doing," Jimmy says.

"I've thought about it the whole ride here." I seethe.

"This is what it comes down to. Ya come all this way for what?" Oland pauses as he gets this look in his eyes. "The McDougals sent ya, didn't they?"

"No. They didn't have to. I came on my own."

He snorts in disgust. "Ach, me own grandson. Ya would kill me over some nig—"

He doesn't get to finish his words. I empty the clip in my right hand into his chest. I don't know who the fuck he thought he was talking to.

"Aye, I did."

I walk around the desk and kick his dead body to the floor. I snort as I see the chair is useless. I perch on the edge of the desk instead.

"Ya have two choices, Jimmy. I can retire ya right here and now. Or ya can be a good lad and let everyone know I'm here now and this is my clan. Anyone wants to challenge the O'Brien name, they have to go through me.

"Ya do as I say and yer sons and wife will go unharmed. Ya fuck with me and I'll slaughter everything ya love just as I've done here tonight," I say while taking a cigar from the cigar box.

"Cole, I have no quarrel with ya. I just want ya to understand what ya just did. Everyone in Ireland will be gunning for ya now. Head of the clan or not."

"Is that option *A* or *B*, Jimmy? I have a house to have cleaned up and a flight to catch."

He sighs. "Option *B*. I'll start working on the cleanup. Ya took out a lot of good men."

"Not if they were willing to serve him."

"Aye, but—"

"Shut the fuck up, ya disloyal bastard," I snarl as I put a bullet through his head and end his sorry fucking life.

I don't need his counsel. I did what I came to do. It's better not to have any witnesses anyway.

CHAPTER TWENTY-ONE

Take Care of You

Deja

I've been at Castle Black for five days now. I haven't heard from Cole and that's making me nervous. I never should have called him in the first place.

If something has happened to him, I'll never forgive myself. This is my mess. Actually, it's not, and I still don't know whose it is. I have so many questions and no one to answer them.

"Ye know pacing the halls isn't going to bring my nephew here any sooner," Uncle Finlay's voice booms through the hall as I pace back and forth through the second floor.

I stop and turn to find him leaning up against the wall with his shoulder, his arms folded across his chest. Those golden eyes fixed on me.

Finlay Black is a handsome man, but I wouldn't try him. He's likely to knock your head off. I've seen his temper flare.

"I didn't see ya there. Am I making too much noise?"

"Not at all. I came to find ye to see if ye've eaten."

"No, I haven't. Have ya heard from Cole?"

"Not yet. I'm sure he'll turn up soon. The lad has a lot on his plate. Give him time."

"Maybe I should head back home," I murmur.

"Och, not at all. Ye are welcome here. I believe Cole was right in having ye come here."

"Is there anything I can help ya with to keep me mind busy?"

"Come have a sit with me," he says with a smile.

I stand, wringing my hands. It dawns on me this man might be one of the only people who can give me real answers right now. Nodding to myself, I follow him downstairs.

"What's on ye mind, Deja. I can hear the wheels turning," he says as we get to the study, and he sits in front of the chessboard.

I take the seat across from him and think of what I want to ask first. He sets the board for a new match as he waits me out. I don't want to ask the wrong thing and have him shut me down before I can get any answers at all.

"How about this? I will fill in some blanks and ye can go from there," he says with a warm smile as he gestures for me to take the first move.

I make a move and listen as he begins. "Yer mother asked me to bring ye to Scotland to yer great-gran. She didn't tell me where she was going or when she would send for ye.

"I got the feeling she wouldn't be returning to Scotland herself. Yer mum was a special woman. She wanted ye safe."

"From what?" I cut him off.

"There are some bad people out there who would love to hurt yer mum. They would just as soon hurt ye to get to her. Yer great-gran and uncles are powerful people in our world, and they wouldn't allow anything to happen to ye.

"I believe that's why she left ye in their charge. That and Ewan has certain skills that I ken have come in handy for ye," he says.

"All the training."

"Aye."

"What does any of that have to do with Cole? Why didn't he know where to find me? Why did he think I was missing?"

"Ye play a way bigger role than ye ken in something that hasn't been revealed to ye yet. Yer importance to Cole has shaped a lot over the years.

"It was best he didn't know where ye were. He has Da's temperament. Things wouldn't have gone as they should had Cole known where to find ye."

"Okay, say I follow ya and all yer saying. What has changed?"

"A lot. Da's death made a lot of people bold. The plan was coming into alignment. The time was already nearing for him to find ye."

"Does anyone around here give straight answers anymore?"

"Ye will have all the answers ye need when the time is right," he says and smiles. "Checkmate."

I groan and shake my head. I can't focus on the game and deciphering his words. My heart sinks as I think of my next question.

"Is she alive? Will I ever see her again?"

His smile falls. "That I cannot answer for I dinnae ken."

Disappointment fills me and I drop my head. I thought he would be able to answer more. Especially concerning Mum.

"Oh, okay. Do ya mind if I go for a walk?"

"Not at all, love. I'll send for ye if I hear anything from my nephew."

"Thanks."

I stand and move to give him a hug. I don't want to break down in tears, so I pull away quickly and turn to leave. I head down to the lower level to the pool.

For some reason, it feels like I'm more connected to Cole while I'm down here. I smile when I see they didn't change the place from our date. Nothing is lit, but it's all still in place.

I go over to the satin padding and pillows and sit down cross-legged to stare at the sparkling water. My mind goes to the night of that date. Things were so much simpler then.

My only worry had been whether or not I could trust Cole. Now I have men coming to kill me. I get so angry every time I think of it.

It was my first time in real-life combat. If I'm not mistaken, it was for Blair and Callum too. I wish I'd had time to tell them both how proud I was of them.

All I got the chance to do was pack a few things at the cottage and run. I didn't want to stay at Gran's longer than I needed to in case more men were coming. I've been calling to check in on Gran to make sure she's okay.

It sounds like Uncle Duncan is there with her. I don't think she has the strength to head to the castle with him. I'm so frustrated. This isn't how I wanted to leave.

It feels like I'm being forced from my home once again. My head is spinning and I'm getting tired. Taking out my phone, I start some music through Bluetooth.

That seems to settle my nerves a bit. I should probably go back upstairs and finish tending to this hair. I got it washed, oiled, and in Bantu knots, but that's as far as I got.

It's dry, but I'll need to straighten it. With plans to go flat-iron it, I release the knots as I get lost in thought. Once I have all my hair down, I can barely keep my eyes open.

I lie down on the pillows with the thought that I only plan to close my eyes for a few minutes. However, moments later, I can hear myself snoring over the music, but I can't wake myself up.

Brooklyn

"Och, it's good to see ye, nephew," Uncle Finlay says as he pulls me into a tight hug as I enter the castle.

"It's good to see ya too."

I couldn't come straight here after handling Oland. I had to get shit in order. I didn't much care if the oul bastard was buried, but repairs needed to be done to the manor, and I needed everyone to know who is now in charge.

"How are ye holding up? Ye look tired."

"Never better," I snort.

"Och, are ye sure? He was yer granda."

"And?"

He releases a chuckle and slaps my cheek. I haven't lost any sleep over what I've done. Anyone waiting for that will be waiting a long time.

"Don't get me wrong. I know he needed to die. I've wanted to do it myself for years, but ye understand what ye have done, don't ye?"

"Aye, I know exactly what I've done. The Kaseys and O'Donalds have tried me already. I shut that shit down hard and fast," I grumble.

"Och, I'm not surprised. The Kaseys have been vying for power since yer uncle married Cass. Joe marrying the lass and killing off the heads of their family after they targeted Cass and the kids, placed them at the bottom of the barrel."

"Well, after fucking with me, they're now under the barrel," I scoff.

"Things will remain volatile until ye assert yersel as the new Lord. They're not going to lie down and give it to ye."

"Aye, I know. I had to call in reinforcements, but I'll get things under control. I'm not going to leave this to snowball for everyone else.

"Och, I didn't think ye would. Ye were the right one for the task," he says with a smile.

"I thought Uncle Jonah was calling to ask for it. He only wanted to offer to have my back," I say in frustration.

Before I left Ireland, Uncle Jonah reached out to let me know the McGowans have my back if I need it. I wasn't expecting that.

This would be the perfect timing for them to move in and take over. They're family, I wouldn't have put up much of a fight if they wanted it. I had thought Jonah was reaching out to negotiate.

However, he wanted to show his respect. I didn't turn down the offer. What I've done has revealed how much my woman means to me. I now have to protect her and my niece from being used as pawns against me and my brother.

"Och, I wouldn't expect anything less from Jonah or Cianán to tell ye the truth. This has Da written all over it."

I sigh. "Aye, I see that now."

To be honest, thinking of Granda Ian is the only thing that kept me from shouting from the rooftop that I killed the oul motherfucker, and anyone else who wants to challenge me can bring it on. Instead, I'm going to handle this with a clear head.

It's time I begin to play chess and not storm the China shop like I normally would. Logan isn't the only one Granda kept under his wing. I paid attention and learned too.

"Ye did the right thing. Ye have my support whenever ye need it. Have ye spoken with LaSalle?"

"Aye, he says things will change with the Alliance for me again. I now get my very own seat at the table, not just the title of my brother's right hand. I've become a different kind of captain.

"One with say and rank. As I understood it before, I would go back to being silent once Logan returned," I answer.

That option is now long gone. I'm not sure how I feel about that. I'm not complaining. I just haven't wrapped my head around any of it.

What a fucking mess I have on my hands. It took all of a day—if that long—for word to get out and those motherfuckers to come to challenge me. I don't much care about that. However, I do realize the magnitude of the target I've placed on my back.

Ireland is indeed now unstable. I've seen firsthand what the McDougal brothers meant. I can't leave things and go back home like nothing is happening. I'm now an Irish lord and I have to enforce my power there.

"It will all work out, lad. Ye can handle it. She's downstairs.

"I won't hold ye up any longer. Ye have a good night and get some rest. Dinnae fash yersel while ye're here."

With that, he pats my shoulder and walks off. My mother's brothers love her and will do anything to protect her and her kids. I never had a doubt about whether or not I would be safe here.

Exhausted, I take a deep breath and head for the stairs that will lead me down to the pool area, where I'm sure I'll find DJ. As I jog down the steps, the sound of low-playing music floats up to me.

When I get to the pool area, I smile as I find her fast asleep on the makeshift bed from our date. I told the staff to leave the place like this before I left. Uncle Finlay doesn't come down here much.

I had a feeling I would be able to bring DJ back sometime soon. Granda left this place to me and my siblings. Logan will have the run of the place for the most part, but it belongs to all of us.

Uncle Finlay is sort of a keeper for now. My mind goes to the O'Brien Manor. Connie and Nakim are there holding things down for me for now. No one is going to fuck with my sister and live to breathe about it.

Nakim might be in a wheelchair, but his mind is still sharp. He has a knack for building structure. Besides, I know him living in the manor and helping me to get things settled would be an extra fuck you to Oland.

I would say it would cause him to roll in his grave, but by now those hogs should be shitting his ass out. I didn't have enough respect for him to bury him in a proper grave. Besides, it was satisfying to chop his ass up then toss him in the pen for chow time.

"So much shit to do," I mutter to myself.

Kate will arrive in Ireland with Shauna in a few days, but they won't be going to the manor. I don't want anyone getting wind of my niece just yet.

As exhausted as I am already, I'm not going to fail her or DJ. Looking down at DJ, I can't help but think about all the things this changes for us. I want answers before I throw her into the fire in America.

I can't ignore the fact that she's been here in Scotland for a reason. My gut is telling me Oland wasn't the only reason. However, she gets so angry anytime I ask about her mum. I fear that something else was going on when DJ was sent here.

"For now, I will keep ya hidden," I murmur to myself.

She looks so adorable in her sleep. I kick off my shoes and pull off my socks, then lower to sit beside her. As I stare down at her, I push a lock of hair from her face.

The thick, dark locks are lying around her head like lush cotton. Her bangs have curled up into springy spirals.

As she sleeps, I think about our future and the things I want for us. I want to buy her a house in New York or a luxury apartment. We'll get married and have kids.

Once I get things settled in Ireland and Logan is home, we'll be able to live our lives in New York without having to worry about a thing. We can have it all.

My mind goes back to when I thought she would be coming to New York the first time. I had been so close to kissing her that night. The alcohol coursing through me had me not giving a fuck. She was mine then and I thought she would be with me soon.

I reach for my phone to change the music to my phone and pull up the song that has stayed with me all these years. "Addicted" begins to float through the speakers.

I put my phone down and lie next to her, not able to take my eyes off her gorgeous face. I only keep my hands to myself because I don't want to wake her. I'm just going to lie here and sleep off some of this exhaustion.

I close my eyes as the music plays. I'm close to drifting off when I feel her soft hand on my face. I open my lids and our gazes lock.

She gives me a smile as she searches my face with her soft brown eyes. Instantly, I reach for her waist and tug her into me. I take her lips in a passionate kiss and devour her.

She cups my face and whimpers into my mouth. I allow my hand to roam her back as we get deeper into the kiss. I break the seal of our lips and look into her eyes when she begins to unfasten the buttons on my shirt.

She's biting her lip and looking back at me with so much lust. I brush her hair back from her face and take her lips again, this time in a more all-consuming kiss. When she finishes with the buttons on my shirt, she sticks her hands inside to run them over my torso and chest.

"Cole," she moans as I move my lips to her neck and run my hand over her soft skin.

I push the strap of her thin tank top down her arm and continue to kiss my way down to her breasts. Once her nipple is exposed, I pull it into my mouth. She cries out and bucks into the air, her voice echoing through the cavern-like space.

I pull away and shake my head clear. "Maybe we should head upstairs."

"No. I mean, do ya think anyone will come down here?"

"Ach, I can't say, but I don't think so."

"Then I want to be here. I want this to be the time and place," she whispers.

"Are ya sure? I can light a few candles in my bedroom."

"This place is perfect. Come here, Cole. I want ya."

I don't think twice. I move in and capture her lips with mine. As I drink from her mouth, I shove my hand into her leggings. I find the fabric of her panties wet and her pussy soaked.

"Please, Cole," she whimpers into my mouth.

I've been wanting to push my fingers into this tight pussy again for months. I love the way she rides my hand and tightens those thick thighs around me.

I return to sucking her peak into my mouth as she moans and begs for more. I can feel her about to come already. Once I begin to move my fingers in a come-hither motion, she explodes, crying out my name.

Pulling my hand from her pants, I then bring my fingers to my lips and suck them clean. Her juices are like candy to me. I can't get enough.

She sits up and reaches to push my shirt off my shoulders. I shrug out of the shirt and let it fall to the floor. DJ then reaches for my belt and releases it.

I pull my wallet and toss it beside my phone. I'll need that in a bit. I look her in the eyes as she bites her lip while pulling down my zipper.

A grin comes to her face, and she lifts a brow when she sees I'm not wearing any underwear. I spring free from my slacks, and her eyes grow wide before a full smile hits her face.

I chuckle and grasp her throat as I lean and take her lips. As I kiss her deeply, I kick my pants the rest of the way off. Then I reach for her leggings and peel them down her legs.

She reaches for her top to pull it up over her head. I can't even stifle the groan that leaves my lips. She's beautiful from head to toe.

I lick my lips and reach to stroke myself. In the back of my mind, I chant a reminder that I need to take my time. Kissing my way down her body, I then take my time planting kisses over the waistband of her panties.

She locks her fingers into my hair as she moans. I chuckle as she begins to push my head lower. Slowly, I peel her panties down and toss them aside before settling onto my belly.

Instead of going right for her core, as I know she wants me to, I turn my head and begin to feast on her inner thigh. I lick then suck the skin into my mouth.

"Cole, please. I need—"

She gasps and doesn't finish her words as I push two fingers into her tight pussy. I pump them in and out as I continue to suck on her thigh, leaving my mark.

Pulling away, I stare at her dark skin as my love bite blooms on her flesh. She whimpers under my touch as her juices grow increasingly loud, causing me to look at her wet center.

I lick my lips in anticipation and then dive in for a taste. I hum as her flavor hits my tongue. My mouth is watering for more.

I don't deny her or myself. Removing my fingers, I dive in with my tongue. My groans and her moans of pleasure begin to blend together.

I keep feasting until a shrieking like sound comes from her lips. I look up her body and find her looking back at me in awe. I narrow my eyes at her as I begin to rub at her pussy. Just as I thought, she begins to squirt.

"*Fuck*," I hiss.

Reaching for my wallet, I pull out a condom and bite into it. She lies watching me with a drunken smile on her lips. With the condom in place, I hover over her and take her lips in a searing kiss.

DJ runs her hands over my skin as she kisses me back. I guide my way to her pussy lips and tease her as I run my length back and forth through her slit, making sure not to enter just yet.

Her pussy heat is enticing me to push in, but I restrain myself from doing so. I want her dizzy with want by the time I enter her for the first time.

"Cole, please. I want ya so much. Please," she begs, breaking my restraint.

I push down on my tip and begin to move into her. She bites down on her lower lip as she looks up into my eyes. The feel of her tight heat pulling me in is like heaven.

I rock my hips gently a few times, testing her resistance. I'm not going to break through like this, and I can see the discomfort on her face. I grunt in frustration.

"I'm sorry, baby. This is going to hurt," I breathe.

She pulls my head to her and kisses me hard. As our tongues dance together, I hook my arms under her thighs and thrust into her with a bit more force this time.

She cries out into my mouth as I break through, and her pussy opens for me. Damn, she feels so fucking good. As I work my hips into her, I have one thought.

This pussy is mine.

Deja

Oh my God, he's so thick and I'm not just talking about his dick. His body on top of mine feels so warm and big. He's filling me up so much and the weight of him is only turning me on more.

"Cole," I moan as I close my eyes and throw my head back.

"Look at me," he growls.

I pop my eyes back open and look into his green ones. The look in his eyes has my juices flowing even more. This intense sensation fills my belly and my toes curl. He tightens his hold on my thighs as he thrusts down into me.

It feels like he's dancing in my pussy as he bounces his hips, moving in and out of me. It feels so damn good. He slips out and that intense feeling pops as my legs begin to shake.

I look down as he does and see I'm spraying all over him. He looks back up at me with a smile and rubs my juices all over his torso. Then he taps his length against my pussy and pushes back in.

"Oh yes, yes," I cry as he continues to rock into me.

"This pussy is better than I thought it would be. Ya have me so hard right now. Are ya okay, love? Is it too much?"

I lock my ankles over his ass as I shake my head no. Too much? Maybe, but I'm not telling him that. I don't want him to stop.

"Please, Cole. Don't stop. I'm fine. I just want ya."

He kisses me hard. "Ya have me. Ya always have me. I love ya."

I reach for his hair and grab a handful as I kiss him with as much passion as he's giving me. Licking his lips, I taste myself on his mouth. He takes over the kiss and bites my lower lip as he gets so deep in my guts he takes my breath away.

I didn't know he could go that far, but the more I breathe and relax, the deeper I feel him go. He lifts up and sits back on his heels, not pulling from my body. I bow my back, pushing my breasts in the air as I feel him rocking into me.

Cole looks back at me with so much lust on his face. Reaching between my legs, he rubs his thumb against my clit. My eyes roll back and I start to convulse.

He stops massaging my clit to run his hand up the center of my body, moving his hand to my breast. He squeezes the mound, then pinches my nipple, sending me into another spiral. My heart is beating so fast. The sound of my juices squirting all over him fills the air again.

However, this time, instead of pushing back into me, he drops down on his belly to feast on me once again. All I can do is clinch the satin beneath me into my hands and hold on for dear life.

My mind is blown. I don't think I will ever be the same. When I come again and he lifts to thrust back into me while kissing me passionately, I know for sure I've changed for life.

As he continues to make my body his, I give myself over to him, mind, body, and soul. Every time he presses his sweaty forehead to mine, I feel more connected to him. Each kiss is an exchange of our souls.

I don't know what I was expecting, but this wasn't it at all. I think I've found something I love more than swinging a baseball bat. Riding one.

CHAPTER TWENTY-TWO

Leaving Scotland

Deja

Cole kisses my shoulder as we lie in bed up in his room at the Black Castle. Last night was amazing. I can still feel him inside me this morning.

If I had to do it all over again, I would still wait for him. I don't regret not having an active love life before Cole. He tightens his arms around me as he nuzzles my neck.

I don't believe either of us has slept much all night. I feel so safe in his arms now that he's here. I'm so happy this morning, I could burst.

"When will we leave for New York?" I ask happily.

"Leave for New York? What about yer gran?"

"I don't want to go back there and bring any more drama. She could have been hurt if they had come to the cottage and not the castle."

I still don't mention my training to him or how I helped to kill all those men. I'm not sure if I want him to know that. I'm not sure how he will react to that information.

"About that. I've caught you mentioning training. What happened when Oland's men arrived?"

I sigh. "Since you insist on sounding like an American, I guess I should work on losing my accent too. I've practiced over the years while watching American shows, you know," I tease.

"Not bad, now answer my question," he snorts and kisses my temple.

I release another heavy breath. I don't know why, but I have this deep feeling I shouldn't tell him what I'm truly capable of. It's a part of who I am and I'm not going to stop training once we get to America.

"I run a pub. I like to stay fit. Big lads come in all the time. A girl has to protect herself."

"You're still singing," he murmurs into my ear.

"Huh?"

"We Irish sing. Our words dance when we speak. New Yorkers' words are spoken hard and with confidence. Take the song out of your speech."

"Oh, I think I know what you mean. How about this? Is this better? When do we leave? Will we live close to Kate?"

"Fuck, baby, we're not going to New York. Not yet," he says in frustration.

I turn in his embrace to look up at him. His face looks as frustrated as his words sound. I'm confused.

"Gran says she wants me to go. She doesn't want me to wait around for her to die. Why don't you want me to come to America?"

He kisses me hard. "I never said I don't want ya to come to New York. I said we aren't going there yet."

"Why not?"

"I killed Oland, DJ. Someone has to take over in his absence. That's me. However, there are plenty of people who would love for that to be them.

"What I did was impulsive and revealed how much you mean to me. People know what Oland did and I responded immediately. The underworld talks.

"Now, everyone knows to hurt me, they only have to come after ya. Until I establish myself in Ireland, I have to keep ya hidden. I'm not going to chance bringing ya to Dublin, and I can't send ya to New York where I don't know what threats are hiding in wait."

"Then I'll go live with my uncles."

"No, no, ya won't. Ya will be with me. When I can't be there, I have people I trust to watch over ya where I plan to put ya," he says sternly.

"Put me? Put me? Cole, what the hell?"

"Now that was dead on," he chuckles and pecks my lips. "Might make a New Yorker out of ya yet."

I roll my eyes. He rolls onto his back and tugs me down on top of his chest. Then he begins to rub my back soothingly.

"I'm only trying to keep ya safe. I have a place for ya to live that I can trust. It will be our home until I can take ya home to New York.

"I'll have to spend time in Dublin at the manor, but ya will be secure at the safe house where I plan for ya to be. Trust me, DJ. All I have done has been for ya," he says.

"I'm starting to feel like a caged bird. I learned a few useful skills in my last cage. I hope you plan to teach me something too," I mumble.

He reaches for my bum and squeezes it. Then he places his fingers under my chin and lifts my head. We search each other's eyes for a beat.

Cole leans in and takes my lips. It's a hungry kiss that gets my juices flowing like this man didn't spend the night fucking me senseless. My bits begin to pulse as if looking for him.

"Aye, I have something I plan to teach ya. Can ya handle another lesson before I make ya breakfast?"

"Maybe," I say with a cheeky smile.

"Maybe I should just go down to make breakfast."

"Shut up, Cole, and come shag me," I say as I reach to wrap my hand around him.

He's already hard as steel. I love the feel of him in my hand. Knowing he's this hard because of me fills me with something I haven't put a name to yet.

He groans, then pushes me onto my back and pounces. I'm a bit disappointed about not going to New York, but at least we will be together. I couldn't be happier about that.

Brooklyn

"No. Come on. Use yer noodle. It isn't safe for them to live anywhere near each other," I sigh into the phone at my sister.

I get it. Kate wants her best friend back. In her mind, I should place Shauna and DJ in the same place so she can be there with them both. That's not smart.

Besides, I don't plan to tell DJ about Shauna yet. I can't risk someone getting ahold of her and torturing the information from her. The less she knows the better.

"Fine, I have a nice place in Cork. I'm going to meet with Aisling when I get to Ireland. I think I can trust her, and the money won't hurt," Kate says.

"I need ya to know, Kate. Not think, know," I bite out.

"I understand how important this is, Brooklyn. I'm not trying to place my niece in danger. Stop biting my head off."

I roll my eyes as my nostrils flare. Kate only calls me Brooklyn when she's annoyed with how bossy I am. This is important.

I need her to take everything seriously. We don't have room for error. Logan has lost enough.

"Can I at least speak to her?"

"Ach. Are ya sure yer not going to slip?"

"Ugh, fine. I can't wait until all of this is over. She's my best friend, I miss her. I lost her too, Cole."

"I know, love. I'm not trying to be a dick. I'm just trying to keep them safe."

"I get it. I heard ya have five guys on Con and me at all times when we're with the wee one. So unnecessary, but I get it."

"Unnecessary to who? Ya both mean the world to me. Granda would have done the same even after all— Hey, I need to go. Talk to ya later. Call me if ya need me," I say quickly as DJ enters the room.

"Hey, ya really made me breakfast?" she says with a smile on her lips.

"Yer stomach was talkin' in yer sleep. I couldn't leave ya like that. I was just about to come to wake ya."

I place the two plates down on the countertop, then open my arms for her to come to me. She's wearing my shirt from last night. It's swallowing her, but she looks sexy as hell in it.

I wrap my arms around her and dip my head to take her lips. The memories of this morning and last night have me hard all over again. I've never been like this for anyone else.

"How are ya feeling?" I ask as I break the kiss.

"I'm grand. Yer right though, I am hungry."

"Ach, come eat."

I take her hand and lead her to take a seat. I can't keep my hands off her. When I release her hand, I reach for her neck and massage it as I sit beside her. She begins to eat, and I place my hand on her back to rub it up and down.

DJ looks at me with a smile and reaches to place her hand on my thigh. I smile back and tuck into my own plate. This feels so natural, like we've done it a million times before.

"Who were ya talking to? Was that Kate?" she asks, breaking the silence.

I nearly choke on the food I just shoveled into my mouth. I punch at my chest, then reach for my glass of water. I don't want to lie to her, but telling her I was on the phone with Kate could lead to questions.

Questions like when she can see my sister? Logan should be home soon now that we know where he is and LaSalle is working to get him out. I only have to keep DJ and Shauna hidden until he's back home.

"No, that was Dylan," I mutter, the lie tasting like shit in my mouth.

However, she's less likely to care about talking to my younger brother. My stomach sours, and I no longer have an appetite. LaSalle needs to get Logan home soon.

"Oh, he must be so grown up now. Did he ever hit that growth spurt?"

I relax and smile. "Aye, he did. The lad is taller than me."

"No, ya tell a fib."

"I don't. He's taller than us all."

"He was such a cute kid. That seems like a lifetime ago."

"Aye, it does. We don't leave until the morning. What do ya want to do today? We can do anything ya want. A date, stay in and chill, whatever ya like," I say as I try to change the topic.

Right as the words are out of my mouth, Uncle Finlay and Morgan, one of the castle hands, walk in with the flowers I ordered for DJ. Four dozen burgundy and white roses. Two dozen in each vase.

"These just came for the lady," Uncle Finlay croons with a smile.

"For me?" DJ says then looks over at me.

"Aye, for ya," I say and wink.

The beaming smile that comes to her face warms my heart. She lifts from her seat to lean in and sniff them. I place a hand on her back to keep my shirt she's wearing from rising too high.

"I'm heading out for a bit. Do ye need anything before I go?" Uncle Finlay asks.

"No, I'm all good. Thanks."

He nods and turns to leave. DJ turns to me with that bright smile on her face. I lean in and peck her lips.

"What's on yer mind?"

"Why burgundy and white?"

"The burgundy roses represent deep passion, intense love, and romantic devotion, if I remember right. The white ones represent innocence, purity, and new beginnings.

"I deeply love ya and I have so much respect for the gift ya gave me last night. I wanted ya to know how I feel and give ya one last reminder of yer innocence before I truly ruin ya," I reply.

She laughs and leans in to kiss me. I cup the side of her face and kiss her passionately. She moans into my mouth and pulls away, still smiling.

"Thank ya. That's actually really sweet. Although I think I might be the one who's going to ruin ya."

I snort. "How so?"

"I know what yer capable of now. I plan to have my fill of ya whenever I can."

I laugh. "Careful what ya ask for. I've been taking it easy on ya. Ya have no idea what I'm capable of, love."

"Um, sounds good. I want to go to the pictures. Is that on the table?"

"Aye, a movie it is."

CHAPTER TWENTY-THREE

Life is Grand

Brooklyn

Eight months later …

"Aw, love. Shh … me wee, lass. Ya have to stop the tears. I can't bear to leave ya like this," I coo as I bounce Shauna in my arms.

I'm here for my weekly check-in. I just landed in Ireland from New York. I've been needed there as much as I've been needed here lately.

Felix has moved Kaye back to Cali, so that's one less thing on my plate, but it seems ten others have been added in her place. If I'm in Ireland, I check in with Shauna at least once a week.

At eight months old, my niece is a cute little thing. Her tiny fingers are so adorable, and she has the sweetest smile.

Every time I'm here, I think of what my babies with DJ will look like. We've been going strong and my love for her is only getting stronger. I'm trying to leave now so I can get to her.

"Ya can go, I've got her," Aisling says as she takes Shauna from my arms.

Shauna gives me that little face that asks where I'm going and why aren't I holding her still. It breaks my heart. I wish I had more time today, but I've been away for too long.

DJ needs time as much as Shauna does. I thought Logan would be back by now, but he's not. I'm growing irritated with how long it's taking for them to release him.

They have nothing to hold him on. He shouldn't be there in the first place. Each day he's there, he's missing out on a day of this wee one's life. Another day that he doesn't know she exists.

I'm tired of all the lying. Which is why I have a big surprise for DJ tonight. It's our anniversary and I'm growing tired of feeling like I need to hide her away.

I've rented out a club in Belfast to throw a party. It's by invitation only. All my guests are flying in by helicopter, including DJ and me, after I take her to dinner.

However, first, I need to fly to London, where our home is. I haven't been able to move her to Ireland yet. Things are still volatile here.

"Thanks, Aisling. She hasn't been giving ya any trouble, has she?"

"Not at all, she's the sweetest babe ever," she says while smiling at me.

Aisling takes good care of Shauna, but I still think Kate could have found a better option. This one eye fucks me whenever she sees me. Aisling is a pretty woman, but I'm not interested.

"How do I look?" Kate says as she comes out dressed in a tight black dress.

She looks like a supermodel. Both of my sisters are gorgeous. Kate is the taller of the two, with her long, dark hair and green eyes. I'll have my guys keep an eye on her tonight.

Kate has been here with Aisling to protect my niece if anyone were to stumble upon her existence. Connie should be here soon to help out for a bit. She was just in California with Dylan for Felix's proposal party.

I have to give the lad a call. I heard things didn't go as he planned. I was sorry to hear that.

"Ya look gorgeous. Seán is downstairs, he's going to ride to Belfast with ya."

"Oh, I get the big security," Kate coos and shimmies her shoulders.

I chuckle and shake my head. She comes over and begins fussing with the lapels of my suit jacket.

"Ya look handsome, yerself."

"Thanks. I try."

"Ya don't have to try much," Aisling says with a goofy smile on her face.

I don't reply. Instead, I walk over and place a hand on Shauna's back before I kiss the top of her head. She turns to look over her shoulder and begins to blow bubbles at me.

"So adorable. I'll see ya soon, love. Ya be good," I say, earning me a gummy smile.

"Ye guys have fun. I wish I could go," Aisling says as she looks me over from head to toe.

I fight not to roll my eyes as I turn to leave. As I walk out, I nod my head for Kate to follow me. Once we're out the door, I look back to make sure we're not followed.

"Ya know ya could have found someone who doesn't want to fuck me to do the job, right?"

"I chose her for exactly that reason. Her obsession with ya makes her willing to give her left tit to please ya. She'd die sooner than disappoint ya."

I make a sour face. I don't want her left or her right tit. What I want is for her to take care of my niece and make sure no one makes the connection to who she is. Aisling can move about with the babe and not need to look over her shoulder.

"Bad idea, Kate. She doesn't know anything about tonight, does she?"

"No, I'm not crazy and neither is she. If she hurts Shauna, ya won't get a chance to make her pay for it. She'd already be earth salt under my boot."

"Hopefully this won't be for much longer."

"LaSalle offered to take her in. Do ya think she would be safer with him?"

"Ach, maybe, but she's our charge. Our blood."

"I hear ya. I was only thinking. I would go with her. She wouldn't be a burden. I would—"

"Kate, Logan is already going to be furious with us. LaSalle has enough on his plate, and he needs to remain neutral when Logan finds out."

"Okay, yer right."

I turn to kiss my sister on the cheek before she climbs into the waiting car. Once she's in the car, I tap the roof. The driver pulls off, and I go to climb into my own vehicle to get to the chopper that's taking me home to DJ.

I miss her and can't wait to see her. I hope tonight makes up for some of the bullshit I'm putting her through. I can tell she's beginning to get frustrated.

"I'm coming, baby. Tonight is all about you," I murmur as I press my foot on the gas.

Deja

"Don't hurt 'em, love," I say to my reflection as I look myself over one last time.

I can't stop smiling. Cole is on his way back to London. I knew he would be back tonight, but what I wasn't expecting was for him to send a dress to the house for me and a note to tell me to be ready for a date when he arrives.

I've been so excited. I showered and did my hair and now I'm standing here in the bluish-gray dress he sent for me. It's sexy but classy.

It's a halter dress. My back is bare down to my waist. Cole loves the tat down my spine, although I've never told him what the Japanese letters mean.

He's asked, but I've told him I'll tell him someday. For now, it's my secret. I'm sure when he picked this dress, he chose the bare back so the tat would be on display.

As I'm sure the slits up the thighs were meant for his pleasure. I turn to the side and smile wide as I look down at the sexy clear stripper-looking heels on my feet, which I already had.

I can't wait to see Cole's face when he gets a look at them. The shoes that came with the dress were cute, but this looks better to me. I'm sure he'll agree when he gets here.

Speaking of which, the alarm system lets me know he's arrived. I turn and head for the front door. When I get halfway there, I stop in my tracks. Cole wears anything he puts on well, but tonight he looks amazing in a suit that matches my dress and a pair of shiny black full brogues.

He's not wearing a tie, and the top three buttons of his shirt are open. I bite my lip as I look the big lad over, knowing what those powerful thighs under that suit are capable of. The fit of the jacket is chef's kiss and the waistcoat beneath is his signature stamp on the perfection that is Cole O'Brien. He looks damn good.

"Are you just going to stare at me, or are you going to come kiss me?"

"I don't know. I think ya were gone too long," I say and give him a sideward glance.

"Get yer sexy arse over here," he growls, his accent proper this time.

I laugh and rush into his arms. He cups my face between his palms and kisses me like a man starved. At first, I think he's going to take things further, but he breaks the kiss and pecks my forehead before he places his forehead to mine.

"Happy anniversary, love. God, I've missed ya. We should go. We have a tight schedule."

"Yeah? Where are ya taking me?"

"It's a surprise. Ya look great by the way. It's going to be torture trying to keep my hands off ya."

"Let's hope whatever ya have planned doesn't keep yer hands off me for too long," I say and smile at him.

He gives a slight chuckle and shakes his head. "I've created a monster, I have."

"Ya love this monster."

"Aye, I do."

He holds my head between his palms and pecks my lips. I pout when it's only a quick kiss. Taking my hand, he then leads me out to the car and opens the door to help me in.

I'm so excited I feel like I'm going to burst. I sit in the passenger's seat and chat his head off as he drives. He doesn't seem to mind.

He never does. Cole is always willing to listen to me and my rambling. He never makes me feel like I'm talking too much or as if he's not listening.

In fact, I know he's listening because he will bring things up days later and he always knows all the details. I've been falling deeper and deeper in love with him.

When he pulls up in front of a restaurant and the valet comes to open my door for me, I think I fall in love with him all over again. We don't go out much. Maybe I should say we don't go out together much.

Cole is always on the move. I, on the other hand, sometimes go out to handle little personal things. It wasn't like that in the beginning. He's been easing up a lot.

This … a date at a real restaurant shows he understands I'm growing tired of being in that house all by myself all the time. Don't get me wrong. It's a gorgeous house.

I have everything I could need and want, but I get so lonely there. I didn't know we would be here in London for this long.

"Come on, our table is waiting," Cole says as he places a hand on my back to lead me inside.

I look up at him and smile. His warm hand against my skin causes my stomach to flip and butterflies to take flight. I can't wait to get him out of that suit later.

He drops his hand lower to rest on my bum. I move in close to his side and rest my head against him. I don't get a chance to settle in as we're taken right to our table.

I'm impressed. This place is nice. I smile when Cole orders a bottle of wine and then proceeds to order for me.

He has come to know me so well. I can't believe we've been dating for a year now. Well, if you ask him, I've belonged to him way longer than that.

Honestly, there's no point in arguing with him. Cole O'Brien gets what he wants. I still can't believe that all this time that has been me.

"What are ya smiling about?" he asks over the rim of his glass.

I've finished my meal, but I'm not ready for the night to end and I don't want to go back home yet. I'm enjoying being out and about. I can't stop smiling because I have the best boyfriend ever.

"Nothing. This is nice. I've missed ya."

"I've missed ya too." He looks down at his watch. "Would ya like dessert? If ya do, we should order it now. We need to get to our next stop soon."

"There's more?"

"Aye, there is."

I bite my lip in indecision. The chocolate mousse that went by looked delicious, but I'm excited to know what's next. Cole laughs and lifts his hand to call for our waiter.

"She'd like the chocolate mousse with the raspberries on top and you can bring the check, please."

"Aye. Can I get anything else for ya, sir?"

"No, I'm fine."

The waiter nods and turns to leave. I look at Cole and tilt my head to the side. He looks back at me, amused.

"What?" he murmurs.

"Ya think ya know me so well."

"Aye, I do."

"How did ya know I wanted chocolate mousse?"

"I heard ya when ya saw it earlier. *Oh, that looks grand. I love chocolate mousse*," he mocks.

"I don't sound anything like that. And ya should mind yer own business. I was talking to myself."

"If yer man isn't listening to ya, ya need to let him go. I'm never going to give ya a reason to free me."

"What if I get tired of ya?"

"Never, what is there to get tired of? I keep ya wet and coming, I give ya everything ya want and need, and I love ya."

"Maybe."

"*Maybe*," he mocks with a smile on his lips.

"Whatever, Cole," I laugh and roll my eyes.

CHAPTER TWENTY-FOUR

Old Friends

Deja

He has done it again. Just when I didn't think it was possible to fall in love with him anymore, he goes and has a helicopter fly us to Belfast.

My cheeks are hurting from smiling so much as we ride in the chopper. Cole places his hand into the split in my dress and rests it on my upper thigh. I look at him and stare into his green eyes as I catch him watching me closely.

"What are we going to do when we get there?" I ask.

He smiles and shakes his head. I poke my tongue out at him, causing him to laugh. His voice rumbles through the headphones in answer.

"Go on, keep yer secrets. We'll see how far that gets ya."

Something crosses his face quickly. The next thing I know, my back is pressed to the cool window behind me and he's devouring my lips. I tangle my fingers in his hair and open for him.

When he pulls away, both our chests are heaving. I don't know where that came from, but … wow. He sits back in his seat and tugs at his jacket, then fixes the rest of his clothes.

I clear my throat and place a hand on my belly. My mind drifts as I wonder what that was about. Soon, we begin our descent.

I shake my thoughts off, not wanting anything to ruin this night. Cole is a passionate lover. That's all.

We exit the bird, and he takes my hand to lead me to the waiting car. Excitement fills me all over again. As we settle into the back of the car, Cole pulls out his mobile and shoots off a text before placing the device back in the inside pocket of his suit jacket.

I don't miss the gun holstered on the inside of his suit. It's not the first time I've seen him wear one. If I'm right, there's a second one on the other side and one at his ankle.

The reality of who he is is always there. Cole has killed for me. His own grandfather.

My earlier thoughts become silly as that reality comes back to me. This man loves me and he's doing all this for our anniversary.

"This is all so exciting. I wasn't expecting any of this. Thanks, Cole," I sing excitedly as I come out of my thoughts.

"Ya haven't seen anything yet."

"How can ya top all ya have already done?"

"Ya will see," he says with a huge smile.

I move to scoot closer to place my head on his arm and wrap my arms around him. He wraps me in his embrace and holds me close. However, I don't get a chance to get too comfortable.

The car stops in front of a club. I look to Cole with wide eyes. I love music and I love to dance. I can't believe he's taking me dancing for our anniversary. The door opens and he steps out. Then he holds his hand out for me. I place my hand in his, feeling like a princess being taken to the ball. Once out of the car, we head for the entrance of the club.

I stumble to a stop when a tall brunette in high heels and a black dress comes running out of the club. I stop and turn to look up at Cole, then I release his hand.

It takes a moment, but when I see her smile and her green eyes, I know it's Kate. I rush into her arms and wrap mine around her. We squeeze each other tight.

"Deja," she squeals as she rocks me from side to side. "It's so good to see ya, love."

We begin to bounce on our toes as we hug and squeal like we're still teens. I tear up and squeeze tighter. So many emotions fill me. I can't believe Cole.

This is the best anniversary gift ever. I had been asking a ton of questions about Kate before he left for New York. Now she's here.

I couldn't love the man more. I feel bad for thinking he was up to something nefarious after that kiss. I'm so happy right now.

"Oh my God, Kate. Ya look good. I've missed ya so much."

"You missed me? My heart was broken when we came home, and you were gone. I didn't know what happened. Da said he didn't know anything. You went with your mom or something," Kate says as tears flow down her cheeks.

I jerk my head back, her da was right there when Uncle Finlay picked me up. I don't get a chance to say a word as Cole comes to move us along to head inside. From the tension in his body, I know he wants us out of the open.

Brooklyn

"Everything is ready in the VIP," Seán leans in to whisper in my ear.

I nod as I keep moving behind DJ and Kate. The smile that has lit up DJ's face since we arrived at the helicopter has my heart full. This is the happiest I've seen her in a long time.

Now seeing her with my sister and how happy she is, I know I'm doing the right thing for her. It's been eight whole months. I'm not going to keep punishing her or Kate.

They miss each other. The two bounce forward while keeping an arm around each other's waist. I chuckle to myself as Kate towers over my girl.

I can't take my eyes off DJ in those shoes and that dress. Those aren't the shoes I sent for her, but I'll be damned if they're not perfect with the dress. She looks so fucking sexy.

"That's yer girl?" Seán asks, sounding like he's about to get his ass kicked.

"Yeah, that's DJ. Find something else to do with your eyes before you lose them," I bite out.

"No disrespect. I didn't know she would be Black and I had no idea … damn. I see why ya keep her hidden, but I don't see how ya stay away," he mutters.

He holds his hand up in front of him when I turn to glare at him. If she weren't mine, I probably would have the same reaction, but she is mine and I don't like the thought of anyone else looking at her like they want to fuck her.

However, I know that's insane because look at her. How can you see her and not think about being wrapped in those thick thighs with a handful of that big fat ass? I'm going to fuck her senseless later tonight.

I've missed her so much. I hate being away from her. I'm going to make up for every moment that I've been gone this time.

I smirk at my own thoughts. I shake my head clear as I see Kate leaning to whisper in DJ's ear. I trust my sister.

She has had time to prepare herself not to overshare or tell DJ anything I don't want her to know just yet.

I have business associates and a few friends here tonight. Only people I could trust with the location and the fact that I'm having this event. My crew from New York is here.

They travel with me more often than not these days. I think it's best if they learn the new operation. Not to mention, I trust them the most.

"Cousin," is crooned just as we're nearing the VIP, pulling my attention as we move through the crowd.

I turn to see none other than Noah Black. I smile and tug him into a one-arm hug, clapping him on his back. I didn't know he was coming.

"What are you doing here?"

"Kate knew I had a case out this way and told me to swing by. Then I heard some noise that had your name in it. I thought I'd detour to drop in and make sure the night goes as you planned," he says.

I frown. Things haven't been quiet, but these motherfuckers have been less bold in trying me. I guess the silence has found the volume.

I look at DJ and how happy she is. I'll kill anyone who ruins this night for her. Maybe doing this was a mistake. However, I'm not about to live my life like a pussy. This shit is going to stop.

I'm the head motherfucker in charge and they all need to get used to it. I can question myself, or I can accept that I'm going to have to shut this bullshit down sooner or later.

"Don't look like that. I didn't come to bring the party down. I've got your back. She'll be fine," Noah leans into my ear to whisper.

I nod and move to place a hand on DJ's back. She looks up over her shoulder at me. Her gaze then moves beside me.

"Noah?" she says with her brows drawn.

"Hey, DJ."

"You remember her?" I say.

"Yeah, I do," he says and moves to pull her into a hug.

I almost forgot how much DJ used to be around. My life seems like I've lived it in compartments. I forgot that at certain points, certain compartments have crossed.

"Let's get to the VIP where we can sit and hear each other," I say to everyone.

Kate grabs DJ by the hand and they move forward once again. Noah and I follow close behind them. I note where my guys are standing and shoot them all nods.

We get into the VIP and the music isn't half as loud. I chuckle to myself as Kate and DJ sit talking at top speed. If you're not Irish, you're probably not catching a word of what they're saying.

"That's hilarious," Noah laughs as he nods at the two of them.

"Come over to the bar. We can talk over there," I say as I shake my head.

I want to give them space to talk and catch up. We turn to head for the bar. Looking around, I can't help but feel like I did the right thing here. DJ is happy. That's all I wanted.

Noah and I spend time at the bar shooting the shit and fucking about. I have my eyes on DJ the entire time. She and Kate have been talking nonstop.

I haven't missed the looks DJ keeps shooting my way. I'm not sure how much time has gone by when Seán comes to whisper in my ear again.

"You have company. He says he only wants to talk," he whispers.

I look over to where he's nodding. Devin McCarthy is sitting at a booth surrounded by a bunch of women. I keep my face expressionless.

Whoever invited him can kiss their ass goodbye. I guess someone has shown they can't be trusted, and now I know what the noise is. This will be another lesson for everyone.

I hadn't planned on doing any business here tonight and this motherfucker hasn't said shit I want to hear any other time we've crossed paths. He's always worried about shit that has nothing to do with him. He reminds me of a snake.

"We have a problem?" Noah asks beside me as he follows my gaze.

"Not at all," I mutter.

I glance over at DJ. She looks so fucking happy. Kate looks happy too.

I feel a little selfish for taking so long to bring them back together. Then I look back at Devin McCarthy and I'm reminded of my reasons for all I've done.

Had I known Logan would be gone this long, I would have gone a different route. Now I'm feeling trapped by what I started. I hate feeling trapped.

However, I'm not about to show any weakness tonight. Instead, I turn to head to an empty lounge sofa across from where DJ and Kate are. I take off my suit jacket and toss it over the back of the sofa. My guns are now exposed, but I couldn't care less.

Fuck the laws here and fuck anyone who has a problem. I dare someone to say something. The law enforcement here has long been under my family's thumb.

Noah and I sit, and Seán moves to stand beside the sofa. I throw my arms over the back of the sofa, not having a care in the world. Devin nods at one of his guys and they stand to come over.

First rule. Always make them come to you. If you can change the setting and move them away from their original place of comfort, you've already won. It's like a mouse moving in for the cheese.

They're as good as trapped. Whatever McCarthy wants, he's not going to get it. However, showing up here to force me to meet with him is going to cost him.

"O'Brien, I was hoping we could talk," Devin says as he and his guy stop in front of my table.

"Your lips are moving, but you haven't said shit worth hearing yet."

"I think that's one of the problems."

"Who has a problem?"

"Ya do. Ya come here and try to take things over with your American ways and that's not how we do shit around here."

"Um, I see."

"Do ya now?"

"Aye, you let someone put a battery in your back and now you have the balls of a man who wants to challenge me.

"The problem with that is I don't give a fuck where I am. My balls hang the same wherever I stand. I'll smack the shit out of ya here, in Dublin, New York, or fucking Portugal.

"I don't discriminate. You disrespect me, I'm laying a boot to your ass. So are we really going to have this conversation?"

"Aye, ya need to under—"

The song changes and my eyes lock onto DJ's. I don't hear another word this motherfucker says. As "I Gotta Be" by Jagged Edge plays, I stand.

"Is he … yer just going to walk away?" Devin says in exasperation as I saunter away.

I remove my cuff links and pocket them as I go. Not taking my eyes off DJ, I roll up my sleeves to the elbows as I move to the dance floor, where I crook a finger for my girl to come to me.

Deja

I smile as Cole crooks his finger for me to come to him. I love this song. I noticed they've been playing a lot of what sounds like my playlists.

I stand and move to the dance floor as Jagged Edge croons about needing to be the one. When I get to Cole, he pulls me into his arms and begins to sway with me in his embrace. He looks me in the eyes as if he's trying to tell me something. I'm lost in his green gaze as he keeps a tight hold around my waist.

As I smile back at him, I reach for his face to run my fingers over his beard. He nips my finger and smiles around it.

"Thank ya," I say softly. "Ya didn't have to do all of this."

"When are ya going to get that I'd do anything for ya?"

I get so choked up I can only nod. I turn away from his intense gaze because I feel myself becoming too emotional. He kisses the top of my head.

I'm caught up in the moment. However, something catches my attention. The guy who had been standing over at the table talking to Cole is now on the other side of the room speaking heatedly with three other guys.

Then it's like time comes to a halt. I blink and watch what I'm seeing click into focus. I reach for one of Cole's guns, push by him, and fire before one of the guys with the angry lad gets off a shot. He drops to the floor, and I take out two more who have pulled guns. Suddenly, I'm grabbed by the back of the neck and shoved behind Cole's big body.

"Lock the fucking doors. No one leaves until I know they're all dead," Cole roars after he puts a bullet in the head of the angry talking guy.

That seems to be the wrong thing to say, as more guys pop out shooting. I fire at one who aims at Cole. I only hit him in the leg as Cole begins to use his body to back me out of danger.

Cole finishes the job, putting two in the guys chest and one in his head. I nearly trip over my dress. As I stumble backward, Noah appears to help me catch my footing. Cole takes out three more guys before he turns to set his eyes on me.

"Go on, get her out of here. I've got this. Take my bike, it'll be faster," Noah says as he tosses Cole his key.

"Where's Kate?" Cole demands.

"In the trenches." Noah nods.

I barely get a glance at my best friend standing in the middle of a gunfight before I'm over Cole's shoulder as he storms out. I don't want to leave Kate in the middle of that, but I don't have a choice as Cole leaves through a back door one of his guys is standing in front of.

Well, I guess the night is over.

CHAPTER TWENTY-FIVE

Unfinished Dance

Brooklyn

I pull the bike into the garage of the house we keep here and park next to Logan's Bentley. This is his place, but we all have access. I had planned to come here for the night after the party.

Cutting the bike off, I pull out my phone to send a text for an update. DJ climbs from behind me on the bike and pulls her helmet off. Setting my phone down in front of me as I wait for a reply, I take my own helmet off.

My phone buzzes as I tuck the helmet under my arm. I grunt as I read that they got all the guys. But Walter, one of my guys, was hit. Noah is taking care of him and helping Seán clean that mess up. Emory and Arnez are getting Kate back to Cork.

"Is Kate okay?"

I look up to find DJ watching me. She's chewing on her lip as she looks nervously back at me. I scan her body with my eyes and freeze with rage.

There's blood on the side of her dress. I put the helmet down and hop off the bike. In the next breath, I'm standing in front of her.

"You were hit?"

She looks down then back up at me. Without waiting for her to answer, I reach to tear the dress open to get a view of her skin. She gasps and takes a step back.

"I wasn't shot, Cole. I think I nicked my side when I almost fell. There was so much adrenaline running through me, I didn't feel it until now. It's just a scratch, I'm fine."

"*Fuck*," I roar and spin away from her.

I grab the helmet from the bike and toss it at the wall. This is exactly why I've kept her hidden. I can't believe I allowed this to happen.

She comes up behind me and wraps her arms around my waist. I close my eyes as I try to see straight. If McCarthy wasn't already dead, I'd kill his ass again.

"Hey, I'm fine. Ya really know how to throw a hell of a party," she jokes.

I turn and place my hands on her hips, pushing her back until her back is against the Bentley. I kiss her hard, needing to feel her lips against mine.

Breaking the kiss, I pull away and look down at her torn dress. Reaching for the soft fabric, I rip the rest from her body and toss it to the floor.

All that's left is the piece around her neck. She's now standing in front of me in those sexy-as-fuck heels and a high-waisted thong. I know it's a thong because I felt it earlier this evening when I slid a hand into the slit of her dress to see if she was wearing any panties at all.

"I liked that dress," she pouts.

"I'll get ya a new one."

"What about my dance? We didn't get to finish it. I was hoping we'd get to dance to our song," she says with a little smile on her lips.

As she looks me over from head to toe, I know exactly what song she's talking about. It's the song we fuck to a lot. I look her over as she stands before me.

I would have liked to dance with her to that song too. With a grin on my lips, I saunter over to the key holder on the wall and find the key to the Bentley. Making quick work of the task, I open the car and link my phone.

Once I have my phone synced, I pull up the song she's talking about. "Hold You (Hold Yuh)" by Gyptian begins to play through the garage. I unfold from the driver's seat and make my way back around the car, where I left her standing.

"Come here, love. I owe ya a dance. No interruptions."

She's hesitant for a beat. I lift a brow as I hold out my hand. She lifts her hand and smooths it down her bangs.

I love the cute ponytail and bangs she has tonight. There are pieces curled on each side of the bangs and the ponytail is curled as well. It's perfect for her face.

DJ gives me a nervous smile. I look her in the eyes, wondering if this is when she's going to fall apart after what happened tonight. I'd understand if she did.

"I'm sorry if I caused trouble. I just saw him getting ready to shoot ya and I—"

I close the gap between us and dip my head to take her lips again, cutting her words off. I groan into her sweet mouth. I was not expecting what she did tonight, but I'd be lying if I said it didn't turn me on.

She pulled the trigger without thinking. Her aim was dead on too. Once she took the first one out, she kept going until I pulled her out of the way and shoved her behind me.

Her words are the last thing I expect. I have no doubt that DJ can handle being a part of my life. She owes me no apology.

I'm the one who's sorry. I hadn't considered what any of the changes to that part of my life meant to my being her man. Now my head is filled with nothing else.

"I need ya," I growl into her mouth.

I kiss her deeper as I think of the constant danger she will be in even after I get her to New York. However, she's mine, and I am who I am. My best guys will be with her once we're home, but DJ proved tonight she can handle herself as well as my sisters.

She'll make a fine O'Brien. I grow harder as I think of her with my last name. As I drink from her lips, I run my hands over her soft skin, from her waist up to her nipples. I take her peaks between my fingertips and pinch then roll them.

"Cole," she calls out as I move my lips to her shoulder.

She works on the buttons of my shirt as I continue to knead her breasts. I take her lips once more and reach between her legs to prime her fat pussy for me. However, as always, she's already wet for me.

I tease her lips, not pushing my fingers into her right away. She whimpers and throws her head back. I go for her breast and suck the flesh into my mouth as I finally push my digits into her tight heat.

With my thumb, I rub her nub. I groan when she comes for me. It feels like it's been forever since the last time I was inside her.

As if reading my mind, she reaches for my belt and tugs it loose. I pull a condom from my back pocket and bite into it. She looks back at me with a sexy smile on her lips.

I free myself enough to roll the rubber on. Once it's in place, I then reach for her and lift her onto my waist as I take her lips for a searing kiss.

She breaks the kiss and moves her lips to my ear. "Fuck me, Cole. I've missed ya. Don't hold back."

"I didn't plan to."

I bounce her in my hold to shift her weight and reach to move her thong aside before I guide my way into her body. I groan and press my forehead to hers. She tightens her pussy around me and a shiver runs through me, causing my balls to jump.

Pressing her back to the car behind her, I begin to nail her to it. The Bentley begins to rock with the force of my thrusts. I lick from the base of her throat up to her lower lip as she cries out in pleasure.

"Fuck, Cole. Yes."

I bite her lower lip as I pump my hips into her. I want her so much and I'm already balls deep inside her with a rock-hard dick. She palms the back of my neck and starts to fuck back.

"That's my girl. Give me that pussy. Keep fucking me back, baby. Show me how good that shit is."

"It's so good, Cole. Yer so fucking deep."

"Yeah, is it hard enough for ya?"

"Yes, I'm coming," she screams before pressing her lips to mine.

She now has one hand on my shoulder while the other is still pressed behind my neck, gliding into the nape of my hair. I pull her away from the car before we fuck up the shocks from me fucking the shit out of her against it.

I slap her ass then widen my stance and begin to bounce her thick ass on my length. She throws her head back, moans, and calls out my name as she creams all over me.

"*Fuck, Cole,*" she drags out as I begin to swivel my hips in that shit.

I slip out and she squirts all over me. I chuckle darkly and place her back down on her feet. Then I turn her and place her palms on the roof of the car. Looking her over, I stroke myself.

Her ass is amazing. Her brown skin is so fucking soft and looks as smooth as it feels. Those heels.

Needing back inside her, I kick off my shoes and then my pants. Then I pull off my socks and drop them on top of my pants. Slowly, I then move behind her and place my hand on her hip.

With my other hand, I guide my way back into her from behind. I can't help watching her ass as I pound it out. The sound of my hips slapping her skin rings out in the air along with our panting, moans and groans.

As if that's not enough, her ass begins to clap around me. I drop my gaze to watch the magnificent sight. She has my length glistening with her juices.

DJ reaches back for my ass and begins to grind on my length. I pulse inside her, hard as fuck. The car is rocking again, but I can't think straight to figure out how to stop it.

I slap her ass and take over once again. Cupping a hand under her chin, I tug her head back and take her sexy lips. I growl into her mouth as I slap her ass a few more times.

My eyes roll back as her pussy starts to ripple around me like a heartbeat. No pussy should be this good. I think I love fucking her because she loves taking me so much and isn't afraid to show me she does.

"Cole, Cole, Cole," she cries as I shift angles, grab the fabric around her neck, and really give it to her.

I dip my head and lick my way up her spine, over that tat that drives me crazy. She begins to squeeze her pussy around me. I bite her shoulder and keep thrusting.

"So fucking good," I hiss in her ear. "Always so fucking good. Come for me, baby."

"Not yet," she pants.

"Now, DJ," I growl. "Be a good girl and come now. I'm not done with ya. I'm still going to take ya inside and fuck ya until the morning."

"Oh my God," she screams as she comes.

A satisfied smile comes to my lips. I kiss the top of her head and wrap my arms around her. This is going to be a long night.

CHAPTER TWENTY-SIX

What You Want

Deja

I have a little extra bounce in my step today. Cole might not like this, but I can't stay locked in that house all the time. I'd rather him be cheesed at me than lose my mind sitting in that house all alone.

At thirty, I'm used to working and being busy. I'm used to training, taking care of my gran, and working at the pub. I used to have an active life.

As the sun warms my face while I walk down this street, I can feel the life coming back into me. I need sunlight, I need to talk to people. Aye, I get that talking to people allows them to get close, but I need to be social.

I thought things would change once Cole moved me here to Ireland. It's still not New York, but something about coming home to Ireland gave me hope. However, nothing has changed.

"He'll get over it," I sing to myself as I skip a step when my destination comes into view.

Cole has been busy with business. I don't know how he does it; he seems to always be on the phone. I know he tries not to be when he comes to the house, but I understand, he's running things on two different continents.

That's why I've found myself a job. I'm so happy with myself. I found a cute pub to work at. Today is my first day, but I haven't told Cole about it.

He has enough on his plate without having to worry about me. I think my party caused him more problems than he's admitting. He's always tense and grumpy these days.

Besides, I can handle myself. I think I'm going to like this place. Larry, the older gentleman who owns the pub, was warm and sweet when I went in for the interview.

He said his nephew normally helps him run the place, but he went away on holiday and decided not to return. I'll be happy to help him. He reminds me a bit of Uncle Ken.

"Ah, there ya are. Hello, love. I've been waiting for ya to arrive, me wee angel," Larry croons with an excited smile on his face.

I smile back but can't help pulling a little face. I'm thrown. He was really nice during the interview, but this is beyond that.

You would think I just walked in with a barrel of the black stuff just for him. He's smiling from ear to ear. When he pulls me into a hug, I'm really confused.

"I'm excited for my first day too, but am I missing something?"

"Oh, sorry, sorry, lass. I'm just so excited. I've wanted to retire and move closer to me brother for years.

"I didn't think that would ever happen. Now, thanks to ya, I'll be on me way in a few days.

"Thanks to me? Huh? So yer closing the pub?"

My shoulders slump. I'm so confused.

"No. I'm not closing the place." He digs into his pocket and pulls out a set of keys. "I was told to give ya the keys when ya arrived," he says happily.

I take the keys and stare at them in total confusion. Larry begins to ramble about vendors and deliveries, but I'm still lost. The bell over the door chimes and I turn to see who's coming in.

A tall ginger comes in. He looks familiar, but I can't place him right away. He has his hazel-blue eyes locked on me.

"Ach, Mr. McGowan, I've handed over the keys as told," Larry says.

"Hold on. Can someone explain to me what's going on?"

The ginger smiles. He has a nice smile. "Hello, Deja. It's been a long time. It's me, Carrick McGowan. Cass Black's nephew."

"Oh my God. Hello, how are ya?"

I go to give him a hug as it clicks into place where I know him from. He's one of Kate's cousins through marriage. However, the last time I saw him, he wasn't this large.

"I'm grand. Brooklyn asked me to come by and make sure ya settle in."

"Huh? He knows I got a job?"

"Aye."

"Mr. O'Brien came in and offered me double the value of the place if I gave it to ya. The pub is yers. I'll be around for a few days to make sure everything goes smoothly. This is such a dream come true for me," Larry gushes.

I'm stunned. Cole bought me this pub. It's only been three days since I came in for the interview.

"Put me to work. I can help wherever ya need," Carrick says, pulling me out of my shock.

"Oh, I think I get it. Yer here as my bodyguard," I say.

Carrick shrugs. "We'll all be around to make sure yer safe."

"We?"

"Aye. Graham, Malcolm, Jeremiah, Reilly and me. Da and the others might stop in from time to time."

I groan and palm my forehead. I can't believe he's done this. Shaking my head, I reach for my mobile to call him.

"Hello, baby," he answers with a smile in his voice.

"*Cole*," I drag out.

"Aye, ya have my gift."

"Yes, but why would ya do this. I just wanted to work. I didn't mean for this to become a problem for everyone."

"It's not a problem. Carrick and the others have already been watching over ya. Now they can get a pint of the black stuff while they do it."

"Cole, this is too much," I groan.

"Nah, baby, it's not. Ya want something to do, now ya have something."

"Thank ya. I love ya," I murmur as I smile.

"I love ya too. I'm sending ya a few new hires. If ya need anything, let me know. I'll be by the house later."

"Okay. Thanks again."

I hang up, smiling so hard my face hurts. I have my own pub. Not the uncles' pub, but my own.

I clap my hands together. "Okay, let's get started. Larry, tell me everything I need to know. Let's get ya retired."

I inhale deeply and lift my shoulders to my ears. This can't be real. I love that man so much.

***

I stumble into the house exhausted. The pub was busier than I thought it would be. Carrick stayed around until closing.

I sent Larry home around eight. He looked excited but tired. He didn't need to stick around all night. He should be packing for his trip.

I drop my shoes by the door and make my way to the kitchen for some water and a snack. After I down the glass of water, I stand at the island with my palms flat on the countertop.

"I missed ya," Cole says into my ear as he comes up behind me and wraps his arms around my waist.

I smile, melting into him. He kisses the top of my head. I could fall asleep right here in his arms.

"I missed ya too."

"How was yer first day?"

"Well, I got the surprise of my life as I was handed the keys to my new pub. I thought I was going to be a barmaid, not the owner."

"Ya would have known if ya came to me first. If ya want or need something, ya can talk to me. I want ya to talk to me."

"Aye, noted."

"Ya sound wrecked. Come, I'll draw ya a bath," he says and kisses my neck.

His mobile buzzes on the counter where he placed it. He snatches it up, but not before I get a glance at it. I'm thrown by the text and how fast he reaches for the phone as if he's trying to keep me from seeing it.

A: *Sorry I missed your call. Was in the shower. I got the money. Thanks.*

"On second thought. Forget the bath. I'm going to bed," I say as I turn and head for the bedroom.

My mind is spinning with who *A* could be. I laugh to myself when I think of Arnez. That had to be him.

CHAPTER TWENTY-SEVEN

Called Away

Brooklyn

Six months later …

"Fuck," I roar after I hang up the phone with LaSalle.

They still haven't released Logan and now motherfuckers want to test me just because my brother isn't around. Wrong fucking move. Logan is the sane brother and that's saying a lot.

I'm the brother who's coming for your head first, then I'm showing up at your funeral to ask questions to see who else needs to die with you. It seems while I've been dividing my attention, some motherfuckers have forgotten.

I'm Brooklyn O'Brien. It's important you think twice before coming for what's mine or anything connected to me. If not, I'm going to answer accordingly.

"Let Christian and Arnez know we're heading out," I bark at Emory on the other end of the phone.

Seán needs to remain here this time. It's fine, I don't need many for this. I plan to make my message heard myself.

He sighs. “Yeah, all right.”

I get it, my guys are exhausted. We’re always on the move. Before that call, I had planned to remain focused on DJ for the next few days.

The guys thought they would get a few days off. Not anymore. Everyone’s plans will have to change.

Pissed as fuck, I head to the bedroom and get dressed, ready to deal with this shit. I need to head back to New York. LaSalle should never have to call me about shit in my own backyard. I’m taking this one personally.

I’ve been riding a pendulum. I get one place under control and the other starts acting up. Ireland is on its way to being stable again, but not without consequences. I’ve buried a few of my own and caused twice as many funerals in return.

Dressed in a fresh suit, I head back out into the bedroom. DJ is in bed, fast asleep. I frown.

Our situation is becoming a different kind of problem for me. I’ve had less and less time to spend with her. Shauna needs more with each day.

At fourteen months old, she’s walking and starting to talk. I’ve had to keep Aisling on for much longer than I had planned. I just changed their location.

I now keep an apartment next door to theirs in case of an emergency or if I want to stay overnight. Some mornings, I don’t know where I am when I wake.

I needed this weekend with DJ. Having her around grounds me. I mutter a curse under my breath and go to lean in and kiss her temple.

She only stirs enough to turn on her other side and snuggle deeper into the bed. I nod to myself. That’s for the best.

I turn and leave, grabbing my dress coat to throw on as I exit the house and jump in my car. I turn the radio on to distract my thoughts as I head to the airport.

I only get halfway to my destination when my phone starts to ring. I groan as I see its DJ. I guess it’s better to do this now before I board the plane.

“Hello, baby,” I say tiredly.

“What happened to ya?”

"Something has come up. I need to head back to New York."

She sighs heavily. "I thought ya were going to spend the weekend with me."

"I still plan to. I'll be in and out. I have something I need to take care of."

"And ya couldn't take me?"

"No, baby. Not this time."

"Why am I not surprised? Be safe, Cole."

"*Fuck*," I snarl as the call ends.

My instincts are telling me not to take her to America just yet. Every time I think of changing my mind, I get this sick feeling that it's not the right move to make.

The Alliance isn't dead, but things have slowed down with Logan in jail and no real release date in sight. LaSalle has almost gotten him released twice now. Then, at the last minute, something has come up to stall everything.

"Be patient, baby," I mutter to myself.

***

Phelim O'Doherty has lost his fucking mind thinking he can strong-arm anyone under my protection. As if I wouldn't respond, as if I wouldn't find out.

I step out of the back of my SUV in front of his club in Brooklyn. His guys see me coming, but don't have the balls to make a move to stop me. I walk right by the bouncer and head inside.

I move straight for the private room. Just as my guy said he would be, he's there as he has been for the last hour. His back is to me as he dances with some chick.

I'm not going to shoot him in the back, so I go and grab his ass by the back of his hair and drag him from the room, kicking and shouting.

His guys in the room go to pull their guns, but I'm faster. I put a bullet in one of their heads and train my gun on the other. He looks like he's going to piss himself as he holds his hands up.

"What the fuck? Shoot him," Phelim barks.

“Shut the fuck up,” I bite out.

Phelim stiffens as he hears my voice. Ah, he finally realizes it’s me. I keep dragging his ass as I head to the loading dock of the club.

When I get there, I throw his ass into a wall. He smacks into it then falls on his ass with his face busted open. He looks back at me with wide eyes and fear in them.

“Yer not so fucking bold now, are ya?” I snarl.

“Br … Brooklyn. What’s going on, man? What did I do?”

Pissed off that I’ve had to come all this way for this, I shoot him in the knee. He howls in pain as he cradles the wound. I flip out the tails of my coat and squat down in front of him.

“Do ya want to keep playing with me?” I hiss in his face.

“It was just a talk. I heard your interests were elsewhere. I thought I could earn a little something extra.”

“Yer a fucking idiot if ya think I believe that.”

I stand to my full height and put my gun to his forehead. I have no patience for this. Besides, I want to get back on the plane to get back to my woman.

“I’ll make sure your piece-of-shit brother joins you,” I say and pull the trigger.

“Anyone locate the other one?”

“He’s at some chick’s place in Dumbo. Word is she’s Fitzgerald’s daughter. He’s been fucking her for months,” Christian replies.

“Isn’t she like fifteen?” I ask in disgust.

Tiernan O’Doherty is Phelim’s older brother. He’s in his fucking thirties.

I know Fitzgerald’s daughter’s age because she wanted a summer job, but I said no because I didn’t like how she flirted with some of my guys while with her da at one of our stores.

I wouldn’t put my guys in that type of position, not knowing her age. Her father is an eejit.

I heard he gave her an apartment of her own in Brooklyn. There’s no way in hell I’m giving my fifteen-year-old an apartment of her own where she’s not supervised.

I think of DJ. If I want to ever have kids of my own, I need to be back on that plane. I can still spend the day with her if I move my ass.

"Let's handle him. I want to be back on that plane within the next hour."

Deja

Something has to give. Things have changed so much since that night I saw that text. I've noticed that Cole leaves the room when he receives certain calls.

He's spending less and less time with me, and he never takes me on his trips to New York. The more I think about it, the more I wonder if there's someone else in America.

It's not like I would know. She's over three thousand miles away. I'm here, alone and frustrated.

I took off a whole weekend for this. Pricillia, the new barmaid I hired, was supposed to cover for me while I spent the weekend with my man.

Now I'm sitting here with nothing on my mind but Cole O'Brien and how he could be playing me for a fool. I hate feeling like this. A glance at the clock only feeds my anger.

"My whole day," I growl.

I get up and stomp my way into the bedroom. I'm going to take a bath to clear my head. Hopefully, when I get out, I won't have Cole on my mind, and I can find something to do with the rest of my evening.

I smile as I think of watching a few American shows to work on my accent. *New York Under Cover* comes to mind. I still have a few episodes of that to catch up on.

I get my bath milk into the water and go to undress in the bedroom. I yelp and nearly jump out of my skin as I find Cole walking in.

Jesus, Mary, Joseph, this man shouldn't look this good. I want to run into his arms, but I'm still angry at him. I place my hands on my hips.

"Did ya handle yer business, or will I wake to ya missing from me bed once again?"

"I took care of what needed to be taken care of. I'm all yours," he says tiredly.

I slump my shoulders, feeling bad. He does have a lot on his plate. He looks exhausted.

I walk over to him, swaying my hips. He gives me a tired smile. Wanting to be near him, I wrap my arms around his waist.

"Were ya going to take a bath? I smell that shit ya love."

"That was the plan."

"Come on then. I had planned to pamper ya for the day. Looks like I'm right on time."

"Not really, but I'll let it go for now."

He releases a tired laugh. Feeling sorry for him, I push his coat from his shoulders and begin to help him out of the rest of his clothes. Once he's standing in his slacks and socks, he cups the side of my face and kisses me.

"Ya know I love ya, don't ya?"

"Yeah, I do. I love ya too."

He takes my lips again and things begin to heat up. When he begins to massage my bum in his big palms, I think our bath will be forgotten. However, he breaks the kiss and pecks the tip of my nose.

When we're both undressed, we make our way into the bathroom and get into the tub together. Cole massages my back and asks me about my week. After a while, I can't remember why I was so angry with him.

After our bath, when he wraps me in a towel, he then takes me into the bedroom where he puts a face mask on me, then paints my toes—I don't even care anymore. Cole shows me he loves me all the time.

I need to stay out of my own head. Things will get better. I just need to be patient.

CHAPTER TWENTY-EIGHT

Our Time

Brooklyn

"What are ya up to?" DJ giggles.

"Stay still, they're not dry."

I sit on my knees on the bed with a towel around my waist as I have her foot in my hands. Music is playing in the background as I blow on her toes that I just finished painting. I'm no fool.

Things are becoming strained between us. DJ needs more and I can't give that to her right now. I know she's pulling away, and the distance has been growing between us.

I hate it, but I've buried us in this secret and it's too late to change that. I still don't want to burden her with the details that could become weaponized against us. I'm doing this as much for her safety as I am for Shauna's.

I want to make this right, but I need more time. I wish I knew how much time that is. However, everything is up in the air with this Logan shit.

I promised her I'd prove that she can trust me, but I've been lying to her all this time. I need to find a way to fix this. I can't lose her, and I can't allow anything to happen to her or Shauna.

"Cole," she moans as I begin to massage her foot.

"Ya have the cutest toes I've ever seen in my life," I say as I look her in the eyes.

She looks back at me with a smile on her lips. I bring the sole of her foot to my face and ghost my lips and nose against her skin. Her body quivers enough for me to take notice.

I smile and kiss the bottom of her foot. I then begin to ghost my face against her skin, moving up her leg. Lauryn Hill and D'Angelo are singing about how nothing even matters.

We need this time and this connection. Pushing aside all exhaustion, I focus on her and only her. If I can show her how much I care, she'll understand everything I've done for her later.

Biting my lip, I move up her body to hover over her face. I don't go in for a kiss; I ghost my lips over hers. Then I drag my nose from her chin, over her lips, over the bridge of her nose.

"Cole, please," she whimpers.

Placing my finger over her lips, I shake my head. There aren't words for what we need right now. I need us to feel.

If she can feel me, she will know. I'm all hers and always will be. I'm taking her home as soon as the time is right.

Tugging the towel from around my waist, I toss it to the floor and settle between her legs. As I press the tip of my nose to hers, I look into her eyes, silently asking her if she's with me.

She nods her head. Reaching for the side table, I grab a condom and place it on. I then take my time kissing my way down her neck. I'm in no rush.

This requires we take our time. I'm not trying to fuck. I want to make love to her.

I tease her pussy with my length as I move to hover over her face once again. I move to her ear as if I'm going to speak into it. However, I just breathe.

Then I drag my nose across her cheek until our lips are a breath apart. Her chest is heaving and she's running her hands slowly down my back. I nip at her lower lip before taking her mouth in a passionate kiss.

As we kiss, I reach for her arms and pin them above her head. I then drag my fingers over her skin until our fingers are laced together. Our eyes remain on each other's as I tighten my hold on her hands and finally slide into her body.

She gasps and throws her head back as I slowly rock into her. I roll my body into hers as she tightens her walls around me. I dig my toes into the mattress and fight not to start moving too fast.

DJ locks her legs around my waist tightly, trying to hold me off with her thighs. I keep driving into her, getting harder by the second. Releasing her hands, I reach for her thighs and open her legs so I can move freely.

She throws her head back with an open-mouthed silent scream. This is more intense than I was going for. Not wanting this to end, I begin to stroke more slowly.

Dipping my head, I pull her nipple into my mouth and gently suck on it. Her walls ripple around me, causing me to begin to suck harder.

I lift my head and look into her eyes. I silently tell her that I love her. I'd die for her. Nothing in my world matters without her.

She nods as if in understanding. That's all I can ask for.

Deja

It has never been this way between us. This connection. I'm speechless.

It's like he's become a part of me. The music is only intensifying the moment. I feel Cole's love for me.

All my frustration with him takes a back seat to this moment. He pulls out and rolls me onto my stomach. Straddling me, he thrusts back into me while dragging his face against my skin. I become lost in him. He's so hard, yet gentle.

My senses are on overload. His breath fanning my skin, his hard dick moving in and out of me, the wet feel of his tongue as he licks between my shoulder blades—it's all taking me higher and higher. I'm no longer sure where he starts and I end.

Even our panting is in sync. I want to whimper his name, but that feels like it might break this spell he has me under. Instead, I clench the sheets, bury my face in the pillow, and silently scream.

I don't know how long we're at it, but once he spills into the barrier for the final time, I can barely keep my eyes open. I drift off feeling satisfied and connected to him in an all-new way.

Nothing but Cole, Nothing but Cole, Nothing but Cole.

I giggle in my half-sleep state as I sing the words in my head.

CHAPTER THIRTY

Tell Me Why

Deja

A year later …

I've been waiting for Cole to arrive. This was his idea. He wanted to take me to dinner, yet he's not here.

I've been waiting for over an hour. I'm beyond pissed. It's been getting worse between us. I don't know if I can keep doing this.

It's been two years, and I've still never been to America. Cole has been plenty, but he never takes me. Again, I'm starting to think I'm the other woman.

Something is just off. I wanted to listen to music in his car the other day while he jumped out to pump gas. I was confused and annoyed when his password he gave me didn't work.

I tried to shrug it off as him getting a new phone, but it went off in my hand with a text as I sat there. I sat in complete shock, dropping it back into the holder when he went to get back in the car. I can still see the words in my head.

A: *Our girl is missing you. She wouldn't go down for a nap without me sending you a pic of her new dress you bought her. She loves it. Isn't she cute?*

I never got to see the picture. I don't think I would have been able to remain as calm as I did if I had. I don't know much about Arnez, but I know the text wasn't from him, as I had thought the first time I saw a text from *A*.

He and Seán were in the other car, as they had been in the last year. I played it off as if I didn't see it when Cole picked up his phone and smiled as he checked his text. I was too shocked and sick to my stomach to ask about it, so I didn't say anything.

Cole always makes sure to use condoms with me. When I mention babies and when we'll start to have our own, he always says he wants to be married to me first. I've accepted that.

I never fought him on it. However, now I have to wonder if he already has a baby with someone else. Is that the reason he doesn't want them with me?

Let's face it, we're not using condoms because I might give him an STD. Cole knows where I am at all times. I've never even thought about cheating on him.

Although if he knows he's sleeping around, that could be the reason he doesn't forget to use them. How kind of him.

He would be late for our date. I had planned to confront him tonight. I've had time to calm and gather my thoughts.

This is the end, I want out. I grab my mobile to give him a piece of my mind. I don't even care if he answers. I'll leave it all in his messages.

"Hello, baby," he answers to my surprise.

I pause, feeling bad as his tired voice comes through the line. Maybe I should cut him some slack. He does have a lot on his plate.

There could be a reasonable explanation for all of this. I spend a lot of time alone when I'm not working at the pub. I could be allowing the drunken stories I've heard to influence my thoughts.

"Deja? Baby, ya there?"

I go to answer, but a child's cry in the background cuts me off. Suddenly, I can hear him moving away from the sound quickly. I knit my brows.

"Um, yeah. I'm here. Where are ya? Will ya be here soon? If not, I'm thinking about heading to the pub."

"I'll be there soon. Give me another hour, two max."

"Cole," a female calls in the background.

"Baby, I need to take care of something. I'll text ya when I'm on my way."

"Yeah, okay."

"I love ya. I'm going to make up for today. I promise."

I roll my eyes and hang up. My mind darts in a million different directions. My mother's words begin to ring in my head.

I don't know why I allowed myself to trust him so easily. Something isn't right and I refuse to allow myself to ignore it any further.

***

"Yer not dressed," Cole says as he enters the house.

I glare at him like he's crazy. I put on my pajamas not long after I hung up with him. I'm not interested in going anywhere with him.

I plan to pack my things in the morning and find a new place to live once I get to the pub. I've even thought about heading back to Scotland.

He sighs heavily. "Deja, something important came up. I would have been here if it hadn't. Did ya eat? I can order something and we can talk."

"I don't want to talk, Cole. Yer only going to make me broken promises and feed me lies."

He comes to sit down on the couch beside me. I frown as the scent of another woman clings to him. It's not his cologne.

It's too soft and sweet. He places a hand on my knee. I snatch it away and stand. He tries to reach for me, but I dash out of the way.

"I'm going to bed. Maybe we can talk if yer around in the morning and ready to be straight with me," I bite out and storm off.

Brooklyn

I groan and run a hand through my hair as Deja storms away. Today has been the day from hell. Both Kate and Connie were needed back home, so Aisling had to call me when Shauna spiked a fever and took a spill.

Aisling was afraid Shauna had broken something. She was fine. The fall and the fever were because she had an ear infection. DJ had called right when Shauna was being a bit fussy.

I didn't mean to miss our date. I had been on my way when Aisling called in a panic. I dropped everything to get to Shauna.

I think I fucked up today. DJ has put up with this for over two years. However, today I can see it in her face.

"Fuck," I groan.

CHAPTER TWENTY-NINE

Busted Windows

Deja

I should have packed my things and left, but I couldn't just walk away from two years of my life. I've given Cole my all. So nope.

I didn't pack and leave like I should have. Instead, I slipped an AirTag in his pocket and one in his car so I could get some answers for myself.

I've been watching his location all day. For the most part, he's been at the O'Brien Manor. However, an hour ago, he moved from there to Cork.

This has my attention as it's not in the direction of our home in Galway. When I google the location, it comes up as some swanky apartments in a little quiet-looking neighborhood. My gut is telling me this is where I need to be; these are my answers.

"Hello?"

"Hey, Pricillia, I need a favor," I say as I move through the house to head for the storage room where my old things have been since I moved here.

"Hey, boss. What's up?"

"I will pay ya double yer shift if ya cover for me tonight. If anyone asks ya, I'm in the back handling the books and I don't want to be disturbed. Oh, and I need to borrow yer car," I say with a smile on my lips as I get my hands on my old bat.

"No problem. I'm there," Pricillia sings.

"I'll meet ya up the road from the pub. Park in front of O'Malley's."

"Got ya."

I hang up and call for a car to get to O'Malley's. Checking the AirTag one last time, I nod my head as Cole hasn't moved. I will have answers before the night ends.

Brooklyn

"Yer so good with her. I know she's happy ya stopped by again today," Aisling says as we walk back to the apartment building after getting Shauna an ice cream cone.

"I'm happy to see her too. Isn't that right, love?" I croon as I lift Shauna into my arms.

She gives me that bright, pretty smile, looking so much like both her mother and father. My brother is a lucky man and doesn't even know it. I wanted DJ to be my wife by now.

She should be pregnant with our second baby at this point. However, she's not even speaking to me. She barely allowed me to kiss her goodbye this morning.

The only reason I'm not home trying to make things right is because I think I need to give DJ and that temper some space. Besides, I wanted to come and check on my niece. I plan to hang out in my apartment here for the night.

I need to plan the move to New York. I don't think I should move Shauna. No one has found out about her as far as I know. The McGowans will watch over her if I ask and one of my sisters will be back here before I leave.

I need to give DJ something tangible. No more empty promises. However, I know the moment she hits the city, she's going to be a target.

For years, people have looked for my weakness. I've never had one, not until now. When I first got to America, everyone thought my accent was my weakness.

Then they thought I couldn't fight back. I proved them wrong on both accounts. I became a terror in those Brooklyn streets and earned the name. There wasn't a place in Brooklyn I couldn't go.

After all the trouble I've caused, those streets are just waiting for me to offer up a soft underbelly. If I'm taking DJ home, I need to have a plan to keep her safe. Add the Alliance and those I've pissed off here who have family back in New York, I have a lot to think about.

It's not like I can be everywhere at once. Still, there's no doubt about it, I'm taking DJ home. We're not going to be apart like this anymore.

"Sorry, Uncle 'ole." Shauna pouts as the rest of her cone lands on the ground, but not before making a trip down my shirt.

I smile and peck her cheek. She's still trying to learn to say my name, but gets tripped up on the *C*. The tears that well up in her eyes take a stab at me.

Placing her back on her feet, I then hand her my half-eaten cone. She smiles brightly as Aisling takes her hand. Placing my palm on the top of her head, I then smooth it over her curls.

"Phanks," she sings as she smiles up at me.

"Yer welcome, love."

"Do ya want to have dinner with us?" Aisling asks.

"I'll think about it. I have some things I need to handle."

"Oh, okay."

I purse my lips and shake my head. I will not miss this one when Logan does get home. I swear her ass called my name on purpose yesterday while I was on the phone with DJ.

This shit is becoming the problem I told Kate it would be. I'm not here for her, I'm here for my niece. I wouldn't feel comfortable having dinner with her with no one else around.

***

I didn't have dinner with Shauna and Aisling. Instead, I've been in my apartment next door making calls back home to check the temperature on things. I want to get DJ out of here as soon as possible.

LaSalle believes things are going to heat up soon with Logan's return. Apparently, they are getting closer to getting him out. This could be good.

"You want to tell me what all this is about?" LaSalle asks on the other end.

"It's … it's nothing," I murmur. "Just have some things I want to move around."

"You know you can talk to me. I'd rather know now than later when you need me to step in."

"Aye, I hear ya. It's fine. I—"

I knit my brows as the sound of my car alarm goes off. Shirtless and shoeless, I rush to look out the window. It's been raining for the last hour. Now it's not as heavy as earlier, but I can still see the mist falling.

"Fuck, I need to go," I rush out as I focus on the sight before me.

Deja

A fucking girlfriend and a baby. He has a girlfriend and a baby. Not any girlfriend either. He's fucking Aisling.

My old friend from the softball team. The way she used to drool at the mention of his name makes me sick to my stomach. I can't believe he did this to me.

I watched from Pricillia's car as they walked down the lane like a little family. I've been stewing in her car for hours waiting for him to leave, but he's been here all this time. Hours, he's been here for hours.

I've never felt so hurt in my life. I've gone from hurt to confused to raging mad. He needs to feel how I feel.

I put in my EarPods and play "Bust Your Windows". Then I saunter toward his car with my bat in hand. As Jazmine Sullivan sings, the rain is falling, and tears are streaming down my face.

I wind my wrist as I get to the car then swing with all my might at the driver's side window. My insides are crumbling to pieces as I see images of them walking together in my head.

I swing again and again until all the windows on the driver's side are smashed out. Then I climb onto the car and get on top of the roof.

I then beat the hell out of the windscreen. I lift the bat over my head and bring it down as hard as I can. I have loved that man for most of my life.

I gave myself to him despite my mother's warning. He didn't take my life, but this feels like he did. I trusted him and he hurt me.

I've taken lives for him, and this is how he repays me. How could he? What didn't I do for him?

Why come to find me and destroy me like this? That little girl looks to be about two. He's been fucking around behind my back for as long as we've been together.

"Ya love me? This is yer love?" I sob as I beat the doors in after jumping back down to the ground.

I swing at the passenger's side windows and take them out, then I walk around the car and examine my work. With my chest heaving, I toss the bat into the back window and walk off.

"You're motherfucking right, I bust the windows out your car," I say in my best New York accent. "Fuck you, fuck New York, and fuck your car."

Brooklyn

I'm standing in the rain, no shoes, no shirt. Staring at my trashed car as the woman who trashed it tosses her bat into the back window and walks off with her hips swaying as she shakes her neck, talking to herself.

My hair is plastered to my face, but all I can do is throw my head back and laugh. I thought I loved DJ before. Now, I know I'm *in* love with her.

I press the key fob to turn off the alarm. I continue to laugh and shake my head at the rage she just took out on my car. I lift a brow as she speeds away in a car I don't recognize.

"So you're jealous, baby girl," I snort to myself. "I love your ass too."

I smile and laugh some more. We'll see about that temper. I can't wait for the makeup sex.

CHAPTER THIRTY-ONE

Step Back

Brooklyn

I sit in the car Seán brought to me as my wrecked car was hoisted onto a flatbed. After changing into dry clothes, I drove here to the house, hoping Deja would still be here. She is, but I'm not sure for how long.

From the cameras in our home, I can see she's packed her things. I can also see she has passed out face down on the bed. She's lying there in her nightgown with her arm hanging over the side of the bed.

I want nothing more than to climb out of this car, go inside, and climb into the bed with her. Then fuck her until she understands she's the only one for me. However, I know how angry she is and that wouldn't be fair.

"Keep your head, Cole. This is your girl. Handle her with care," I mumble to myself.

I want us to sit calmly and talk this out. She deserves that much, but I'm still not willing to tell her everything about Shauna, so I don't know where that leaves me.

I still believe I'm doing the right thing. I can't let this change my mind and jeopardize all I have done to keep my girls safe. My niece is my heart and DJ is my world.

It would kill me to lose either of them. I'd rather be safe than sorry. I can't risk telling DJ the whole truth. Not yet.

I stare at her sleeping form in our bed, wondering how I got here. I love this woman more than anything, but life keeps getting in the fucking way. Just when I think this will be the time for me to make things right and take her home, this happens.

"Fuck this," I grunt and go to get out of the car.

We can fight, we can fuck, but by morning, we're going to set this all straight. I reach for the door handle, but my phone begins to ring. I curse under my breath and look at the caller ID on the dash.

My brows draw in as I look at the name of the caller. My chest tightens. This is not someone who calls me often, if ever.

Why now? I glance at the tablet in my hands at DJ. She still hasn't moved.

"Hello," I answer the call.

"Hello, Brooklyn."

"Phoebe. How can I help you?"

"Oh, no. I'm calling to help you. Although you're not going to like this."

"I'm listening."

"Are you? Because it's important that you do. You will lose everything if you don't. The crown, the empire, the clan, and most importantly to you, the girl."

"Yes, I'm listening."

"Good, I need you to step back. Don't enter that house. Leave her to her anger for now. She will learn the truth when it's time.

"If you ignore my warning, your tempers will get in the way, and she will never arrive in the place that matters."

"The place that matters?" I ask in confusion.

"Ah, yes. You are to be king—one of the various Kings of New York, and one of the most powerful there is. Your brother will lean on you when times call for it, and you will need to lean on your queen.

"A queen meant to be one of the Bellas. Not just any Bella, but the right hand of Death herself. You will resist at times, but this is the way it must be.

"Congratulations, King Cole. You're in the major leagues now. Make the right decision. I will be in touch when the time is right."

With that, the line goes dead. I sit staring out of the windshield. I know not to ignore the old gypsy. However, her words don't entirely make sense to me.

I glance down at the tablet, unseeing. The one thing to stick out from Phoebe's words is that I'll lose DJ if I enter that house.

"*Fuck*," I roar and punch the steering wheel.

Before I pull off, I take a screenshot of DJ lying in our bed. Then I do the hardest thing I've ever done in my life: I drive away.

CHAPTER THIRTY-TWO

A Gift for You

Deja

Three months later . . .

I've been going through the motions for the last three months. Nothing matters. I'm putting one foot in front of the other.

I had planned to leave, but Carrick and Graham showed up at the house the next morning—after I had beaten the hell out of Cole's car—to let me know the house was mine and I didn't have to leave.

I thought long and hard about whether or not I should leave. In the end, I decided to stay as long as Cole stays away from me. Now I'm not sure if I'm happy that he has or disappointed that he didn't even fight for us.

I should feel silly for that, but here's the thing. Cole was my friend way before whatever we became. When we were younger, he was someone I could trust, someone I would talk to. I can't believe this is who he turned out to be.

"Hey, Deja, earth to Deja."

I'm brought out of my thoughts as I stand behind the bar in the pub. I should be getting ready to open. I look up to find Graham McGowan staring back at me.

I smile and tilt my head to the side. Graham is handsome. That red hair suits him. His hazel-blue eyes always have mirth dancing in them.

He's a big lad, but something about his presence is welcoming and calming. I don't mind that the cousins still come around. They make me feel like I did gain something from coming here.

"What about ye?" I say as I focus.

"I have something for ya. He-who-shall-not-be-named sent it for ya. Where should I put this?" he says as he holds up a long box.

I frown, knowing the gift is from Cole. So much for him staying away. At least he knows not to come around here himself.

I point for Graham to place the box down on the bar top. He places it down then stands there with his arms folded across his chest. I snort and lift a brow.

"Well, yer going to open it, aren't ya?"

I laugh and shake my head. "It could be something private," I mutter.

"I doubt he would have had it sent here if it were," he says pointedly.

"This is Cole. I'm sure he wouldn't give a shite either way."

"Ya have a point. If it's a replica of his bod, just shut it back and I'll go mind my own business."

"Or ya could mind yer business now and I could open it when I feel like it," I say.

"Aye, but we both know I'm not going to do that."

"Ach, yer doing my head in. Fine."

I open the box and can't help the smile that comes to my face. It's a new matte-black-painted baseball bat. There's a metal plate fixed to the end.

I bring the bat to my face to read the inscription on the plate. My smile wobbles a little.

DJ and Cole. A force together.

The year and date of our anniversary are under the message. I frown and toss the bat back into the box. I don't even bother to pick up the note that's in the box.

"Ya told him about last night, didn't ya?" I hiss.

"Ach, we told him some guys tried to get out of hand. Aye."

"What don't ye get? Ya and yer brother and cousins need to understand Cole and I are done. Stop involving him in my life.

"This is my pub. My business. Take it back. I don't want it."

"But—"

"Are ya deaf? I said I don't want it."

He stands staring at me like I've lost my mind. I can handle myself. I don't need or want Cole's stupid bat or his help. I kicked those guys out myself before Carrick or Malcolm could interject.

I warned them to keep their mouths shut last night. I can't believe they went behind my back and told Cole anyway. All at once, it all comes crashing down on me.

I grab my things and storm out of the pub. I can't do this. I never should have stayed. I can't breathe here. He's everywhere. I need a break from all things Cole.

Brooklyn

I pinch my eyes closed and throw my head back against the headrest as I sit in the back seat of the SUV. I just watched DJ storm out of the pub. I figured she would be angry after receiving my gift.

However, I wanted her to have it. Keeping my distance in the last three months has been harder than I ever thought it would be. Every time I get ready to say fuck it, Phoebe Romaine texts my phone to stop me.

It's eerie that she knows every single time. For that reason, I listen—because how in the fuck does she know? I play her words in my head daily.

You are to be king—one of the various Kings of New York, and one of the most powerful there is. Your brother will lean on you when times call for it, and you will need to lean on your queen.

A queen meant to be one of the Bellas. Not just any Bella, but the right hand of Death herself. You will resist at times, but this is the way it must be.

I'm still trying to understand what she meant by the Bellas. I have no idea who they are. The right hand of Death? I've been circling that part most.

"Should I follow her?" Emory says from the driver's seat.

I shake my head. "No, let her go. I'm of more use in California. Let's head back."

CHAPTER THIRTY-THREE

The Lesson

Deja

I walk into my great-gran's bedroom and go to take the seat next to her bed. My heart aches to see her like this. She looks so frail. Much worse than when I left.

My anger grows all over again. How did I allow this to happen? I feel so selfish and stupid.

"I'm so sorry," I whisper.

She opens her eyes, and they are unfocused at first. It takes a moment before she's able to train her gaze on me. A smile comes to her lips.

"Aye, she told me ye were coming," she says weakly.

I purse my lips. If she's talking about that gypsy friend of hers, I don't want to hear it. I left in the first place because of her.

"Och, and she told me ye would be angry. Listen to me, Deja. Ye did the right thing.

"Dinnae fash yersel. I am auld. My time grows near whether ye be here or not but ye should not be here."

"How can ya say that? Where should I be if not with ya?"

"Ye should be where ye will unlearn—" She begins to cough midsentence.

I have to fight against my tears and frustration. What am I supposed to be unlearning? Why do I have to leave to unlearn it?

"It's okay, Gran. Rest," I say softly.

"No, I'm fine. Ye need to understand. It's important. Yer destiny awaits ye.

"This will always be yer home, but yer life is tied to where Phoebe has seen ye."

"Where has she seen me?"

"Ye belong in the Big Apple. Yer destiny lives in New York. However, the time hasn't come for ye all to be there. It is coming. They will be there when ye arrive."

"They who?"

"Hush—" The coughing begins again.

"I'm sorry, Gran. I will sit here and be silent. You sleep."

She gives a laugh and her eyes twinkle. "Och, love. No. I don't mean for ye to hush. That is who will be there when ye arrive. Hush and the Black Death. They will teach ye to trust.

"This is the lesson. This is what you will unlearn. This mistrust. When ye learn this from them, the lad will reappear and ye will know the truth."

"What if I don't want him to appear?"

"Aye, ye say that now, but is that what ye heart says? Phoebe has told me a lot. Ye aren't seeing the whole picture.

"He needs ye to trust him. That's going to save ye all. The trust of a real family. Not one born of blood but one forged in it. I believe those were her words," she coughs the last part.

I sigh. "I don't understand."

"Ye will. Go back to the life he has given ye in Ireland. Ye will know when to leave. Yer king will do the rest."

"He's no king of mine," I mutter to myself.

She chuckles. "Aye, love, he is. Ye will see."

CHAPTER THIRTY-FOUR

New Land

Deja

Six months later …
My feet hit the pavement in soft taps as I make my way toward the house. I've been running in the mornings to clear my head. Every morning, I wake with anxiety.

Ye will know when to leave.

But I don't. That's the thing keeping me anxious and feeling crazy. How will I know?

What will it be? A sign or something. This is driving me mad.

I push harder, wanting my life to be normal again. Nothing feels normal anymore. I'm living in his house and running his pub. None of it belongs to me.

I shake my thoughts off as two figures appear on the front steps of the house. I pull my gun and rush up behind the two.

"What do ye want?"

They both turn slowly with their hands up. I cock my gun and keep it aimed. The one on the right pushes their hood back.

"We've been missing ye and this is how ye greet us after all this time?"

"Callum?"

"Aye, it's us. Put the gun away," Blair says as she tugs her hood off, revealing her dark blond, almost brown hair.

I place my gun on safety and nod my head at the black gift box she's holding. "What's that?"

I'm not sure why the two are here or how they knew how to find me, so I'm reluctant to embrace them. Old habits tend to die hard, especially once you've been burned. This is what Cole has left behind.

"They said ye would be like this. We come in peace. This is a gift from Gran," Blair says.

"Aye, let's go inside and we'll explain," Callum says.

"Is she all right?" I say as panic fills me.

"Aye, she's fine. Well, enough to order everyone around," Blairs says.

I move past them and head into the house. The two follow me inside. I go to the fridge and grab a bottle of water.

"Can I get ye anything?"

"No, we're fine. Ye should open this. Gran said ye shouldn't wait."

I walk over to the island where she has placed the box. Placing the water down, I then reach to take the lid off. I gasp and step back once it's open. Then I toss the lid aside and peek back into the box.

"Damn, that's morbid," Callum mutters.

"Gran said ye would know what it means."

I knit my brows. In the box on a black velvet pillow sits a gold crown. On the pillow, in the center of the crown, is a black apple with worms crawling out of it. Beside the apple is a timepiece, and resting against the side of the box is a pistol with a suppressor.

"Well, what does it mean?"

"Um, I think the apple symbolizes New York. The Big Apple. However, it's black and rotten and the worms are coming out. A sign of death.

"It's black, so Black Death. The pistol and suppressor, that's a symbol of silence. Hush," I mumble to myself.

"If he's my king, that makes me ... It means it's time. I'm finally going to New York," I say with a smile.

"Ach, our bags are in the car. We'll be waiting," Callum says and turns to walk out.

"I'll help ye," Blair says excitedly.

I look between the two as Callum walks away. I think I'm still missing something. What are they doing here?

Brooklyn

"We're boarding the plane," Callum grumbles.

"Good, everything is taken care of. I'll send you a text with where she needs to be for her interview. Someone will meet you when you land with a care package."

"Fine. Thanks," he says and hangs up.

I haven't made up my mind about the kid yet. He has a bit of an attitude. Given who he is, I'll give it a pass for now.

Only for now. I was surprised to get a call from Phoebe Romaine with instructions on what to do next. Everything was so detailed.

I followed her instructions right away. Ewan seemed to be waiting for my call. He informed me that the two trainees Phoebe had him raise beside DJ would be accompanying her to New York, Callum and Blair.

My head is still spinning. How long has this been going on? There is way more going on here than I know about. I still have more questions than answers.

Once I hung up with Ewan, I made my next call. I contacted my cousin Felix to have him call in a favor with Valentina Donati. I need her to hire DJ when she arrives.

This was a nonnegotiable for Phoebe. She said it had to be Valentina Donati. She also said it would all work out once the two met.

I only hesitated for a moment as her words came off cryptic. However, I have done all of this because Phoebe Romaine has saved my life within the last month. One phone call kept me from losing my life.

I haven't questioned a word she has said since. I may not know Uri or Val well, but I've heard the names. If she says DJ needs to work for them, I know it's for a reason. A reason that might save her life someday.

I will never ignore anything that could save that woman's life. Deja will be here soon, but I still have things to do. I clear my thoughts and look across my desk.

Nakim is on his tablet, carrying out the tasks I've given him. He was already with me when Phoebe made the call. I'm at one of our Cali warehouses making sure shit is running as it should while I'm in town.

"Have a dozen burgundy roses sent to the apartment. I want them waiting there when she arrives," I say.

"You want me to handle anything else?"

"Nah, head out. Thanks."

He nods and drops his tablet into his lap before he turns his wheelchair around and heads out of my office. Nakim will always have a place with me. I take care of my friend, and he takes care of me.

Once he's gone, I shoot off a text to check on progress with the living arrangements. The apartments need to be ready for her and her bodyguards when they arrive. I nod at the response as it comes in.

Next, I move on to a little research. I have yet to be formally introduced to Uri Donati, but I'm going to make it my business to know all there is to know about him even if I don't understand why Phoebe insisted I place the love of my life in his and his wife's hands.

"Our time is coming, love. It won't be long now."

I grin and throw my drink back. It's only a matter of time now. I miss my girl like crazy.

CHAPTER THIRTY-FIVE

Don't Lie

Deja

I sit here in this home office with my stomach bubbling. I'm interviewing with Mr. and Mrs. Donati. Their daughter is adorable.

"Uri, do you mind if I have a moment with Deja alone?" Valentina says as her husband, Uri, wraps up the interview.

"Sure, love. I'll be upstairs when you are done."

I like Uri's blended accent. He sounds as if he's from London, but there's something else. Italian.

It's a cross between a British and Italian accent. I love it. He gives off such a cool vibe, but make no mistake, the two come off as dangerous.

I've never been a nanny, but I'm trusting the process. When I arrived in America, there was a fully furnished apartment waiting for me and another for the twins.

I'm still confused about why they have followed me here. Callum seems to have an attitude about it, but Blair couldn't be happier. I've been too nervous and confused to figure out what's going on with Callum.

Then there's this interview. Uri and Val have been kind, but I'm not sure if I should reveal anything about myself. Which is why I've been trying to hide my accent.

I think I'm doing a good job. I might have slipped once or twice, but it didn't cost me the job. In fact, they hired me on the spot. I'm sort of excited.

"I like you. There's something about you. However, I don't like liars," Val says once Uri is gone as she narrows her eyes at me.

"I haven't lied," I say as I bristle.

She walks around the desk and leans her bum against the front. Locking those blue eyes on me, she seems to stare right through me. I begin to get deflated.

Everything had been going so well. I fold my hands in my lap and curse my having listened to that old gypsy I've never met. She's done nothing but ruin my life.

"Omission is a lie. You are leaving a lot out. It's okay, you don't have to tell me your secrets today, but you will come clean."

She reaches to cup my chin and lift my head, then continues. "Trust is everything to me and Uri. You will have to learn to trust us as we will learn to trust you."

"So you're not taking back the offer?"

"No, I'm not. Like I said, there's something about you. Your face, something about it is so familiar."

"I don't think we've ever met. I was born and raised in Ireland. I've lived in Scotland most of my adult life. For about a year, I lived in London."

"No, that's not it. It will come to me, Deja."

Hearing her test my name on her tongue causes me to want her to remember. I want to help her remember. Val has something about her that draws you in.

"DJ. You can call me DJ," I say.

She smiles. "Okay, DJ."

I lick my lips nervously. I don't think I've ever met her before, but she sounds so certain. Suddenly, her expression changes and she's smiling at me.

"I'll have someone show you to your room. Settle in. When you're done, we can play with Vita for a while, let her get used to you. My gym buddy is gone.

"You will take her place. In the morning, I want you to come to train with me. Uri hates that I'm pregnant and still training"—she shrugs—"how else do we killers stay in shape, right, DJ?"

I sit with my mouth hanging open. Val winks at me and saunters out of the room. I stand and look after her.

"You're the new nanny?" A tall lad says as he appears in the doorway.

He's cute. Dark hair and bright gray eyes. He's not as big and thick as Cole, but he's not bad to look at.

"Aye, I mean, yes. I'm Deja."

"Mattia, come."

This one is a bit cocky, but I keep my mouth shut and follow him. I'm here, I'm in New York. I'm walking in my destiny.

Now to figure out who this Hush and Black Death are. I wonder if Cole knows I'm here. Ugh, never mind.

He can keep his cheating arse right wherever he is. I'll be just fine without him.

"Damn."

I turn to find Mattia watching as I walk by. His mouth open as he stares down at my bum. When he catches me catching him, he smiles and his dimples pop.

I smile back. Cole would lose his mind. I wink and sway my hips as the thought crosses my mind.

Brooklyn

I pick up the wedding invitation on Wyatt's desk and stare at the name on it. Luca Donati. A grin comes to my lips.

I think it's time I make my presence known to Donati and DJ. No one needs to get any ideas. The sooner it's known who she belongs to, the better.

"You know the Donatis?" Wyatt asks as he nods to the invitation in my hand.

"Nope, but I'll be coming to the wedding with you." I shrug.

"What? It's by RSVP."

I grab a pen and the RSVP card then write three on the card for the number of guests coming. The invite was addressed to Wyatt and his wife, so I make sure to count Nellie. I then toss the card down.

"Bro, you know you're damaged, right?"

"Tell me something I care about. How is Nick? Anything new on Bailey and Mark?"

"Yo, Wyatt. I need that file. Come on, man. I want to get out of here," Noah calls through the office.

"Nick's good. I'll catch you up on the rest after I get this shit done. You coming out for drinks or heading out?"

"Jet's waiting. I'll have to catch you next time," I say and pat him on the back.

"Yeah, I figured. Let me know if you need anything. It's about to get real," he says.

"See you at the wedding."

He laughs. "Yeah, see you there."

CHAPTER THIRTY-SIX

Deja

Nine months later …

"What's the deal with you and Brooklyn?" Val asks as we leave the shops we just cleaned out and walk toward the car park.

I bite my lip as I think of the wedding. I hadn't known he would be there. I was there to work, not as a guest.

When he came up behind me and wrapped his arms around me, I was startled. Mattia looked like he was going to come to my rescue until Uri pulled him back and whispered something in his ear. Needless to say, Mattia hasn't spoken to me since.

In fact, I haven't seen him much lately. After getting caught checking me out on my first day, we've talked a few times, and I had planned to go on a date with him. Cole blew that out of the water.

"Ya owe me an apology and makeup sex," Cole had breathed in my ear.

I was so angry with him and myself for allowing my body to melt into his. I didn't get to respond because Vita started to cry. I had to tend to my charge, but not before Cole left me with something to think about.

"My own granda is dead because of ya. Imagine what I'll do to someone who's not my blood and tries to touch what's mine. Don't get someone killed because ya couldn't trust me.

"When ya know the truth yer going to be angry with yerself for missing out on this dick all this time for nothing. I want ya, DJ, but I'll wait. Make no mistake, baby, I'm coming for what's mine," he whispered in my ear before releasing me.

I haven't been able to get his words out of my mind since the wedding. I clear my throat and glance at Val. She's become my friend. I don't want to lie to her.

She and Uri have been showing me what it's like to trust, whether they know it or not. I love watching their relationship and how they are with friends and family. They have pulled me into that trust.

"I don't know Brooklyn."

Val's face hardens as she glares back at me, looking like she's ready to kick my ass. I sigh and hold my hand up. I want to be here, so I've been honest with Val about my life.

"I don't know him as Brooklyn. I know him as Cole. I grew up with his family.

"His sister, Kate, was my best friend. Cole and I were dating until I found out he cheated on me. Then I busted all the windows out of his car." I shrug.

Val bursts into laughter. "I knew I liked you. Mattia was one of our best guys. When Uri said he was sending him away to save his life, I wondered what the deal was, then I saw O'Brien looking at you like a hot piece of meat."

I roll my eyes. "Wait, that's why I haven't seen Mattia. Really?"

Val shrugs. "If Brooklyn says you're his … my husband isn't going to get in the middle of that, and Mattia didn't need to die for something he couldn't have."

I burst into laughter. "Maybe he could have. Cole should know how it feels."

"Are you sure he cheated? He doesn't strike me as the type."

"I caught him walking with her and their daughter outside their apartment."

She looks at me with wide eyes. "That doesn't sound right, DJ. Do you mind if I look into this? If you're right, I'll make sure Uri knows to keep him away."

"You don't have to do that. I doubt I'll see him again."

"Yeah, okay, I'll look into it. The look on that man's face said he plans to be all up in your life. Just you wait."

I laugh and shake my head as we move through the car park. Uri has the kids today, so against Uri's wishes, we're traveling a little light on security.

"Deja, get down."

I duck down as a bullet bursts through the window of the car we're in front of. I drop my bags and pull my gun from my purse. Val insists that I carry at all times.

I look around to see where the shot came from. I already know that voice that called out the warning. It was Callum.

I spot him and Blair heading my way with their guns drawn. Gunmen appear out of nowhere. I look to Val, and she has two guns out.

She takes a step to fire back and groans in pain. "Fuck, I think I twisted my ankle," she whimpers in pain.

I look down at her foot, and she's not putting her weight on it. She's a mother of three. The last thing she should be in is the middle of a shootout. The twins and I can handle this.

"Stay here," I command.

"What?"

"Stay here, we have this," I repeat.

I signal for Blair and Callum to follow my lead. I then round the car we're hidden behind. I take out two heading my way.

Valentina

Everything in me wants to run out and lie down, everything not mine. However, Uri would be pissed, and I'm not about to leave my babies behind trying to be the hero.

DJ has proved to be a skilled fighter. She's a good shot, but I've never seen her use more than one pistol at a time. I've been telling her we need to work on that.

She's just not able to flip that switch to override her dominate hand. It took me time to master the skill, so I get it. I'd just prefer if she were ambidextrous.

Being able to use both hands has saved my ass more times than I can count. Right now, it would come in handy for sure. However, my nanny and her two angel shooters shut my injured ass up real fast.

DJ rounds the car and takes down two guys. She then tucks her gun away and runs toward a car a few paces away as the girl angel covers her.

DJ flips and lands on the hood of the car in front of her. She kicks the gunman at the side of the car in the head before he can turn to face her. He drops his gun and DJ lands on her feet in front of the car.

The guy is taller than her, but she doesn't hesitate. The guy moves in, throwing a punch, but DJ blocks it. He goes to throw another combo, and she ducks those too. She jumps in the air and kicks him in the chest, sending him flying back onto the hood of the Mustang in the parking spot next to them.

The guy kicks back up onto his feet and shakes his head. Meanwhile, angels one and two are picking guys off as they run through the parking garage like two little demons.

I might take their angel titles back. One of the gunmen runs out from behind a car and aims at the demon boy. I snap into action and send a shot through the guy's head.

Demon Boy turns and sends me a nod. I turn my attention back to DJ just as she kicks the guy, sending him flying back onto the hood of a car, his legs hanging off one end and his head hanging from the other. She moves quickly and pins him down with one arm. Then, with all her might, she brings her arm down on his head, snapping his neck over the edge of the car.

"Nasty." I wince and bob my head appreciatively.

Pulling her gun, she takes out another two guys as Demon Boy moves swiftly, taking out another three. Demon Girl is a few cars down from me. She pulls a knife across another guy's neck.

She then drops to the ground and shoots two of the guys in the ankles. Then finishes them off as they drop to the ground.

"Well, damn. Who the fuck did we hire?" I murmur to myself.

The three might seem like they're working separately, but they move like a well-oiled machine. The two blonds are vicious as hell. They've earned my respect.

DJ moves down a few cars and stealthily climbs up onto a van parked there. Once on top of the van, she crawls as silently as she can to the front.

At the last second, as her weight rocks the van, the five targets she's after turn and look up, giving the two demon shooters a chance to come up behind them as DJ rises and shoots.

They take out the final group together. DJ then slides down the windshield and lands on her feet in front of the van. The smile on her face says it all.

I pop out as I note the coast is clear. Pulling my phone, I shoot off a text to get a cleanup crew in here. Micheal needs to be involved in this one. Hopefully he and Sim have come up for air.

"Where the hell did that come from and who are you two?" I say to DJ and the other two as I hobble over to them and glare down at one of the dead guys at my feet.

"You said I have secrets; now you know most of them, like you wanted. This is Blair and Callum. Although I'm not sure what they're doing here," DJ replies.

"Let's get ye out of here first. We can talk about the rest later," the Callum guy says.

"Who were they and what happened to Eddy and Tank?" I ask with a frown as I look around for the guards who came out with us today.

I told them to keep a distance, but this is too much of a distance for my liking. I know they know better. My frown deepens.

"One dead, the other down. Ye might want to get him some help. We watched them pick them off," Blair answers.

"Um, interesting. Let's go. You two, SUV with us," I bark. "I'll handle the rest."

Brooklyn

"Where is she?" I bark as I storm into Uri Donati's home.

When I got the call from Callum that there had been an attack, I thought I was going to lose my mind before I made it here. I just spoke to Uri yesterday and told him I had planned to come for DJ.

After that call, there was nothing that could stop me from coming. Not a text, not a call, nothing.

"First of all, who do you think you are coming up in my home barking out demands?" Val says as she appears with one of her little boys in her arms.

She hands the boy off to another woman and then stands with her hands on her hips. I look around for DJ, wondering why she isn't with the baby. My frustration grows as my eyes don't land on her.

"She's not here. I sent her and those two demons home for the night."

"Take this as her resignation," I bite out and turn to leave.

"They weren't after me, Brooklyn. Uri and Micheal are out making a visit to your problem because she's my friend."

I stop in my tracks and spin to face her. I narrow my eyes. Val sighs and rolls her eyes.

"Lynch, the guys were some of his low levels. I say he was testing the waters. Too bad your girl is a bad motherfucker and drowned their asses."

I knit my brows. "What do you mean?"

"That girl is no joke. I would work with her if the need arose. She has my loyalty for life for protecting me."

"Aye," I murmur.

I think I finally understand what Phoebe has guided us to. The fact that she hasn't texted to stop me from coming here gives me the feeling that the path has been fulfilled and this was the desired outcome.

"Do you? Because I've never been afraid of the big bad wolf. If you hurt my friend, I will hunt you down, and I never miss my prey. I put a dog down when I find one."

"Aye, I know who ya are, and I know who yer husband is, but I've never been afraid of death. And if I have noise to make, I'm going to make it with my whole chest and dare a motherfucker to try to hush me.

"Apparently, DJ has told ya about what she thinks I did. She's wrong, and you would be making me implode this whole alliance over a lie. Everything I do is for DJ.

"The girl isn't mine. If I told ya who she belongs to, I'd have to kill ya. I think I might like ya and yer husband, so thank ya for being DJ's friend and tell yer husband I owe him for Lynch. Good night."

With that, I turn to leave. I have someplace to be. Enough is enough.

CHAPTER THIRTY-SEVEN

The Truth Is

Deja

I step out of the shower and wrap myself in a towel. My head is still reeling with the fact that Callum and Blair followed me to America to watch over me. They were sent by Gran and Uncle Ewan because of this Phoebe woman.

I have so many unanswered questions. I mean, I know I work for a mob family; I put two and two together. Uri and Val move like the uncles and Cole.

I figured out a while ago who I was dating and living with. It's not something I've said out loud, but I know. I think I've always known who the O'Briens are.

My questions come when it comes to why Val? And how does she and Uri connect to Hush and Black Death? I'm so deep in thought as I grab my lotion and walk into the bedroom that I almost don't feel his presence.

I look up right as a thought clicks into place. Val and Uri *are* Hush and Black Death. I stumble to a stop, but my mouth isn't hanging open because of the revelation.

I'm gobsmacked because Cole is sitting shirtless in the accent chair that normally sits in the corner of my room. His legs spread wide and his hands resting on the arms of the chair. His hair is a little messy, but sexy.

"Don't look so surprised, love. I told ya I was coming for ya."

"Get out, Cole," I growl.

"Not before ya look at the file on the desk. Ya want the truth, I'm here to give it to ya."

I purse my lips and walk over to the vanity where he placed a file. I pick up the file and open it. There's a picture of a little girl inside.

Tears fill my eyes. She looks so much like Cole. I swipe my hand under my nose, not sure why he wants to keep hurting me like this.

Then I flip to the next picture and my cousin's face smiles back at me. I flip from Raven back to the little girl and my brows knit. I'm suddenly confused as I take in the fact that the little girl looks like both Cole and Raven.

"Ach, Logan and I do favor each other, but I'm not the lass's father. Oland had Raven murdered the same day he sent that army for ya.

"Yer call sent me to check on her. I found her dying and that little one hidden in a closet. Raven died in my arms.

"I've been protecting Shauna to make sure no one tries to finish the job. I wouldn't tell ya about her because I know our enemies would use ya to try to find her—to destroy me and my brother. I needed to protect ye both. The less ya knew, the better," Cole says into my ear.

"Why tell me now?"

"Blair and Callum. Ya have also made powerful friends willing to kill for ya and from what I hear, yer no slouch yerself."

"Why were you guys with Aisling?"

He snorts. "We needed someone who could move about with Shauna and not be detected. Kate chose her. She's not even my type, goofball."

"Oh my God, Cole. I'm so sorry. I'll pay for the car. I … I … I don't know. I got so angry."

Cole grabs the back of my neck and turns me to face him. In the next motion, he has his lips crushed to mine. He kisses me like a man desperate for air.

He's taking all of mine as he deepens the kiss. It sinks in how wrong I had been and how much I miss him. I throw myself into the kiss and allow him to devour me.

He reaches for my bum and pulls me into him. Groaning into my mouth, he pulls my towel from around me and tosses it to the floor. Lifting on my toes, I try to get closer to him.

"How should I punish yer little ass?"

"Huh?"

"Ya didn't think it was going to be that easy, did ya?"

"Come on, Cole. You weren't spending time with me, you wouldn't bring me here with you, and you came home smelling like another woman after I heard one calling your name over the phone. I saw you with them. What was I supposed to think?"

He grasps my throat and looks down into my eyes. The fire in his eyes should scare me, but it only turns me on. He moves his face closer to mine and I stick my tongue out to flick over his lips.

"You're hiding the accent well, baby. Good girl. Your ass was supposed to think that you trust me.

"That I love you too much to hurt you like that. That I'd die before I see you hurt. Instead, you chose to get jealous and trash my car, which could have exposed you and Shauna," he breathes against my lips.

My eyes go wide. I never would have forgiven myself if I got that baby hurt. I should have given him a chance to explain before I went all bonkers on his car.

"Aye, now ya understand, don't ya? Now, baby, how should I punish ya?"

"I don't know, but I'll take it. I'm so sorry, Cole."

"I've missed you so much. It's good to have you home."

"Cole, the other closet isn't under construction, is it?"

"Ach, not at all. If I couldn't have you in my arms, I wanted you in my bed. It took everything in me not to come home when I knew you were here."

I lower my head, feeling ashamed of myself. I should have trusted him. An idea comes to me, and I look up at him through my lashes.

"I think I know how to make some of it up to you," I say.

"Aye, I have some ideas too."

He begins to back away from me as he frees his belt from around his waist. He then sits back in the chair with his legs spread wide. Then he loops the belt like a pair of cuffs.

"Come here, DJ," he croons.

I smile and go to turn on some music. "Unholy" by Sam Smith and Kim Petras begins to play as I turn and saunter my way over to him. Cole breaks into a smile as he takes my naked body in.

"Turn around and bend over," he commands as I reach him.

I turn and bend at the waist. He slaps my bum then leans in and kisses the sting away. I moan and bite my lip.

"Reach through your legs and put your wrists together," he says.

I do this and he fastens the belt to my wrists. He then grabs the belt like a handle and dives his face into my core. I cry out as he feasts on me.

"Mm," he hums as he pushes in deeper.

With his free hand, he opens me for him to do that thing with his tongue. Then he starts to suck on my lips as he groans and moans in satisfaction. It feels so good.

I start to circle my hips and grind in his face. Cole slaps my cheek and places a hand on my hip to still my motion. I pout, but not for long.

"Oh shit, Cole. I'm coming."

He continues to feast on me. Then suddenly, he pulls away right as I'm about to climax and sits back in his seat. I scoff. He can't be serious.

"Is this really what we're doing, Cole?"

"Keep talking, love. I like the sound of it."

"Cole, please don't do this. I need you."

He growls and stands to his full height. In a series of fluid motions, he drops his pants, puts on a condom, and drives into me. Grabbing my waist, he holds on to me to keep me from tipping over.

"Keep begging me, I might let you come," he says.

"Please, you're so hard. I missed you so much. I need you, Cole. Fuck me, please."

"Good girl," he groans as he bends his knees, presses down on my waist and swivels his hips as he thrusts.

My eyes roll back. His dick is so big. He's stretching me so good.

I start to wind my hips again. He tightens his hold on my waist and growls. I bounce back on him, and my cheeks start to clap.

"I love this fucking fat ass. Who the fuck else could I want when I have you? I have it my way, I'm going to die in this pussy.

"You're mine, DJ. Only mine. You always have been," he says tightly as he continues to stir my insides.

I'm so wet and he's so hard. Just when I'm about to come, he pulls out again. This time, he pulls my hands from between my legs and lifts me into a standing position.

He dips his head to breathe me in, hovering his lips over mine. I look into his green eyes, pleading with him to give me what I'm longing for.

He pecks my lips hard then takes a step back and sits in the chair once again. I look over my shoulder and smile. Two can play this game.

Brooklyn

I'm torturing us both. Her tight pussy has me right on the edge. I bite my lip as I look her over. DJ turns to face me and drops to her knees.

She's only gone down on me a few times. I'd rather have my face between her legs for her pleasure, but I'm interested to see what she's going to do with her wrists bound.

"What are you up to?"

"I want to tell you how sorry I am. Let me talk to you," she purrs as she pulls the condom off.

I open my mouth to say something, but drop my head back and groan as she takes me into her mouth. Placing a hand behind her head, I relax and allow her to bob on my length.

"That's it, baby. Good girl. Just like that. *Fuck*," I hiss.

She rolls her neck as she bobs. Resting her bound wrists on my abs, she then claws her nails against my skin. Not able to hold back, I lift my hips and pump into her mouth until she starts to choke.

I relax back into the seat. She lifts her head, allowing her saliva to drip all over me, then sucks some of the moisture back into her mouth. Tilting her head to the side, she spits on it and then sucks on my girth.

Knowing I'm a bit wide and long for her mouth, I release her hands for her to work with them. She wraps her hands around me and continues to suck, getting me sloppy wet. My eyes roll back.

She holds up my dick and sucks on my balls while stroking me. The sounds coming from her sucking, slurping, and gagging are driving me crazy.

I bite my lip as I look down at her. When she takes me in deep and holds me in her mouth, I can't help bouncing my leg like that's going to help me hold back from coming.

It's the smile on her face as drool drips down her chin for me. This is the best head she's given me. After she works me like she owes me, I come down her throat with a roar.

"Fuck, baby, come here," I murmur as I pop free from her lips.

She lifts my pants and pulls out the other condom I have in my pocket. Standing, she turns and sits in my lap. The music is still playing on repeat as my girl decides to put on a show.

She throws her arms over her head as she looks back into my eyes and grinds her hips on me. I'm already growing hard again. I lean in to kiss her, but she turns her head at the last minute.

I chuckle and palm her breasts. DJ has a nice pair of double *D*s. Nice, firm, and perky. I could spend days getting lost in this curvy body.

"You sure you want to play this game with me?" I breathe in her ear.

"Mm," she moans.

I grin and pinch her nipples. She rolls her body over mine then slides down, using my thighs to hold her up as she dances between my legs.

Lifting and bending at the waist, she claps her bubble ass at me. I groan. I haven't had enough of her yet.

As if reading my mind, she turns, squats in front of me and rolls the rubber into place. I stand and grab a handful of her hair, walking her back toward the bed. Lust fills her eyes, bringing a smile to my face.

I nip at her lips as I get us across the room. To my surprise, she turns me and pushes me back onto the bed. I laugh and lie back as she climbs onto the bed and up my body.

She takes my lips into a kiss as I run my hand over her soft skin. I groan into the kiss as she claws her nails over my chest. Swiftly, she breaks the kiss and turns her back to me, straddling my hips.

Reaching between her legs, she seats herself on my hard length. We moan in unison as she slides down. I sit back and watch her enjoy herself. Her ass bouncing on me hypnotizes me.

The scent of her bodywash fills my nostrils and makes my mouth water. Reaching for her waist, I guide her up and down. I tighten my hold as she really gets into it.

Running her hands up her sides, lifting her arms in the air, all while grinding on my cock. I run my hand up her back and grasp the back of her neck as she goes from grinding to bouncing.

She leans forward and starts to rock back as her pussy sucks me in. The sound of her wet heat fills the room, sounding creamy and drenched. My brows crease as I watch her ass bounce and ripple.

"Fuck," I hiss and slap her cheeks one after the other, making them ripple some more.

Then she kills me. My girl looks over her shoulder and sticks her tongue out the side of her mouth as if to taunt me with the visual of her enjoying how much she's loving this.

I growl, sit up, grasp her by the throat and take her mouth in a searing kiss as I wrap the other arm around her waist and take over from beneath.

"I fucking love you," I growl into her mouth.

"God, I love you too. You feel so good, Cole."

"I'm going to make you feel good all night. You ready for that, baby?"

"*Yes, yes, yes, yes,*" she screams as I finally allow her to come.

CHAPTER THIRTY-EIGHT

Her Happiness

Deja

Since that night Cole showed up at our place, we've been inseparable. At least when it comes to where we live, we have. I was a little miffed with him for resigning for me.

I liked my job, but I got over it as Cole promised he had something better suited for me. He has taken me to his parents' place, and I got to spend time with Aunt Kara. Uncle Dougie has been traveling, so I haven't seen him yet.

I've been spending most of my days with Kara and Kate, Cole drops me off with them when he goes to work. Blair and Callum usually tag along. It doesn't make sense for them to hide in the shadows watching anymore.

I know why they are here. It feels weird knowing all this time they've been trained to watch over me. I had thought we were just learning together.

Today I'm excited because Cole says he has a surprise for me. He told me to get dressed up for a date. I've gone through everything in my closet and still can't decide on what to wear.

"This is insane," I groan and stomp my foot as I stand in the closet, still in my panties and bra.

All I did while working for Val was shop. I have more than enough clothes and shoes. Heck, the woman still sends me shoes and bags when she thinks of me.

My friend thinks of me often. When I'm not hanging out at the O'Brien home, I'm with Val and her adorable children. I love Vita, and the boys have me wrapped around their little fingers.

I can't lie, now that I know about Shauna and who her parents are, I've been thinking a lot about having babies with Cole. I'm not rushing him to get married, but I can't help wondering when that time will come so we can start our own family.

"Yer not ready? What are ya doing in here?"

"I can't figure out what to wear. It's our first date since I've been here. I wanted to look nice."

"The way your drawers are all up in that ass, you could stay just like that. I wouldn't complain."

"Shut yer gob, Brooklyn," I snap and roll my eyes at him.

He laughs and comes into the closet to wrap his arms around me. He then kisses the top of my head. I melt into his arms as his cologne surrounds me.

"Brooklyn? Mm. I don't know how I feel about that," he murmurs into my neck as he buries his face there.

"I'm the only one who calls you Cole besides your mother and siblings."

"I know. I don't think I want that to change. Not yet anyway."

"Then behave. Or Brooklyn it will be."

He sighs. "Let me help you. We need to go."

"You're going to help me pick something to wear, really?"

I pull a face and crane my neck to look back at him. He pecks my lips, then releases me to walk through the closet.

I watch as he fingers a few items then pulls a couple to look them over before putting them back. He then grabs a cute sundress that has an open back. Next, he grabs a denim crop jacket.

I take the items as he hands them over and hold them up. It's a cute outfit. The dress is colorful. Pink, orange, and yellow, the jacket is a light-blue denim wash.

Putting on the dress and then the jacket, I wonder what shoes I should wear. Cole turns to me and holds up a pair of denim wedge sneakers that are perfect. I grin and take the sneakers from his hand.

It is in this moment I note he's wearing light-wash jeans and a fitted T-shirt under a black leather jacket. Black construction boots are on his feet.

"Thank you. This is cute," I say once I have the shoes on and I take a glance in the mirror.

Cole takes my hand and leads me out of the closet. I can't help but wonder what this date is that he's in such a rush. There's something about his demeanor I can't put my finger on.

Oh well, we shall see.

***

The drive here has taken some time. Cole won't tell me where he's taking me, no matter how many times I ask. Now that he's parking, I'm totally confused.

We're in a nice-looking neighborhood, from what I can tell, but there are mostly shops lining the lane. However, I don't see a restaurant other than Chinese, but it looks more like a takeout place, not someplace to sit down for a date.

"Come on, get your ass out of the car," he says with a smile on his lips as he opens my door.

I roll my eyes at him, but take his hand and step out. That's when I see the awning. My mouth falls open, and tears burn my eyes.

Walsh's.

"I couldn't decide on a name at first. I thought of calling it DJ's, but it's an Irish pub. O'Brien's would have brought too much attention, so I went with Walsh's," Cole says as he wraps his arm around my waist and leads me to the front door.

"What have ya done?" I choke out.

"It's yours. You like working in pubs. I thought this would be a place that would make you feel at home."

"Have I told ya how much I love ya?" I say as I leap into his arms.

"You're adorable when you're happy. This is nothing. Come on, I want you to see inside."

He pecks my lips and gives me a squeeze. When we step inside, I'm in awe. The place is much bigger on the inside than it looks from the outside. It immediately has a homey feel.

I might give him some slack on his accent because he nailed the Irish pub vibe with this place. I couldn't have designed it better myself.

My heart fills as I realize Cole never fails to show me how much he loves me. I feel bad for not trusting him. I learned a lot about a loving, trusting relationship from being around Uri and Val.

I look behind the bar and smile when I see the bat he gifted me mounted to the wall. As I see it, I realize how long I've had that type of relationship.

"I love it. Thank you so much, Cole."

"Anything for you, love."

Brooklyn

I'm happy to give this place to DJ. The smile on her face made it worth it. Although it broke my heart when she saw the framed picture of her and her parents.

She broke down and sobbed in my arms. I wish I knew more about what happened all those years ago. I've had to swallow down that need to know because I'm not going to ask her.

I see how much pain it causes her. If I'm meant to know, the answers will come to me without me having to add to her hurt. All I want is to make her happy.

"That was delicious," she sings as she finishes the meal the chef I brought in prepared.

I'm leaving the decision to open a kitchen here to her. Pubs with kitchens in this area do better. However, of the pubs I've seen her manage, they didn't have one.

"We should christen the place," I say with a grin.

"Ach, really? I just ate. Can I digest my food first?"

"I'm not talking about sex, butthead. Is that all you want me for?"

She laughs. "I think I would be a dickhead if you're going to call me names and I do want you for more than sex. You're my favorite dance partner.

"Queue the music. I think christening the place is a grand idea," she says with a sly smile then sticks her tongue out at me.

Smart-ass, I should have known she knew what I meant. I go over to the stereo system behind the bar and find something for us to dance to. I smile when I find just the right song.

"I Know What You Want" by Busta Rhymes and Mariah Carey begins to play. I dance my way back to DJ and pull her up from her seat. I spin her around then bring her back to me by her waist, sticking my thigh between her legs as I hold her close.

I flex my fingers against the soft skin of her back as I dip to press my forehead to hers. She cups the sides of my face as a smile comes to her lips. Tilting my head to the side, I take her lips in a firm kiss.

Breaking the kiss, I pull back and allow her to turn her back to me. I wrap my arms around her and hold her tightly, still keeping the two-step sway in play. Splaying my hand over her belly, I lean in to kiss her shoulder.

At six-three, I tower over her, but she fits me perfectly. There has never been a woman who has fit me better. Closing my eyes, I press my nose into the back of her hair and inhale.

"I love you," we state at the same time.

I kiss the back of her head and squeeze tighter. Things feel like they're finally falling into place. This is all I ever wanted.

And then my phone rings.

CHAPTER THIRTY-NINE

Return of a King

Boyle

Seven months later …

"Yes, yes, fuck me harder," she screams as I pound into her tight pussy.

I grab her long blond hair and pound harder. Sweat is dripping down my back and I'm getting so close as I fuck her from behind. I didn't come here for this, but this is usually how things go when I come here.

I've become her fuck toy. That wasn't what I was asked to do, but this woman is a force, and the pussy is good.

I release my load and groan. I needed that. I've been stressed the fuck out.

Sometimes I wonder if this shit was worth it. If not for her, I would be a lost cause. My boss sure doesn't give a fuck about me.

"That was good. You fuck like you have shit on mind," she says with that Russian accent as she lies on her stomach, looking back over her shoulder at me.

"I always have shit on my mind."

Getting to my feet, I then stumble over to the chair in the corner and flop down into it. I grab my smokes and pop one into my mouth, then light it.

Blowing out the smoke, I narrow my eyes at the pretty blond on the bed. She sits up and looks over at me with those cold blue eyes. I still don't know how I've fallen into this shit with her.

"You came to talk, da? Talk. What is problem now?"

"He's not happy. You promised him you'd take care of the girl and stop the Alliance bullshit from happening. O'Brien gets out today, and the lass is still alive," I reply.

"This my problem, why?"

"You made him promises. He doesn't feel like you're holding up your end of the bargain."

"I prefer when I dealt with old man. He was old bastard, but he understood long game. Your boss is only after name for himself.

"He doesn't understand what my family is owed. What we have lost and sacrificed. I want girl die as much as he does.

"I need her to die to get to my goal. Lynch was my mistake, waste of time. Did not get job done, but answered questions for me.

"Bitch I want isn't going to come out of hiding for threat, little bitch can handle herself. He wants Alliance stopped, he has to be patient, da," she says, giving me that cold look of hers.

"He's growing tired of the excuses."

"I would take her out myself, but gets me nothing. Besides, I can't reveal myself yet. My family has more invested here than your boss. Let him play in his shadows, I don't fear him."

"That's easy for you to say. He's growing suspicious of us. We might need to cool things off."

She rises from the bed and strolls over to where I'm sitting. Straddling me as I sit here, she then takes my cigarette and takes a drag. I frown as she blows the smoke in my face.

"He give you trouble, you stay with me. Tell me, what is in this for you? Why you do this for him?"

I look away. I can't tell her that this all started because I wanted Deja Walsh for myself. My boss was meant to kill me that night.

Instead, he saw a use for me and my cousin took my place. I only had to keep my mouth shut for a few days and then disappear as the rest of my family was killed on Oland's orders. In return, I was promised delivery on all the promises Oland made.

However, here we are. Oland is long dead, and I've received nothing promised. I'm the last in my bloodline still breathing.

Deja has a price on her head and I'm no closer to having her or the wealth I was promised by Archie McDougal. I have nothing if I walk, but there's still a chance the boss could deliver if I stay.

"Da, you have secret to keep. Does boss know secret, or do you keep from only me?"

"I have my reasons. I've lost too much to turn back."

"So have I. You stay with me, and we make work. You don't have to be pet. You partner, help with counteralliance. I treat you with respect, da."

Before I can answer, she reaches to stroke me to life and seats herself for another round. I'm going to regret this. I know I am.

Deja

I sit at the bar in the O'Brien Manor in Dublin with my feet up. Knowing who this place used to belong to doesn't really leave me wanting to be too respectful. I was a little surprised when Brooklyn told me he was bringing me along for the trip.

Logan has been released from the clinker. However, something bigger is happening here. There have been a ton of people in and out all day.

"You don't really believe the words on your skin, do you?"

I turn to find an older man looking at my back. Given the fact he has read the Japanese written on my back, I assume he's Japanese. He tilts his head to the side as he regards me.

"I don't believe I still do. I once did."

"Words are powerful. You should think over those and decide how to go about removing them."

With that, he nods and turns to leave. It is then that I notice Cole standing in the doorway, watching me. I have never wanted to cover my back more.

With his face clouded over, Cole turns and storms off. He's been having a hard day with how angry Logan has been. I don't think his brother has said a word to him since he arrived.

Feeling like I should at least explain why I chose the words, I stand and go to follow after him. However, Logan appears and stands in front of me.

"We should talk."

"Why? Ya don't like me?" I blurt out.

He sighs and purses his lips. "When have I ever said I don't like ya?"

"Ya clearly don't. Ya have always tried to keep us apart. Did ya know I was in Scotland?"

"Aye."

"Were ya the reason I was sent there?"

"No."

"But ya know why, don't ya?"

"Aye."

"*Logan*," I drag out.

"I can explain, but ya won't be able to tell Cole. He has already tipped the scales enough."

"Then I don't want to know. We don't keep secrets from each other."

"Then he knows why ya can clear out an army or parking garage without batting a lash? Or are ya saying he didn't just ask Kiyoshi Nash what that tat on your back says."

"Like I said, ya don't like me, so why should I listen to anything ya have to say?"

I turn to walk off. Not even caring that my shoes are still sitting by my seat. I need to find Cole.

"Because I'm trying to keep my hotheaded brother from getting himself killed."

I freeze. If there is any chance Cole could be hurt, I'm going to listen. I turn back to Logan, lick my lips, and nod.

Instead of going to find Cole, I follow Logan. My stomach is in knots. I'm not sure I should have come on this trip.

Brooklyn

I stand outside the manor, staring at the hills. I've been out here trying to clear my head. Logan is one thing, the Alliance is another, but that tattoo.

I probably wouldn't be this angry if she had told me what it said when I asked. So much time has passed, and she still hasn't told me out of her own mouth.

I thought it was something cute she was just too embarrassed to tell me. Now I know what it says, and I don't know how to feel about it. Is that how she feels?

Trust no one, not even your shadow.

I close my eyes and work my jaw as arms wrap around my waist. Then I feel her press her face against my back. I know it's DJ from the way my body reacts to her nearness.

"I've had this tat since I was eighteen. I was alone, scared, and couldn't protect myself. I also didn't know what or who I needed to protect myself from.

"These were Mum's last words to me, I got them to remember. Since you arrived, I've ignored all her warnings, and I've allowed you in.

"Please don't take these words to heart. I trust you with my life. I love you, Cole."

I turn and look down at her. I want to know what happened. It's on the tip of my tongue to ask.

"Can we leave the past in the past for today? Being here has opened so many wounds. I just want to forget it all for a while."

I nod my head and dip in to take her lips. She wraps her arms around my neck and opens for me. The kiss becomes heated as I back her against the side of the house.

Lifting her onto my waist, I press her against the cool stone exterior of the manor. We kiss passionately as I grind against her heat. I want her, but I don't have any condoms on me.

"We can't," I say against her lips.

"Everyone has left. It's just your family and Logan's two friends. No one's coming out here."

"I'm not afraid of getting caught," I snort. "I don't have protection on me."

She looks up into my eyes. "I trust you."

"Are you sure, baby? Don't you want to wait until we're married?"

"I'm already yours, Cole. A party and a piece of paper aren't going to change that."

I kiss her hard. Her words mean everything to me in this moment. I fumble with my belt and zipper.

When I reach between her legs, I find her already wet for me. I groan and kiss her hungrily. I can't get enough of her.

"Cole," she cries out as I thrust into her tight, wet heat.

"Christ, ya feel so good. I don't deserve ya. I've done nothing in my life to deserve an angel like you."

"I was made for ya, Cole. Ya deserve me because I could only be yours."

I latch my lips onto her neck as I thrust in and out of her. Being inside her bare is a feeling like nothing I've ever felt in my life. She's panting softly, trying not to make too much noise.

"Fuck," I growl.

"How are ya this hard? My God, ya seem bigger. Yer stretching me so much."

"Ya do this to me. Ya make me lose my mind just thinking about ya. I love ya so much."

"Yes, yes, I love you too."

I take her lips and kiss her with more intensity and desire than I knew I could. I think it's all the trust she's showing me. In this moment, I want to give her the world.

With my brother home, I can finally start to move forward with my life. It's time I put a ring on her finger.

I pull away to look into her face. The ecstasy I see in her eyes has my balls tingling. I stick my thumb into her mouth and press down on her lower lip.

"Come, I can feel it. Come for me."

She throws her head back and starts to convulse against me. I pull out and come into my hand. She stands on wobbly legs, grinning up at me with a drunken smile.

I dip in and peck her lips. “Mine,” I breathe as I rub my nose up and down the bridge of hers.

CHAPTER FORTY

Crossing Paths

Deja

A month later ...

Noah and Bean's wedding has been so nice. I'm really enjoying myself. I like Nellie, Bean, and Heather.

I think Roni will even grow on me. Although she was a bit curt with me, I don't hold it against her. There was a time when I was the same way to protect myself.

Besides, I know she's focused on watching over Shauna for Logan. I would have done it had he asked, but I guess he's placing me in the pot with the rest of his family. Val has introduced me to many of the women here.

"Ellen, have you met Deja? DJ, this is Ellen, Sam's wife," Val makes another introduction as a tall brunette with dark eyes comes over with a glass of champagne in her hand.

She's pretty. She could definitely pass for a model. She gives me a smile that lights up her face. I return the smile and stick out my hand for hers.

"None of that, come here," she sings and pulls me into a hug.

Once we embrace, she releases a gasp and steps back. With a mix of a sad but excited smile now on her face, she cups the side of mine. I look back at her, confused.

"The girls will soften him. They are meant to be first. He will need them.

"You will name him Patrick, and he will be something amazing and fierce. Younger than my Sammy, but very wise and respected as if he's much older. Sammy will know him as a friend and a brother. They will even out each other's tempers as Sam and Logan do for each other," she says then moves her hand to my belly.

I look to Val then back at this woman. I'm not sure where any of that comes from, but I get the feeling I shouldn't ignore her words. I'm reminded of the gypsy who guided me to New York through my great-gran.

If not for her, I wouldn't have the friends and family I have now. I'm not sure what her words mean, but she's sure of them. She lifts a hand to her lips and rushes off.

I look to Val and lift a brow. "*Ohhh … kaay,*" I drag out.

I look around to find Cole. He's with his cousins, laughing and having a good time. I shake the eerie feeling off and run my hands down my sides.

"You'll get used to it," Val says. "Come, let's have a drink with Paige and the girls."

I smile and nod. Val has endeared herself to me even more in the last few months. After my talk with Logan in Dublin, I shared with her how my mother left me, and she offered to track her down. She hasn't found her yet, but I love her for trying.

CHAPTER FORTY-ONE

Closing a Chapter

Deja

Seven months later …

The death of Ellen Mairettie has impacted so many people. I just met her and then she was gone. I feel horrible for Sam and his children.

Logan has been spending a lot of time with him to help him through. However, tonight, all the O'Briens have come to my bar to be together as a family. I think everything that has happened has caused them to need to connect.

I didn't mind closing down for the night for them. Seeing them all together has brought back so many memories. I'll admit, I'm a little in my feelings to know Ciara doesn't remember me. It feels like so much of our lives have been stolen from us all because of one evil man.

"Can I help with anything?" Ciara asks nervously.

I look up from the glasses I'm gathering to pour a round for everyone. Kate was helping, but she had to go to the bathroom.

Connie has Shauna in her lap as she sits with Dylan, Jamie, and Ciarán.

"I've got it, but if ya want to hang around and talk while I fill, yer welcome to," I say with a smile.

She gives me a relieved smile. I get the feeling she wants to bond, but she's not sure if I want the same. She's my little cousin. She might not remember me, but I remember her and blood or not, I'm here for her.

As we fall into a light banter, I pour drinks. I'm also keeping an eye on Cole. He and Logan still have a ton of tension between them.

I hate to see him hurt like this. He did what he thought was right. I get that his moves created a ripple effect, and we probably shouldn't be together, but Cole has changed my life so much.

My time with Uri and Val gave me something. I have friends and I've learned to trust again. None of that would have happened if Cole hadn't come for me. At least that's what I keep telling myself.

"I'll take those to the table," Ciara says once I have one of the trays full.

"Thanks."

Logan comes over and takes a seat at the bar. I look him in the eyes and purse my lips. He's forgiven the rest of the family, but he's still giving Cole a hard time. I don't think that's fair.

"You need to forgive him or tell him the truth," I bite out in a whisper.

"To tell him the truth, I have to forgive him. I still haven't gotten there," he grumbles.

"He's your brother. He loves ya, and clearly, he loves yer daughter. I understand telling him everything is going to hurt him and make him a madman at the same time, but if ya keep this up, yer only driving a wedge between ye. Tell him the truth, Logan."

"The truth? No one around here knows the truth, only the parts of it they can handle. If ya give a child a toy they can't hold up, they collapse under the weight of it. I'm protecting him more than ya know."

"Are ya saying I still don't have the whole truth?"

He grabs a mug and winks at me. "Aye."

With that, he turns and walks away. Frustrated, I return to my task of filling beer mugs. Now I'm angry because he's withholding information from me.

I don't realize I'm slamming things around until Cole comes over with a concerned look on his face. My face heats with embarrassment. He crowds my space and cups my cheek.

"Are ya all right?"

"I'm fine," I say softly and bury my face in his chest.

He wraps me in his embrace, and I melt into him. Just as I relax, my phone rings. I pull away and look up at Cole with my brows furrowed.

I'm not expecting any calls. Val and Uri are helping Sam out with his kids. Val and I spoke earlier and she said we'd talk in the morning.

Pulling my phone from my back pocket, I see it's a call from Scotland. My breath catches in my throat. I shake my head, not wanting to answer this call.

I already know what's coming. It's like a stone settles in the pit of my belly. I suddenly can't breathe.

Tears are running down my cheeks, and I haven't even answered the call. I feel so sick. Cole pries the phone from my hand and answers for me.

"Hello." His deep voice rambles.

It should comfort me, but I can't find any comfort in the sound right now. I cover my mouth as my stomach turns. It feels like I'm in a box with no air.

"Aye, Ken, it's Cole. She's standing right here with me. What about ye?"

I look up into his face as sadness covers it and he closes his eyes, nodding as if Uncle Ken can see him. Grabbing me by the back of the head, he pulls me into him.

I can't help the sob that rips from my throat. Gran is gone. I've lost my great-grandmother.

"No," I cry into Cole's belly as I double over in pain, clinging to the back of his shirt.

It is one thing to know this day was coming and another for it to be here. I will miss her dearly. We just spoke this morning.

I thought she sounded great. She joked a bit and made me promise to come to Scotland to bring her flowers, which I thought was odd at the time. Now I get that she was saying goodbye.

"Aye," Cole's voice cracks. "I'll make sure she's there in time for the service."

That's the final straw. My knees buckle and I drop to the floor. Cole sits down on the floor with me and wraps his arms around me.

At some point, I end up in his lap as he rocks me and murmurs soothing words. Another chapter is closing and I'm still not sure of my path.

CHAPTER FORTY-TWO

Words of Gypsies

Deja

"What are ya up to?" Cole asks as he enters my bedroom at the castle.

I never spent much time here, but the uncles have always made sure I've had my own space. I love Cole for coming to Scotland with me for this. I've been lost in my thoughts more times than I can count.

"I'm going through some things to see what I want to take with me. Uncle Duncan brought some boxes over from the cottage," I reply.

"You still don't think you're ready to go over there for yourself?"

"No, I know she told me to leave, but I still feel like I abandoned her. I would have so much guilt if I stepped foot into that house. I want to remember the place for my happy memories with Gran."

"Not to mention you sound American now. You can't take that bullshit into her home," he teases, making me laugh.

I smile at him. It's clear what he's trying to do. Cole has proven to be a great boyfriend.

"Look who's talking. I wonder if that friend of hers knew you were a New Yorker who would rub off on me," I taunt back.

He lifts a brow as confusion covers his face. I bite my lip as I realize we've never spoken about Gran's friend and what sent me to New York.

"Gran had a friend. She said she was a gypsy. When I was reluctant to leave with ya or even date ya, Gran told me her friend said I would leave when the lad who loves me showed up.

"Gran also told me I would go to New York because that's where my destiny is. I was to meet a Hush and a Black Death. I hadn't known then who Val and Uri were, but I figured it out right when ya came to tell me about Shauna."

Cole nods his head. "Aye, she was talking about Phoebe Romanie, who was Ellen's grandmother. She passed recently as well, a few weeks before Ellen, Sam's wife."

"Oh my God. That makes so much sense."

"What do you mean?"

"Ellen, at Noah's wedding. She said some things to me, and I thought them odd, but knowing who her grandmother was, it makes more sense now."

"What did she say?"

"Something about naming a boy Patrick. I think she said we would have girls first, but there would be a Patrick, and he would be friends with Sammy?"

I don't get to finish my words fully as Cole lunges at me and captures my lips. He kisses me hard and deep, leading with his tongue. I lace my fingers in his hair as he pushes me onto my back and shoves everything from the bed.

"Cole," I pant as he reaches under his sweatshirt that I'm wearing.

"I want ya pregnant. If I have to get through a daughter or two for my son, we need to start now," he breathes into my ear.

"Cole," I laugh.

My laughter is cut off as he lifts my shirt and captures one of my peaks in his mouth. I'll admit, the thought of having a baby with him does bring a smile to my face, something I haven't had much lately.

Then there's a knock on the door. I sigh and hurry to pull my shirt back down. Cole sits up on the edge of the bed with a scowl on his face.

"Yes?" I call out.

"I'm heading out for dinner. Ye guys still coming with?" Kate calls through the door.

I love her for coming to Scotland with us to be my support, but right now I want to strangle her. Talk about poor timing. Cole pulls a hand down his face and rolls his eyes.

I look down at his pants and see the print running down his leg. Yeah, we're going to need a bit before we can go. I laugh quietly.

"We'll be down in a bit," I call to Kate.

I then lean in and kiss Cole's lips while still laughing. With a growl, he tackles me to the bed and tickles me.

CHAPTER FORTY-THREE

Pandora's Box

Onyx

I jog up the stairs to my fifth-floor apartment. I don't take the elevator to keep from getting trapped. When I step out of the stairwell, I frown and quickly pull my gun as I notice my door has been disturbed.

I move quietly to the door and nudge it open. The scent of a cigar is the first thing that catches my attention. Apparently, I have company.

"What are you doing here?" I say as I place the safety back on my gun.

"Och, hello to you too, Léan," he says like a grumpy big brother.

I roll my eyes as I tuck my gun away. "Hello, Finlay."

"Orla has passed away. Everything has changed."

"Is Deja all right?"

My heartbeat picks up. This is my worst nightmare come true. I thought I was doing the right thing by her.

I didn't know this would take years of my life away from me. Years Deja and I can never get back. She's grown to be a woman without me.

"She is fine, but the auld woman left behind something I think you should have."

"Did Ken and Ewan send you?"

"Och, no. My nephew sent me, but it was Da's words that caused him to."

"Ian?" I ask with my brows threaded.

"Aye, he's still playing a match. He did leave the journals for Logan like he said he would, and they are loaded. Nothing about any of our lives has been by accident."

"Nothing was an accident around Ian Black," I scoff.

Finlay chuckles. "Ye would have been my wife had we not fought like brother and sister from the time ye arrived."

"Is that right?"

"Aye, ye should read the letter and the pages Logan and LaSalle copied for ye. It will all become clear."

I nod and move to take the manila folder he's holding out to me. Taking the pages out, I then take a seat on my sofa across from the accent chair Finlay is sitting in, like he's the owner of the place and I'm the guest. When I see the handwriting on the pages, it's like a punch to the gut.

I run my hand over the page as I close my eyes. I miss Ian. He was the closest thing I had to a father. I learned a lot from him.

Léan

My Léan, my Onyx. From the day I found ye, I knew ye were special. There was something in yer eyes that gave me pause.

I knew that day I would make sure ye were avenged. No young girl, no child should have been in the state I found ye in. When I began to train ye and show ye the love ye deserved from a father, I saw ye had forgotten where I found ye and where ye came from.

Yer brain erased all the horror. Ye might have forgotten, but I never would. The Krupin family had no right to do what was done to any of the girls or boys they took and sold.

I saw a lot of things while in my time of service, but coming across ye and the bodies of yer friends who hadn't survived was by far the worst thing I've ever seen. Ye have lived yer life thinking the Alliance doesn't involve ye. Thinking ye have no skin in the game.

Ye are one of the reasons I started this. Learning about the families connected and how many of them I knew, I was disgusted. But I made note of those who wouldn't touch it, those I could ally with.

Those were the families I could stand with. The families who earned off your suffering, from yer body, will fall once the Alliance is in place. They will never have the power to do to another what was done to ye.

To make that happen, I needed more power. To make this happen, I had to place ye on the board before me. I'm sorry, love.

Angus was waiting in that coffee shop for ye because Lennox and I told him to be there. I needed Léan Black to become Helen Walsh. Onyx was ready to disappear, so I made that happen for ye before I lost ye altogether.

I saw ye ready to bolt. I would have lost a daughter and the wee one ye didn't want to tell me about. Ye had to become Helen.

Ye and the little one were safer that way. I knew ye were pregnant even though ye hid the fact from me. That vacation ye took told me more than ye knew.

I believe with all my heart Angus was the best thing for ye. His love for ye was real. Never doubt that.

Angus cherished ye as a woman, his woman. Finlay wasn't right for ye. The lad loves ye, but as an annoying sister.

My plans for Joe were elsewhere. At first, I didn't think ye had it in ye to fall in love, not romantically. Not after ye walked away from Deja's father.

I had hoped that relationship would stick. Then Phoebe Romaine contacted me and pointed out what threads to pull. I watched and waited.

I saw the moment Cole became infatuated and I nudged that bond as much as I could, knowing Oland couldn't resist triggering ye to take his life and setting ye on a path to finish what I started.

Lev Krupin was the only one from that family who could be trusted. He thought differently from the rest. He didn't believe in all their practices.

The Krupin family is dangerous. Phoebe told me you would hunt them and always find the task just outside your reach until Deja and Cole were together and yer past deeds came back to haunt ye.

I have one more task for ye, love. This one brings the board to a decisive advantage. It's time for the zugzwang. You are my final checkmate before I hand over a winning board to my boys. They will handle the rest.

Phoebe said to tell ye to find the child. The one with the gray eyes that see all. Ye will know it's him because he looks like his father and he will finish what his grandmother and I started.

Forgive me. I didn't want to return yer past to ye, but this is how we win.

Your father, not by blood, but always in heart,
Ian Black

I swipe at the tears rolling down my cheeks. I do remember where and how he found me. I just pretended not to because he was so kind, and he wanted to protect me.

Ian Black saved my life and then gave me the skills to never be taken advantage of ever again. However, I didn't know the family I've been hunting is the reason for how I ended up in that horrible life.

The Krupins haven't made it easy for me to find them or get close to them. They are like ghosts. Pavel is only seen when he wants to be, and even then, it's nearly impossible to get near him.

I guess he learned from what I did to his brother. I'm one of the best and they still evade me. I thought it would end with Pavel. However, once I began to dig, I found I'd only be cutting off one head and there would be another who would follow. Deja and I would forever have to look over our shoulders.

"There is something else ye should know," Finlay says, causing me to look up at him.

"What's that?"

"Misha Krupin has killed Pavel. The sisters have taken things over and they are worse than the brothers. He wants their heads and could get in your way."

This is what I mean. That family is unhinged, but not untouchable. Ian's work will not go in vain.

"Understood."

CHAPTER FORTY-FOUR

Blast from the Past

Valentina

I stand in the viewing gallery of the training facility. DJ and one of the trainees are sparring. I wince as DJ catches him in the throat and he stumbles back.

I'm in more awe of this chick the more I see her in action. She's skilled in combat and will clear a target course with one hand behind her back. If those two demons are with her, forget it.

I love watching them work. With them helping me train the other ladies, I'll have the army we need.

"Hello, Val."

I turn, ready to fight. My mouth falls open when I see who's standing in the room with me. There were certain skills my uncle didn't feel he was the right fit to train me for. That's when I met this woman.

"Onyx? What? Wait … you're her mother. That's why I'm having trouble finding you for her. Helen Walsh doesn't exist," I breathe as it all clicks into place.

"She did once. That is who my daughter knows me as."

"So she doesn't know about what you do?"

"No. You look good, Val. I've heard a lot about you and what you've become."

"I can't say the same about you. You disappeared after training me."

"I did Valentine a favor. I was out of the business," she says as she comes to stand beside me to look down at Deja in the ring. "Look at her. She's good. I couldn't have trained her better myself."

"She moves like you. I couldn't put my finger on it before. She has some of your facial features, but I couldn't put it together."

"That's probably for the best."

"Why are you here now? You're not going to let her know, are you?"

"I'm here for you. The kid says it's not time for her to know I'm here."

I close my eyes and groan. Sammy. What is that kid seeing now?

"Me? Why me?"

"The Bellas are your idea, right? Ian wanted me to train an army for his grandsons. I'm here to help you do that."

"How do we do that without her knowing?"

"You leave that to me."

She pats me on the back and turns to leave as quietly as she entered. I stand with my mind reeling. Then a smile comes to my face.

My girls are going to be lethal. The Bellas. I like that.

Brooklyn

As I stand by the bar at Walsh's, I put my shades on while reading over a text on my phone. It's time for me to head out. I drove DJ to the pub, but I can't hang around like I normally do.

Jamie is here working on the POS system and teaching DJ all the shit it does regarding the family and family business that goes beyond the pub itself. I have a lot on my plate today. Since Orla's death and the black box she left for the Alliance, there's been a lot of movement.

LaSalle will soon be announced as Don, and Logan has officially taken his place at the head of the Black clan. I'm finally settling in as the head of the O'Brien clan in Ireland, and DJ has signed over her assets to the Alliance.

"Hey, you heading out?" DJ asks as she comes to a stop in front of me.

"Yeah, I have to go," I reply and place a hand on her hip as I lean in to peck her lips.

Her soft lips entice me to deepen the kiss. I slide my hand to her ass and devour her mouth as I knead her sexy curves. Breaking the kiss, I peck her lips a few times and then place a kiss to her forehead.

"Be good. No fighting the delivery guy this week," I say and chuckle.

"He's clumsy. I'm not going to keep losing stock because he has two left feet and promises a discount that I never receive." She scowls.

"I have a new vendor for you. She starts next week."

"Thank you. Will I see you here tonight?"

"I'll try. I can't promise anything at the moment. I already have a ton of shit on my plate today."

"Okay, don't let me hold you up. I love you."

"I love you too, baby. See you at home," I murmur and kiss her lips before I tap my hand against her ass and leave.

I step out of the pub with my phone in my hand as another text comes in. When I look up, I frown and scoff. I'm not in the mood for this shit today.

"You three have to be the dumbest motherfuckers on earth," I say as I look between these assholes.

Detectives Vargus, Baker, and Strong have become a thorn in my side. They've been warned, but they don't listen. Because of the Alliance, they are all on the verge of losing their badges.

Fucking with me, it's about to be their lives. I'm losing my patience. Standing here in front of DJ's pub is a different kind of dumb.

"Don't worry, we're not here for your corrupt ass. We have some questions for the owner of this bar," Detective Baker says.

I snort and rock my jaw. "You have the audacity to call me corrupt?" I pause to reel my temper in. "Nah, fuck what you're talking about. You have a warrant?"

"We only have questions for now. Are you the owner?" Detective Strong says, cutting Baker off before he can speak again.

"The only owner you'll be talking to. What the fuck do you want?"

"We have a body and a book of matches from this place was in the vic's pocket."

I shrug. "What does that have to do with me?"

"The name Deja was written on the inside flap. Word is that's your lady and she's the owner of this place."

I keep my calm and remain expressionless. Inside, I'm ready to burn down everything moving. Someone is playing a game of *fuck around,* and I know they don't want to *find out.*

I take off my shades to look them in the eyes. "You boys have seen firsthand what playing with me and mine gets you. You come to me when you find the problem, not with the problem.

"And now, if this becomes my problem, it's going to be yours. You feel me? You boys have a good day and stay the fuck out of this establishment.

"Go near my woman and all the grace that has been given goes up in smoke. I hate repeating myself and you three have brought me to my quota of words for you this century. Have I made myself clear?"

"Whatever, fuck this asshole and his bitch. Let them Russians put a bullet in her head," Detective Baker grumbles and turns to head for their car.

I pull my gun and cock it. "You want to repeat that?"

Vargus jumps in front of me and holds his hands up. Strong restrains Baker as I glare him down.

"This is the shit we have to deal with now? He can pull a fucking gun on me in broad daylight and we're not going to cuff him?"

"Not if we want to keep our badges. We shouldn't even be within a hundred feet of him in the first place," Strong barks.

"Fuck this shit, they can have my badge."

"Listen, we didn't come here to start any shit. We got a lead and came to talk to Deja. If you won't allow us to speak with her, keep an eye on her at least."

"My baby is always good, but thanks," I say as I pat his cheek. I think I'm going to like this alliance. The NYPD has needed some checks and balances for a while.

I hop in my car and call Logan and LaSalle. They should know about the mention of the Russians. I'm not sleeping on that.

CHAPTER FORTY-FIVE

Italian Weddings

Boyle

Seven months later …

"You are sure you want to do this?" I say as we sit in the car watching LaSalle Locatelli's wedding from down the hill.

The place is buzzing with activity. Some powerful people are in attendance. Once this move is made, we're not going to be able to back down. I don't know if she's thinking clearly anymore.

So much has changed now that the Alliance has gone into effect. They may not be at full capacity, but they are still strong and growing stronger. I think this is a mistake.

"Da, now or never. You have said yourself. Misha closing in on truth. Once he returns to Russia, he will know. Those women have made sure of it.

"I am now alone. I have only you. This time. We can hide behind Gormon. They won't know we were here."

I sigh. "Why not just go to Misha? Let him learn the truth from you."

"*Net,* Misha one thing. My revenge another. I don't want him know until I complete my mission."

"But isn't—"

"Enough," she barks loudly, her ice-blue eyes blazing back at me as her nostrils flare.

I sigh. I have officially jumped out of the pan and into the fire. The boss has been calling me to find out where I've been. I go back to where he's hiding and I'm a dead man.

However, I'm watching the woman before me lose everything, including her mind. If I had known then all I know now, I wouldn't have joined forces with her. I get the feeling there is no name, no power at the end of this for me.

"Listen to me, my love," she says as she cups my face and turns it to hers. "I don't need them. I'm better off without those witches.

"He will kill them for me, and I will take what's rightfully mine. Little time and patience will get us everything we want. We find Léan's daughter, I kill her, we go."

"Here's Gormon's people. Let's go."

Deja

I turn to the sound of snickering as I try to creep out of the room where Cole and I were just having sex. Val and Pam are watching me with amused smiles on their faces.

I groan and palm my forehead. I knew we shouldn't have come up here. I mean, it was worth it, but now I feel like a child with my hand in the cookie jar.

However, when Cole comes out of the room with his tux jacket in his hand, his shirt open, and his tie loose around his neck, I want the floor to open and swallow me whole. I even notice a love bite on his neck. I can't say I remember putting that there.

He walks over to me without a care in the world and dips his head to kiss me. It's not a little peck either. He palms my bum and pulls me into his body, bending me backward as he devours my lips.

"See you all downstairs, ladies," he says as he breaks the kiss and winks down at me.

Pam and Val burst into laughter. I bite my lip as I watch him walk away. Am I crazy for thinking he looks sexy with his gun holster strapped across his shoulders?

I shake my head clear and turn to my girls. I don't know why I'm so embarrassed. I've caught them both in similar situations.

"What are you guys doing up here?" I ask.

"Tasha had to pee. She needed help with her gown. It was our turn," Val replies.

"Oh, there's so much to think about with all of this," I say as I begin to daydream about marrying Cole.

"You guys planning on getting married soon?"

"I don't know. Things are always so crazy. He doesn't get to be just Cole. Brooklyn takes up so much of his life.

"I'm not complaining. I'm always here to support him. I know what I've signed up for," I reply.

"It will happen at the right time for you guys," Val says reassuringly.

"Phew, I thought I was going to burst," Tasha says as she comes out of the bathroom, patting at her dress as Camille comes out behind her.

Suddenly, the sound of gunfire rings out through the air. I snap into action and pull the gun from the holster around my thigh. Val pulls two guns of her own.

"What the fuck?" Pam gasps.

"Tasha, get back into that room," I bark.

No bride should have to deal with a shooting at her wedding. Val and I can hold this floor down if any threats appear. Before we can come up with a plan of attack, Cole reappears with his guns drawn.

"All of ye, into the room DJ and I were in, now," he barks.

"I'm not hiding from shit. Where's my husband?" Val growls.

"Heading out front with the others. LaSalle wants Tasha to remain up here. I'm thinking Uri and Nate would want the same. DJ and Cam, don't start with me. In the room now," he commands again.

Before we can all protest again, Blair and Callum appear and the gunfire quiets and comes to a stop. Cole comes to me and pulls my head to him while still holding his gun. Then he kisses my forehead.

"We're leaving as soon as I get word that everything is clear here," he murmurs.

I look up and see the anger in his eyes. I know immediately why he's angry. We played the pull-out game one time too many. I'm two months pregnant.

Cole was so excited when I told him why I hadn't been drinking at the wedding or last week at the engagement party. That's how we ended up in that room up here. He hasn't known for more than an hour, and now this.

I nod my head, not trying to argue with him. It was instinct. I didn't think about the pregnancy.

I did what I was trained to do, but he wouldn't know that. I don't even know why I still haven't told him. I'm somewhat afraid to.

He's seen me in action. Well, not really, but he knows I can shoot. I'm going to tell him.

Brooklyn

As I stand here in Italy, in the study of the Locatelli mansion, it becomes painfully clear how real the Alliance has become—no longer a theory my grandfather murmured in my brother's ear, but a reality. Tonight proves the other side is willing to take risks as much as we are.

Of all places to decide to challenge us—at LaSalle's wedding after the announcement of his becoming the don. Shit is more than real.

However, what's become more real than that is the fact that I'm going to be a father. I had planned to wait for things to settle a little more before I proposed to DJ and made her my wife.

Then we would start our family. Well, I fucked that all up. I think I remember the night it happened. I'd been drinking with my brothers at the bar. Once DJ shut the place down and locked up for the night, I bent her over one of the tables and fucked her right there.

I rolled that same table in the back the next morning because I had my way with her all over it. On top of it, face down, ass up, name it, I gave it to her. Now we have a baby on the way. The timing sucks, but I couldn't be happier.

"I want answers. You have less than twenty-four hours," Logan barks out, pulling me from my thoughts.

Pulling a hand down my face, I acknowledge what I need to do. I can't move the same. Not when it comes to DJ.

I walk over to Logan and look him in the eyes. He looks pissed off and frustrated. I get it, this should never have happened.

"I need to take DJ back home," I say to him.

"With all this going on? This wasn't just an attack on LaSalle. This was disrespect to all of us.

"We need to be here to handle this. He's leaving for his honeymoon. The least we can do is stick around and watch over his family," he bites out in frustration.

I'm frustrated with the entire situation. I just found out I'm about to be a father, and the next thing I know, our friends' wedding is being shot up. My heart was in my throat as I raced back for DJ.

Finding her with a gun in her hand, like she was ready to run out there and get involved, pissed me off for so many reasons. Not only is she pregnant, but I don't want this for her.

"DJ is pregnant. I want to take her back home. I'll be ready for anything you need, but I need to get my family home first," I say, hoping he understands.

Shock comes over his face and then a huge smile. He tugs me into him and gives me a bear hug. I'm a little shocked at first.

While he's been talking to me since our fight after his revelation about DJ and Ciara, there has still been a little tension here and there. Logan can be stubborn and I'm no better.

He cups my face in his hands. "I'm proud of ya. Ya and DJ were meant for each other. I'm happy for ye. Go home, protect our family, aye."

"Aye," I say as I get a little choked up.

Knowing he sees DJ as family means a lot. I wasn't sure how he would feel about us after everything that's transpired. I have to admit, the tightness in my chest begins to loosen up.

"There's no feeling like it. Yer going to make a grand da."

"We'll see," I snort.

In this moment, I feel like I have my brother back. I look up to my older brother. It was killing me for him to be so pissed at me.

I would do it again if it meant him getting to come home to that sweet wee angel. Shauna is everything to him, like I knew she would be. I know he would have been devastated had I not kept her safe.

I can accept his anger. He had every right to it. As long as we're good now, I can handle anything else.

"I love you, man," I say as I clear my throat.

"Aye, I love ya too."

CHAPTER FORTY-SIX

Fire & Rage

Deja

Eight months later …

"Here, you look like you could use a drink," Logan says as he hands me a bottle of water.

"Thanks," I say.

My mouth has been a little dry. I had planned to head over to get a drink, but Shannon stopped me to talk my ear off a few times. I don't mind, I like her.

"Yer welcome. Have ya eaten?"

"Aye, thank ya for asking."

He grunts and nods. I can see his thoughts racing across his face. He has something on his mind.

Our relationship has grown since he told Cole the truth about knowing where I had been all along. I get that he was protecting us both. Even when he pulled Cole away from me during my birthday party, he was looking out for me.

"Mom is having a ball with the girls. She's been texting pictures of them all day. Cole won't look at them because he doesn't want to ruin the night for ya."

"I know, I peeked once at the group chat and almost broke down. I've wanted to go home for hours now," I whisper and snicker.

I'm missing my girls. This is the first time I've been away from them. I had the babies three months ago and Cole didn't want to bring them to the baby shower.

Tasha is so adorable with her belly. LaSalle hasn't stopped smiling. I'm happy for them. They have been through so much.

They're a strong couple and are only becoming stronger. My friendship with Tasha has grown since the wedding as well. She and the ladies are my crew.

If Cole knew of the things I get up to with them, he would flip. Especially if he found out how long I trained while pregnant with the girls.

Logan chuckles. "Almost forgot he added ya to the group chat."

"What's really on yer mind, Logan?"

He opens his mouth to answer, but a commotion breaks out. We both stand to see what's going on. As my eyes land on Tasha, I watch as LaSalle scoops her into his arms.

"Oh no, what's happening?" I say.

"LaSalle has been concerned that she's been in labor this whole time and trying to hide it," Logan replies.

"What can we do?"

"I'm heading to the hospital with them. I'm sure that's where he's headed. Ya and Cole can ride with me if ye want."

"Oh, I have a bottle of whiskey I've been saving for LaSalle. I meant to stop at the bar to pick it up. We'll meet ya at the hospital, yeah?"

"Aye, see ye there."

***

"This is going to be quick. You don't have to come inside with me. I'll be right back," I say as Cole pulls up to the bar.

"If it will be quick, we can both be in and out. The place is closed. I'd feel better if I went with you."

I purse my lips and give him a pointed look. Just as I get ready to tell him I can more than handle myself, his phone rings. He looks at the incoming call and curses.

"Fuck, I need to take this. Hold on."

I roll my eyes because by the time he takes his call, I could be in and out. This is Cole. I should know better. He's always my protector.

He's been extra protective this week as Blair and Callum have been away for a little bit. I'll admit, I do feel strange knowing they're not lurking somewhere nearby. I've grown used to having them around at all times.

"Hey, man. What's up?"

"I'm right behind you. This shouldn't be said over an open line," Czar says right as high beams flash behind us.

Cole sighs. "All right."

He cuts the call and leans across the console to kiss me. "Go on in. I'll be right out here talking to Czar. Get what ya came for and bring your ass right back out."

"Aye, aye," I say with a teasing smile.

He pulls a face that tells me he thinks I'm a smart-ass. His annoying smart-ass, whom he loves. I wink at him then turn to run across the street to the pub.

Brooklyn

Czar told me earlier that we needed to talk. No one was expecting Tasha to go into labor. We all took off to support LaSalle and Tasha.

We had been pulling out when DJ asked me to bring her here to pick something up for LaSalle. I guess Czar took notice that I wasn't heading for the hospital using the same route as everyone else.

Whatever he needs to talk about must be pretty important. I step out of the car and walk to meet him in front of his SUV. The first thing I note is the concern in his blue eyes.

"What's up? What's that look about?"

"Remember that body you asked me to look into about a year or so ago when those cops came sniffing around?"

"Aye, you said nothing came up. Just some lowlife."

"Yeah, at first glance, that would be true. I came by as you asked about a week ago. There was a guy sort of lurking around. I didn't think anything of it at first.

"He was old enough to be my dad. I took him to be harmless. However, this other dude showed up, and he started taking pictures of the pub. The first dude sees him and drags him out of the car.

"You told us not to make ourselves known or obvious when we come around, so I held back and watched. He dragged the guy into the alley and beat the shit out of him, then threw his body in his own trunk and drove off.

"I shrugged it off since you did tell me she has bodyguards, I thought maybe they were back. Then Andrei gets a visit from your NYPD boys while I'm there. They were asking after one of his guys and they mentioned the dead guy you had me look into.

"They think the two murders were connected because—get this—body number one had just started working for Andrei the day before he was killed; body number two had only been with him for two weeks," he explains.

"You're just telling me this?"

"Brooklyn, come on. You know how much shit is on my plate. Listen, I'm not finished.

"I took a picture of the guy they're looking for, but I can't find anything on him. He's like a fucking ghost. The only reason I connected any of it to DJ is because you said her name was found on the first vic's body. I can't say what the connection with him is, but you know we don't believe in coincidences."

"Aye, there's no such thing around here. I'll keep an eye out and inform the others to do the same."

I look down at my watch and then back up at the pub. What's taking her so long?

Boyle

I'll admit we're never going to get another opportunity like this. Deja always has someone with her. We never even got close to her in Italy.

Sending that lad all that information about Deja backfired. It's been over a year, and he's been killing off our guys. I'm still annoyed about that.

I work hard to get them in the right place—and then she sends them in to get killed, like getting them jobs with the Russian mob is so easy.

We lucked out tonight, and we have guys on the way to make sure this job is completed. I will say, I could have been wrong. Things have been looking like they might turn around.

Her connections are never in lack and that has gone a long way for the cause. The Alliance has pissed a lot of people off. Some who are willing to pay to see it fall apart. We are taking the money and doing the jobs to get to our ultimate goal.

"Hello, Deja."

She turns to me in surprise. I swing the bat I've taken from behind the bar and hit her in the head. I was warned not to give her a chance to put up a fight.

As I stand over her, I grin. If I can't have her, no one can. Our lives could have been so much different if she had only stayed away from O'Brien.

Everything was fucked after that bonfire. If she hadn't been flirting with O'Brien, I never would have gone to see Oland and my family would still be alive.

"Hurry, light cocktails. We need leave before he comes looking for her. Men on way, they will hold him off while place burns."

I nod and go to light the rags she stuffed into the alcohol behind the bar. When I get to the final one, I light the rag and toss the bottle a few feet away.

We then run for the back door to get away. Once in the car, I'm grabbed by the back of my neck. The excitement rolling off her is enough to make me hard.

I want to get her back to the hotel and fuck her until the sun comes up. My chest feels tight. I thought I would be happier to know Deja is gone from this earth and Cole O'Brien can never place a hand on her again.

It doesn't feel great at all. I need to get lost in this pussy to fuck the hurt I shouldn't feel away. Nothing is ever easy.

"Let's go. I want you," I say.

"*Da*, hurry up. I have bottle of vodka to celebrate."

She climbs back into her seat and flips her blond hair over to the other side of her face. Then she reaches into her backpack and pulls a bottle from it.

Her eyes are sparkling with happiness. One of her goals has finally been accomplished. She would be happy. I pull off with a bitter taste in my mouth.

Deja

"Micheal, I've found her. I'm coming out. We can't go out the back. It's blocked," Sim says as I lie groaning on the floor.

My head is pounding. I reach to cup it and something sticky covers my hand. When I pull my shaky hand away, it's covered in blood.

"We have to go. The oxygen and fire are causing the alcohol to combust. This is going to get bad, very bad. Can you walk?"

She helps me to my feet, but I feel a little lightheaded. Wrapping my arm around her shoulders, she then helps me to move toward the door. I trip and knock into something.

It's too smoky to tell what. We keep moving forward even though I'm now limping with each step. As the fire hisses and roars, glass shatters and pops, and the wood whines and groans as it burns and snaps. Above it all, I can hear Cole outside screaming my name.

"*Deejay*." His accent is coming through heavily.

I can hear his pain as he calls for me. My thoughts go to our children. My girls need me.

I push forward faster, knowing we need to get out of here if I'm going to get back to them. My chest and lungs are burning but I keep moving with Sim.

Sim tightens her hold around my waist and steps a bit faster as she carries the brunt of my weight. As we get through the smoke and push out of the front door, I'm semi-relieved.

With each step, I breathe a little easier. Right when I lock eyes with Cole and we clear the burning pub, an explosion goes off behind us. My body is propelled in the air.

I feel the moment Cole wraps his big body around us to shield us from the blast. That's the last thing I'm conscious of.

CHAPTER FORTY-SEVEN

All My Love

Deja

Four months later …

"DJ, will ya come on, love?" Cole groans from the other side of the door.

"Hold on, will ya? I'm coming."

I grumble under my breath as I look myself over in the mirror. We're in Ireland, so I'm living out of a suitcase. I'm not really equipped for getting ready for a date like I would be at home.

Cole felt we needed to get away for a bit. Honestly, I can't say I disagreed. Waking in the hospital was scary, but I was happy to have my friends and family surrounding me.

Cole almost never leaves my side these days. When I told him I thought the attacker knew me, he was livid. The servers for the cameras were on site, so the footage burned with the pub.

That hasn't stopped Cole from trying to find out who was behind it. I've heard murmuring around everyone that it had something to do with some Russians or something. Cole won't talk to me about it.

He's been more Brooklyn than Cole over the last few months. Which is why I haven't been able to stop smiling since this morning. Cole woke me with breakfast in bed.

He had the girls strapped to his chest and back while carrying a tray of French toast, bacon, and freshly squeezed orange juice. It was so good.

Watching Cole feed the girls while I ate was icing on the cake. He's such a good father. I know we hadn't planned the girls, but I wouldn't want to change anything that has happened that has brought them into my life. With each day, I fall more in love with them and their father.

"DJ, baby. Come on. We need to go," Cole says with impatience.

I sigh and shake my head. I don't know why he's in such a hurry. Everything in Ireland bows to him and his will. There isn't a restaurant that wouldn't change everything to accommodate us. Besides, he didn't give me much notice.

I roll my eyes at the jeans and crop top I had to settle for. The heels are cute, so there's that. Grabbing my purse, I go to leave.

I step out and find Cassie Black holding one baby as Laoise McGowan holds the other. Cole didn't want to stay in the O'Brien manor on this visit. When Cassie heard we were here during her visit, she offered to have us come to the McGowan estate.

Once Graham and Malcolm called Cole to see if he planned to stay with their gran, he gave in. I have to say, I don't mind. I love Cass and Laoise is a hoot.

"Are ye guys sure ye be okay to babysit?" I ask for the millionth time.

"Aye, lass, between the two of us, we've enough babes for our own softball team. Ye get out of here and show yer lad some love," Laoise says with a smile.

"Aye, she does not tell a fib, she doesn't. Seven lads hell-bent on outdoing me and Joe. We can handle these wee angels. Go on," Cass adds.

I go over to kiss each of the girls. They are so quiet and well-behaved. They took to Laoise and Cass right away.

"DJ," Cole groans.

"What is it with ya? Why are ya rushing me?"

He throws his arms up in the air. "We have shit to do. I don't want to be late. Can ya bring yer pretty ass on?"

I smile and roll my eyes at him. This better be a good date. Only an hour's notice to get ready and now he's rushing me like an impatient child.

Brooklyn

I've been planning this date for a month. We're running late and it's all my fault. I was up all night with the girls so DJ could get some rest.

Then I got up early to make her breakfast in bed. I didn't mean to fall asleep with the girls when I put them down for a nap. I woke with less than two hours for us to get here.

I'm so grateful to Aunt Cass and Granny McGowan for babysitting while I got dressed and during the time we'll be on this date.

I've never been this nervous about a date in my life. I feel like I'm fifteen all over again. After almost losing DJ in that fire, I can't put this off any longer.

"I can't believe we're late," I murmur to myself.

"Is it really that big a deal? I'm sorry. Ya didn't give me much time," she pouts.

I pull into the parking spot and turn to kiss her lips. "It's not yer fault. It's mine. Come, we need to go."

"Wait, *Field of Dreams*. What are we doing here?"

"I called in a favor. That's why we need to be on time," I say before climbing out of the car.

I should have known she would recognize the softball field right away. How could she not? This used to be her dream.

Now I'm starting to sweat as I mumble to myself while rounding the car to let her out. I can't believe I almost fucked this up. She takes my hand as she gets out of the car, but her attention is on her phone.

"It says here there aren't any games this evening, but there's one in the morning. Are you sure our date is here?"

"Give me that," I huff and snatch her phone from her to shove in my back pocket.

She looks up at me with the cutest smile on her face. It takes my breath away. In this moment, I know I'm here to do the right thing.

We get to the field and Seán is standing there with his cousin Connor, who helped make all this happen. My heart is thundering. DJ places her hand on my back as if she knows I need her touch to calm down.

"Okay, I'm about to burst with curiosity. What are we doing here?" she says.

"Do ya think ya can still knock one out of the park?" I ask with a grin on my lips.

"Did ya eat all my favorite crisps and couldn't find them anywhere after to replace them like ya promised?"

I burst into laughter. "Shut yer little ass up. I learned to bake them myself and made ya some, ya brat. It's been almost a year, get over it."

"I'm not over it, Cole. Still not over it," she taunts.

I pull her into my arms and kiss the top of her head. This is why I love her. Swaying her in my arms, I breathe her in.

"Yers were better, but ya didn't have to eat all of my crisps in the first place," she says into my chest.

"Whatever, come on. Yer up." I slap her ass and release her.

"Yer pitching?" she scoffs.

"No, smart-ass."

She's been following a new up-and-coming pitcher. I grin as the pitcher comes out on the field, holding a ball and mitt. She walks over to DJ and pulls her into a hug.

"Ya were amazing. I remember watching ya hit when I was younger. Yer the reason I play," Niamh says to DJ.

"Thanks. Yer amazing yourself. It's so nice to meet ya. I've been rooting for ya."

"That means a lot to me."

"Shall we, ladies?" Connor says.

Seán hands DJ a bat and Niamh heads to the mound. Connor and I step off the field out of the way and Seán jogs after us to follow.

Once we're in the dugout, I stand with my arms folded across my chest as I watch. This is all about timing. I want it to be perfect.

"Here we go," Seán says.

"Aye." I nod.

Deja

I'm vibrating with excited energy. I haven't been on a field in years. To be on this field is a dream come true.

I didn't know I could love Cole more than I already did. Bringing me here has made him a superhero in my mind. Meeting Niamh is the icing on the cake.

"Okay, DJ, this is it. Don't shit the bed, love. Yer man is watching. Show him ya still got it," I whisper to myself.

Niamh throws that crazy screwball of hers. My breath hitches as I become one with the bat. I see myself hitting it before it gets to me and then I swing. The bat cracks against the ball and it's out of here.

I drop the bat and go to run the bases for old time's sake. Before I get to first base, fireworks explode in the air and the cheers of a small crowd ring out.

I stop and look up in the bleachers. All of the O'Briens and a few of the McGowans are in the stands, cheering and pointing. I turn to look at what they're pointing to. Lighting the sky are the words:

Will Ya Marry Me?

The wind is knocked out of me. I drop to my knees, sobbing.

Cole comes to wrap his arms around me. I tuck my face into his neck, not able to stop crying. I can't believe he did this.

"Come on, love. I'm going to need an answer," he teases.

I pull away. He looks into my eyes. It's that look.

The one my da used to give Mum is written on his face. It's the look I always wanted my husband to have for me. The one that tells me without a doubt that he loves me. I cup his face and nod.

"Aye, I'll marry ya."

He crushes my lips with his in a searing kiss. Everyone cheers for us, but nothing else matters in this moment. Cole is everything to me.

CHAPTER FORTY-EIGHT

Making a Play

Boyle

"I still say we should have split up," I mumble as we step off the jet and climb into the waiting vehicle.

We're flying in from Poland, where we've been lying low. When news came in that Deja had, in fact, made it out of the pub, we knew we needed to move and shift the plan.

Manipulating the situation with the Russians and Serbs in New York is officially off the table. I do believe we've burned a few other bridges there after the failed attempt on the Locatelli woman.

"We're using up men. I need you here with me. While Misha in Russia, we hit New York and here.

"This where I need you. Here with me. I can't fail again. I have run out of time."

"Ya have run out of time. This is why I should be in America, making sure the attack is a success."

"It will be success, and we will be able to mend few bridges. I need to pull her into the light now."

"What if she hasn't appeared because she doesn't care, or maybe she's already dead? Shouldn't our focus be on the Alliance and taking the power they have created? We end them and we can take it all," I say.

"*Net*, I have bigger picture. This my life's work. Not time to give up.

"Time to push, get done. When accomplish goal, we have all power. Our love will bring success we need."

I school my features. This isn't the first time she has mentioned she loves me. I don't know if it's a ploy to manipulate me or if she means it.

I can't say I'm in love with her. The sex is good, she has kept me living a comfortable life, but I don't know that I love her. She's ruthless and if I let my guard down, that could be my life.

I've already gotten away from one controlling, manipulative boss. I refuse to become trapped again. As I remain silent, she reaches to squeeze me over my pants.

"We blow off steam in hotel, *da*?" she purrs.

"Aye, not a bad idea."

Brooklyn

I walk through the McGowan estate shirtless with Cara and Liadan in my arms. My girls are so cute. It's the long, full lashes for me.

I feel like I'm walking around with two gorgeous dolls in my arms. They already have me wrapped around their wee fingers. I didn't know I could love anyone the way I love them.

"Daddy did good," I coo to them. "She said yes. Now we have a wedding to plan."

Liadan makes a little shriek that's pure adorable. Cara has been nodding off, so she jumps at the sound of her sister's excitement. I chuckle and kiss each of their cheeks.

"Shouldn't ya be giving the lass a good shag to celebrate?"

I turn to find Granny McGowan looking back at me. I laugh and shrug my shoulders. I love this woman as if she were my own gran.

"They were fussing. I decided to take them for a walk to get them to knock out."

"Ach, hand them over. Ye young ones need to learn to leave them be. They make noise as much as they shit. Ya don't have to jump every time they whimper."

The tiny woman comes over to me and reaches for Cara. Liadan begins to whimper on cue. I frown at her for trying to make me look bad.

"Go on, hand her over," Granny McGowan says.

"I'll carry her for ya."

She puts her hand on her hip and glares back at me. "Do I look oul and banjaxed to ya? Hand me the babe, Cole O'Brien, before I lay boots to ya."

"Yes, ma'am," I chuckle.

"Grand, yer a smart lad. Now go put yer shirt on before my husband gets mauled. I'm remembering when he was yer age."

I suppress my laugh and lean to kiss her on the cheek. I'll come back for the girls after a shower and a few phone calls. It's been a long day.

"Thanks."

"Don't even think about coming back for them this evening, lad. Ya should be working on their siblings."

"Yes, ma'am."

I shake my head and head for the guestroom DJ and I are sharing. She's probably passed out. I can't help smiling as I think of how happy my entire family is for us.

Connor even gave us time to have a quick family game. I haven't had that much fun in years. Today is a day I'll never forget.

I step into the bedroom and look around for DJ. I don't find her, but I get an idea. I pull out my phone and put on some music.

When I look up, she appears from the bathroom in her panties and the crop top from earlier. As I focus on her, I realize it's not the same tee. This one has Brooklyn printed across the chest.

I break into a grin. She has this dreamy smile on her lips. The ring looks great on her.

She sobbed even more after I placed it on her finger. A perfect fit. DJ hasn't stopped smiling since I proposed.

Actually, that's not right. I didn't miss how happy she was to be up at bat. We've talked about why she had to give softball up. I wish I could kill Oland again.

"Where are the girls?" she asks, looking around.

"Laoise insisted on taking them for the night. Tried to clobber me, she did."

DJ begins to snicker at me. Her face lights up with her laughter. My heart swells to see the joy in her eyes.

How could I love this woman any more than I already do? She makes this life worth living. If she asked me to walk away from everything just to be hers, I would.

"What's that look about?" she asks as she crosses the room and wraps her arms around me, placing a kiss against my chest.

"I'm looking at my fiancée. I'm in awe of ya. I always knew there was something special about ya.

"Now I get to watch that magic every day and with each day ya show me yer more amazing than I thought the day before," I say as I wrap my arm around her.

"How did I miss it?" she breathes in almost a whisper.

"Miss what?"

"That look. Ya've always looked at me that way."

"What way?" I knit my brows.

"It's the look I've always associated with love. The way Angus looked at Mum. How yer da looks at yer mum.

"I never noticed it before, not before my eighteenth birthday. Now I can remember all the times ya looked at me with that look. It's been in your eyes for years," she murmurs.

"I've loved ya for years. My DJ, my love."

"Cole, I need to tell ya something."

I cover her lips with my finger as "Ordinary" by Alex Warren comes on. I don't want to lose this moment. This song says all the things I can't find words for right now.

I dip my head to press my forehead to hers. When our lips connect, I feel like she breathes life into me. The connection is more powerful than it's ever been.

She runs her hands up my sides, bringing goose bumps to my skin. I continue to consume her lips as I turn her so her back is to my front. Then I move my lips to her neck and plant a slow trail of kisses against her soft skin.

Reaching under her crop top, I then palm her breasts and groan into her mouth. We continue to kiss as I knead her mounds. She whimpers into my mouth, causing me to pinch her nipples.

Releasing one breast, I glide my hand down the center of her body, over her belly, and shove it into her panties. I find her wet for me already. Groaning, I push my fingers into her.

She lifts on her toes and starts to rock her hips. It doesn't take long before her legs start to shake. I drop to my knees and peel her panties down her legs.

Not able to help myself, I nip at her ass as I smooth my hands up and down her thighs. Pressing my hand to the center of her back, I bend her over so I can feast on her. When she begins to circle her hips in my face, I growl and slap her ass.

Adding my fingers to the party, I eat her pussy until she cries out and her knees buckle. Getting to my feet, I then lift her into my arms and carry her over to the bed.

Once I place her down gently, I shove my sweats down and climb onto the bed with her. DJ moves swiftly and takes me into her mouth. I sit my ass on my heels and reach to lift her hair out of the way.

"Fuck, baby. Just like that. Take your time.

"I'm going to fuck you right. There's no need to rush. *Fuck*," I hiss out.

She keeps sucking and pumping me with her hands. She's so beautiful going down on me. I grow harder from the sight alone.

"Yes," I growl as she rolls her tongue around me.

Lifting my hips a bit, I hold her head in place. She chokes around me and allows her saliva to run down my length. Releasing her so she can move her head, I watch as she runs the back of her hand across her mouth.

Lying back on the bed, she looks back at me with lust in her eyes. "I want ya."

She will never in her life have to ask me twice. I move between her legs and thrust into her tight pussy. I can't believe it's this tight after she pushed out my girls.

It feels even better than before she was pregnant. I look into her eyes as I dive into her, rolling my hips and pounding into her deep.

"God, I love ya."

Deja

As I look into his eyes, I have no doubt that he loves me. Cole has gone above and beyond to show me that I can love and trust him. I had planned to reveal my last secret to him.

I'm hoping it will take some of the stress off his head once he knows. I know since the fire, he's been more concerned about me. I don't think Blair and Callum will ever get to leave at the same time again.

"Oh God, yes, Cole," I pant.

He's so hard inside me. I rock my hips back into him, causing him to growl and kiss me hard. Just when I don't think it can get any better, he pulls out and turns me over. Lifting my hips in the air, he thrusts right back in.

Grasping my waist, he pulls me back to him with each thrust. He then moves his hand to my shoulder and grabs my hair with the other hand. It's so good, but too much all at once.

I reach back and try to hold him off. He growls and knocks my hand away. Then he changes angles and pushes his palm down on my back.

"Don't run. Take that dick. I want that wet pussy to talk back to me," he says and slaps one cheek, then the other.

I'm coming and sobbing at this point. Cole slows down and begins to grind his big, fat dick into me. He's so hard as he pulses inside me.

My eyes roll back. All I can do to stay sane is fist the sheets and try to rock my hips against him. He groans and presses my body down flat as he keeps stroking.

"So fucking good."

"Cole," I whimper.

"You need a break, baby?"

"No. I can take it," I sob.

"Good girl."

He pulls out once again and turns me on my side. Then he lifts my leg over his waist and eases his way into me as we are face to face.

Connecting our lips, he kisses me deeply. Reaching for his hair, I hold him to me as he works my body like only he can. He keeps making love to me as we get lost in our own world.

"Cole, Cole, Cole," I scream sometime later.

I'm not sure how long we've been at it when I feel his hot seed spray my walls as they squeeze around them. My heart is pounding as I come with him.

"That was amazing," I laugh when I catch my breath.

He pulls from my body and moves to spoon me from behind as he wraps me in his arms. I bask in the feel of his warm body wrapped around me.

"You are amazing. I love you. Get some sleep." He kisses the top of my head and gives me a squeeze.

"I love you too." I yawn.

CHAPTER FORTY-NINE

Deja

"I'll see ya later," Cole says as he kisses my forehead.

"What time is it?"

"Four forty-five, I didn't mean to wake ya. Sleep in. The girls are with Cassie and Laoise. Callum and Blair are with them."

"Ugh, I hate that ya have to go out. Will ya be long?"

"No, I'll be back by lunch."

"Okay, I'll miss ya."

"I'm already missing ya," he says and kisses the tip of my nose.

I roll over and try to go back to sleep. About ten minutes later, I know that's not going to happen. I punch the pillow and grumble to myself.

I might as well get up and shower, then go find my girls. I miss their little faces. After I'm showered, I think about going for a run.

Maybe Blair will come with me, and Callum can stay behind with the babies. He loves being an uncle. Those girls have so many protectors.

I dress in a pair of leggings and a running top. After I'm dressed, I head downstairs to find the girls. I'm sure they're up. The time zone difference has thrown their routine off.

Looking down at my phone, I think of calling Val. It's about eleven at night in New York. My mind goes to last night and I smirk.

At this time of night, Val and Uri are probably busy. I'll have to wait for later. I hear the girls before I see them. Cara is squealing her head off.

When she comes into view, I find Callum playing peekaboo with her. Liadan is in Cassie's arms, trying to look around her to see what her sister is excited about with her nosy butt.

I go to take Liadan from Cass, but Cass scowls at me. I laugh and shake my head, but leave them be and go to find some coffee. It's as I drink my coffee that I notice Blair isn't here.

"Where's Granny McGowan and Blair?" I ask.

"Mum is out in the garden before the sun gets blistering. Blair went for a run."

"She still tends to that garden? I can still remember when Kate and I would come to help her."

"She would love that. Why don't ya go out there?"

"I'm going to have to fight ya to get my children back, aren't I?"

"Ye can fight me boys for not allowing me more time with my grands. Besides, Cole is like one of my own and these two are so precious and full of personality already. Are ye planning to have more?"

My entire face gets hot. I think that was Cole's mission last night. Patrick might already be on his way. However, I keep this to myself and give a warm smile.

"Aye, we do. Not sure when, but we will."

"Grand, then ye should enjoy this time I'm giving ye. I don't know how Joe and I found time to have another four after we had the first three. Little fuckers were so damn busy and nosy."

I laugh and go to kiss her cheek. "Thank ya, Cass."

"Ye can call me Aunt Cass, ye know. Always could have."

"Thank ya, Aunt Cass. I'll be in the garden with Granny McGowan if ya need me."

"Is it okay if I run up and make a few calls?" Callum asks.

"Sure, ye go right ahead. Me shoulder isn't what it used to be, but I can still hold me guns, or if I have to, I'll settle for the one like me mum," Cass says.

I jerk my head back, but then I remember Cole telling me she was shot in a shootout in Cali. Good thing we're not expecting any of that around here. I hesitate for a moment before Cass shoos me away to go help in the garden.

"Aye, there ya are. Would ya like some help?"

"Ya know, I have four sons and five grandsons and none of them volunteer to help. Yer a good egg. Cole's a lucky one, he is."

"Put me to work. How can I help?"

"Will ya hand me that?" she says and points to a bag of soil.

I grab the bag she's pointing to and carry it over to her. She pulls a blade from her little boot and slashes the bag open. I get down on my knees to help her.

The task seems to go by faster as we fall into a little banter. It feels good to talk to her in Gaelic. I haven't missed that I've fallen right back into my accent while here.

We're almost done when I hear shots fired. I snap my head up and look in the direction the sound came from. Another shot is fired, causing me to jump to my feet.

"Hurry, in the house," I say to Granny McGowan.

She waves for me to leave her. "Check on the babes."

As we get into the house, I find Cass with Cara and Liadan in her arms. I look around for Callum and remember he went upstairs to make some calls.

"Take cover, I'll handle this," I say without waiting for a response.

I dart for the bag I tucked away in the front of the house in case of an emergency when we arrived. Tossing on the holster quickly, I move out the door. My heart stops when I see Blair moving toward me, covered in blood.

"We're being ambushed. Get back inside. We need to call for help," she says.

I rush to her to help her inside. A red dot appears against Blair's forehead. In a single breath, I push her down, pull one of my guns, flip across her body, and fire at the coward aiming for her. I land on one knee and take out another two.

"Ya come on me property and expect to leave with ye lives? Drop the guns and back away," Laoise says as she pumps her shotgun. "Try me. All I need is one shot and I'll send ya to yer maker, I will."

"And if she misses, I'll pump a hole through ye," Cass says as she comes from around the other side of the house with two shotguns.

I'm in awe, but I snap out of it. Laoise makes good on her promise as the asshole laughs at her. He flies back and hits the ground.

Swiftly, I put a bullet in the head of the other one who had been coming up behind me. More shots are fired from overhead. A glance up tells me it's Callum.

He's on the roof with his semi-auto rifle. As Cass and Laoise help Blair into the house, I help Callum clear the rest out. We're lucky no one else is hurt.

I run inside to see how bad things are with Blair. Callum's footfalls thunder through the house as he comes running. Laoise is holding some towels against Blair's wound.

The babies are crying, so I run to get to them. I can still see Blair from where I stand as I lift my girls into my arms. Tears burn the backs of my eyes.

"It's only a flesh wound. She was just grazed," Callum says with relief in his voice. "I can patch her up. Ye should call Brooklyn."

Logan

An eerie feeling settles in my stomach as both my and Cole's phones ring at the same time. Seeing LaSalle's name, I answer quickly. While it's still early morning here, it's in the middle of the night in New York. Something must be up.

"Hello."

"We were hit. They came to the house."

"Fuck, is everyone okay?"

He scoffs. "We're all fine. Your cousins showed up to save our asses. Sammy knew they were coming and called in the cavalry. Misha, Uri, your cousins, we're all here."

"What?" Cole roars.

I look up from my call and see the dark cloud covering my brother's face. He's vibrating with rage. I know right away LaSalle wasn't the only one targeted.

"Hold on, LaSalle, something is going on here too."

"No, I've got this. Text me the address of where they came from. I'll handle it," Cole barks out tightly.

He won't look at me, so I know he's about to do something crazy. Ireland is his turf. He's a grown man and doesn't have to listen to me.

In fact, I know he won't. However, I need to know what's going on. If LaSalle was hit too, there's no telling who could be next.

"Kill him. He should have come to me first," he says darkly and ends the call.

"What's going on? LaSalle says his home was hit. Do we have a situation I should know about?" I say as calmly as I can.

"Nah, we don't have anything. They attacked my girls at the McGowans. I've got this," he says and storms out.

I sigh. "Did ya hear that?"

"I did. I'll gather everyone here and we'll jump on the jet. I get the feeling you're going to need backup. I have a little surprise for you when we arrive."

"Aye, see ya when ya get here. Let's pray he doesn't get himself killed."

I end the call and pinch the bridge of my nose. This was no coincidence. We're looking at one problem. The attack on Tasha in New York, the wedding, now this, I promise it all stems from the same place.

Brooklyn

You want something done right, you do it yourself. The disrespect—going after what's mine right under my nose—has to be answered right now.

"How are they?" I say to Graham as I drive to the address that was sent to me.

This never should have happened. One of my own men had information about this and didn't come forward until after the hit. It might be time for a little reorganization in Ireland once again.

"They're all fine. Gran is giddy because she got to pull her gun out. I think we can bury the oul lass a happy woman."

"Fuck, I'm sorry I brought this to her door. I should have left more men."

"Ach, ya couldn't have known. From the footage, they were in good hands. Aunt Cass still moves like a spring chicken, and Gran held her own, she did.

"Blew him right down. Aye, blew him down right where he stood, she did. DJ is something else, I tell ya."

"I'm here," I say and hang up.

I already have my vest on, so I load up and climb out of the car to race for the building these assholes are held up in. From my intel, these motherfuckers got in last night. However, some of these guys with them are on loan from cowards who don't want to face me head-on.

I don't care where they're from or who they are. They're going to wish their mothers swallowed them when I'm done. No one goes after my family and lives to see the next sunrise.

With a barrel on each of my guns, I move in. Everything happens in a blur. I clear the front of the building, but in my rage, I forget to use my suppressors, so they're hot on my ass immediately.

"Fuck you," I roar as I step out from behind some crates and blow down another ten or more of their men. I may have lost the element of surprise, but these bum-ass motherfuckers weren't built for this. They can barely shoot.

I move swiftly to get to the upper level, where I have a feeling I will find their boss. That's where I want to be. I want the son of a bitch who had the balls to put a hit out on my family.

Sweat is dripping down my back as rage pumps through my veins. I'm moving on pure adrenaline. Bullets hit the concrete wall I'm standing behind, only making my thirst for blood that much stronger.

I pull a grenade from my belt and toss it around the corner. The explosion shakes the building, but allows me to cross over to the path I need to move forward. I keep moving, gunning down anything in sight.

I know I'm outnumbered, but I'm also getting out of here on sheer will if nothing else. I get down the hall and come to an open door. I move in with caution. There's a blond and a dude who looks familiar standing inside.

"Boyle?" I say and knit my brows.

Boyle McTavish was that little shit my granda was trying to marry DJ off to. Seeing his face sends blinding rage through me. Before I can pull the trigger, I'm hit hard across the back of my head.

Boyle

"Da, this good. I want him alive. She come for him, I finish job men couldn't do. Get him up. We move."

I bite back all I want to say. I told her this wouldn't work, and we've lost two teams. I should leave now. At least with my former boss, he didn't have me on these dummy missions.

"Motherfucker," I bite out under my breath. "Get him up, ya heard her. Let's go."

CHAPTER FIFTY

A Mother's Wrath

Deja

I've been pacing the front room since Logan arrived to say Cole took off to handle the problem on his own. That was yesterday. Cole hasn't returned and Graham was the last one to have contact with him.

I stop and spin for the door when it opens. Ronan is the first one through, followed by Dean. I was told to keep it to myself, but she's Ronan's wife. Next to come through the door are LaSalle and Tasha.

I'm a bit surprised when Sammy and his sisters come through the door with them. I wouldn't have thought any of them would have brought their children with them. Heck, I want to wrap my girls in bubble wrap and send them away.

Roni and John are the next familiar faces to come through the doors, followed by all the other brothers, then Sim, Micheal, Annabella, and Nate. When Kate, Connie, Dylan, Jamie, and Ciara walk in, my knees almost buckle.

Cole has so many people who care about him. We can't lose him. He has to come back to me and the girls.

"You guys can come with me. I think I have a lead on where he is. We can get a plan going and roll out," Logan calls out as he appears.

He's been in the study with the McGowans for the last two hours. I want to follow after them, but Tasha comes to pull me into a hug. "Stay here. We've got you."

I pull away from her and nod. Val comes over once Uri is out of sight. Sim is right behind her.

"Are you all right?" Val asks as she brushes a hand over my hair.

"No, I want to be out there. He needs me."

"That's why we're here. Pam is waiting in the SUV. We'll give it a couple of minutes and head out," Tasha says with a smile.

"I smell trouble, and my middle name is Maker. I want in," Dean says.

"See, I told you I liked her," Val says to Tasha.

"How will we find him?" I ask as I wring my hands.

"Sammy. There's been a development with him and the girls. They work together. We'll explain on the way. We have an exact location," Tasha replies.

"The kid who called me?" Dean asks.

"That's my son," Tasha says proudly.

"Yer not going without us." Blair appears with a determined look on her face.

"You've done enough. Please stay here with the girls. I need to know they are safe so I can focus on bringing their father home."

"I hate it, and Callum is going to be pissed."

"Next time, Demon. We can't take you out there clipped," Val says.

"Fine. Be careful," she says and pulls me into a hug.

"Okay, Bellas. Let's move out," Val says.

Val and Tasha lead the way as Sim, Roni, Dean, Annabella, and I follow. Pam is behind the wheel as we get to the SUV. Sim hops into the front seat and punches in an address as the rest of us load in.

Seeing it's going to be a tight fit, Val tosses Roni the keys to one of the other SUVs, and I follow them and Tasha to climb into that vehicle. Kate and Connie come running out at the last minute.

"Ya didn't think ya were going to do this without us, did ya?" Connie asks as she hops in.

"Not a chance," Val says.

***

We pull up not far from the location Sammy gave to the ladies. Apparently, one of his sisters sees numbers. She then gives them to Sammy and he sees what they mean and how to use them.

That's how he knew what numbers to call. The kid is amazing. There's no telling what he will be capable of when he's older.

We all climb out of the SUV and round to the one Pam and the others are in. Pam pops the boot and there are vests, comms, and firepower waiting for us.

We all suit up and get ready. I fear what we will find when we get inside. I try to push that out of my mind so we can get in there and get to my man.

"Val, you're with me. Sim, you head in with DJ, Sammy is going to lead you to where they're holding Brooklyn. We'll cover you and push in to get you out.

"Connie, Kate, Roni, you do the same from the south side. Annabella will be here as our medic. Pam, you stay with Annabella and cover her just in case."

"Right, stay in the car so my husband doesn't kill us all," Pam says.

"You're as important as the rest of us," Tasha says.

"We all get out untouched. Do as we were trained, ladies. This is what we were built for," Val says.

"Okay, let's go," I say and take off.

Sim is right beside me. I take out two guys as I move forward for the entrance. Sim puts down another two.

"He's on the first level. A large space toward the back of the building. Hurry, you have to be quick. She hasn't made a decision," Sammy says into the comm.

I'm not sure what he's talking about, but I nod and wave for Sim to move with me. I tuck my gun and move to take out the guy ahead of us. Not having a lot of time, I take him out at the knees then snap his neck.

I then pull my gun again and jog toward the back. A door comes into view with two guys guarding it. Sim takes them both down before I can do it myself.

"Time is running out," Sammy says.

"Tasha, Val, what have you done?" Logan's heated voice comes through the comm. "Stand down. We're on the way."

"It's too late, we're here," I say.

"You enter, I will stand guard here," Sim says.

I nod and push into the room behind the door, wanting to groan when I see it's not a room but another wide-open space with crates and cargo everywhere. However, I do see Cole bound to a chair in the distance, his back to me.

I growl when I see a guy standing before him as if he's been beating him. I move behind one of the large crates before I'm spotted. Inhaling deeply, I then peek out to see if I have a shot.

I'm frustrated when I can't find a clear shot. I look up to see if I have any other options. Not seeing any, I decide to get closer. Good thing I do, as more guys come into view.

There are five in all. The one standing in front of Cole and four others. I also note there are two other entrances to the space that I can now see.

"Make the call. Get Deja here and ya can get on with yer life," the guy snarls and punches Cole in the face.

Cole sits unfazed, with a grin on his lips and his head held high. Something about the guy's voice tickles my brain, but I lose that thought as I get around the crates and Cole's face comes into view.

"Ya do know when I get free, I'm going to kill ya, right?" Cole taunts and laughs.

"Shut the fuck up. Ya have none of the power here. I'm not afraid of ya. Everything ya have belongs to me."

Cole rolls his eyes and scoffs. "Yer not man enough for anything I have. Ya can't even throw a proper punch. Do ya really think yer going to get me to do anything ya say?"

The guy pulls a gun and cocks it. Without thinking, I holster my pistol and pull the rifle from my back as I aim and move from cover.

"Looking for me?" I say, shooting two of the other four guys.

The guy aiming at Cole spins to face me. He then rushes to stand behind Cole, using him as a shield as he sits in the wooden chair.

"Boyle?" I say in confusion as I look into the eyes of the asshole holding a gun to my man's head.

"Decision made, they all die," Sammy says into the comm.

I'm distracted for only a moment. However, it's all the moment they need. More men storm the area from one of the side doors and a blond woman appears with them.

"We finally meet," the woman says with a thick Russian accent as she glares at me with her cold blue eyes. "If I knew man all it takes, I would have started with him. Mother should have taught you to be heartless. She wouldn't have come for him."

"Who the fuck are you?" I snarl.

"You don't need to know. You will be dead soon and who I am won't matter."

I can clear this room and get out of here, but Cole is tied to that chair. I'll risk him getting hit if I try something. Suddenly, gunfire can be heard in the distance.

"You two. See what problem is," the blond orders, causing two of their men to leave, bettering my odds.

Boyle laughs, drawing my attention to him. He's still aiming at Cole's head. He's the first one I need to put down.

"Ya let yerself go, Deja," Boyle snarls at me as he looks me up and down with a cross between lust and disgust.

Cole snorts as rage fills his face. "Ya mean, ya have no idea what to do with her. Little dick syndrome, aye? Yer better off with that skinny bitch. She might feel your tickles."

I would laugh if we weren't being held at gunpoint. Only Cole would talk as if he had the upper hand while we're outnumbered. I think I love him more than ever in this moment.

I'm not about to allow this prick to body-shame me. I carry my curves with pride. Even after two babies, I know I look good.

I want to shoot him even more. Why is he even here and who's the bitch with him? My blood is beginning to boil.

"We're cornered. It's going to take a second to get through them. Can you hold on?" Val says into the comm.

"Don't worry, I got it."

I gasp. I know that voice. My hands begin to shake, and tears burn the backs of my eyes.

That's when everything begins to move in slow motion. Looking like a thick Black Lora Croft, my mother appears, wielding two huge axes in her hands. She spins one over her head and then chops off the head of the guy before her.

Not skipping a beat, she spins both axes and turns her body as she moves and chops the next guy's legs out from under him. His upper body drops to the ground like a Jenga tower. It's his screams that draw everyone else's attention away from me.

I glance at Cole. He winks at me as a cocky grin comes to his lips. He then front flips his body and the chair he's restrained to, doing a full rotation then bringing his weight down on the chair as he lands on his back, breaking the chair.

He snaps the zip tie from his wrists and swiftly grabs one of the broken legs from the now splintered chair. With the force of a savage, he drives the chair leg through Boyle's chest. The other end coming through his back.

The blond woman screams and turns her gun on me. I'm still in shock. Not having the wherewithal to move out of the line of fire, I stand here blinking.

My mother places the bloody axes on her back and pulls two pistols to start clearing out the place. She's amazing.

Remember, if I can't fix this and keep it away from you, I will be there when you need me most.

"No," Cole roars, pulling me from my shock.

I feel the impact of the bullet just before he knocks me to the ground with his big body. He pulls one of the guns from my thigh and begins to fire at the blond.

She grabs one of her men by his hair and tugs him in front of her like a shield as she backs away and continues to fire at us. Her human shield jerks in front of her as Cole fills him with holes.

Her gun jams or something, causing her to curse and toss it aside, not that her aim is any good anyway. With the gun forgotten, she drops the guy's body and turns to run. Cole lifts from on top of me and begins to check me over.

"I'm fine. She caught me in the vest," I say to ease his panic.

He stands and lifts me in his arms. "Put me down. We're outnumbered. I need to help."

"Who says we're outnumbered?" Logan's voice comes through the comms.

The sound of the gunfire shifts. I peek around Cole to see Logan, LaSalle, Dylan, Jamie, the Blacks, McGowans, and my uncles rushing the building as they join the Bellas to clear the place out.

"You and Cole get out of here. We've got this," my mum says into the earpiece.

"I was wondering when ye were going to show up," Uncle Ewan says.

"I've been around, but today my baby needed me," Mum replies.

CHAPTER FIFTY-ONE

Gun Smoke

Onyx

Present day ...

I wake with a smile on my face. I have way more to smile about these days. Spending time with Deja and my grandbabies is the highlight of my life.

"Time to go check on my wee monster," I say to myself as I stretch my arms over my head.

I told Deja not to worry about the kids today. I know it's not her real wedding, but she can still enjoy as much of the experience as possible. Besides, I can handle getting three little ones ready for the day.

I'll start with Patrick. I can't wait to see my handsome boy in his little tux. I've missed out on so much, but getting to be there when my grandson was born meant everything to me. Patrick Ian O'Brien is the most precious baby ever.

That smile melts my heart whenever I see it. Deja is such a good mother. I'm proud of Cole too.

He'll do anything for my daughter and their kids. I know Ian would be proud of him. He reminds me a lot of his grandfather.

While lost in my thoughts of how Ian Black's plans have all begun to come into fruition, I shower and get myself ready first. Once dressed in my robe, I go to the nursery where Patrick is.

It's when I'm right outside the door that I hear a young voice inside. Patrick isn't even one yet, so it's not his voice. I stop with my hand on the handle as I listen.

"Hey, Patrick. A lot of people are going to be angry with me after today, but I have to do it this way. I had to lie.

"I've seen all the paths this day could take. This one is the only one where we don't lose anyone. Not permanently.

"In the other paths, you lose your grandma and grandpa. I can't allow that. You will need both lions to roar beside me. I need you like you need them.

"I'm doing this to make it right. I'm still learning, but I know this time I'm doing the right thing. You will see."

Sammy, that's Sammy's voice. I release the door handle and take a step back. I stand wondering if I should tell the others what I've heard.

Then I cover my mouth. This child has never been wrong. If I say something, I could die today.

Deja has spent enough of her life without me. I can't allow that to happen again. However, this child has just admitted to lying, and everyone is prepared to put their lives on the line today based on his word.

Just when I am ready to turn and find Brooklyn, the door opens and Sammy steps out. He looks me in the eyes with his piercing gray ones and lifts his finger to his lips.

"Trust me," he whispers, then walks off as if he has said nothing.

"Your little ass is the reason I have gray hair," I mumble to myself and head into Patrick's room.

Brooklyn

Now that the shock has worn off, I shouldn't be so surprised this woman has defied me and is here by my side. We argued for weeks about her role in all of this. This was not the plan.

Learning what my woman is truly capable of was a shock, but I hate it to this day. Not because she doesn't need me, but the fact that she's so willing to jump into action because she's fucking badass. That's fine, but at any minute, any one of us could take a hit.

I would lose my mind if I lost her to any of this. Patrick hasn't even turned one yet. Yet here we are, explosions happening all around us, gunfire ringing out, and chaos ensuing all over the estate while our family and guests are all underground.

We'll be lucky if any of them show up for the real thing in Scotland. The guest list, the wedding invites, all had to look authentic.

Thank God Sammy suggested at the last minute that we send non-family to another location, only allowing guests who understand this life to be a part of today.

We couldn't have too many in attendance as the weight on the trapdoors had to be precise. Sim and Sammy were geniuses for coming up with the idea to put the scales under the photo step and repeat for everyone's weight to calibrate the door release and ease down of the seats.

Every detail of today was thought out and planned to a tee. Nothing should go wrong. As I have that thought, my clip runs out.

I rush for cover to reload. A flash of white catches the corner of my eye. I take my gaze off my task for a second and find my soon-to-be wife covering me.

God, she's beautiful and so fucking amazing. Shots hit the stone statue I'm behind and I snap back into action. Fully loaded once again, I focus on the enemy ahead.

"Abort, abort. Stop now, da. She's getting away," Misha's voice comes through the comms.

"Ach, then go after her," I snarl.

"*Net,* Czar has been hit. Lovie, get his wife here, now," Misha commands.

My chest grows tight. Czar is Misha's cousin; of course, he's done. Czar's life takes priority.

"Lovie, do you hear me?" Misha says.

"Keep calm. She has taken Lovie and Milanie. They will be okay. This has happened just as I wanted," Sammy says in a static voice. I would think he was asking his parents to go to the park, not talking about a kidnapping.

"What?" Misha roars. "Why would she take them?"

My head is pounding as I put all that has happened together. Czar is down bad enough for Misha to call this all off. Lovie has been caught up in all of this again and Misha's daughter has also been taken, but this bitch is still breathing.

Fuck, my family has just been sucked deeper into this. If I thought I was going to sit DJ's ass down after this, I can fucking dream on now. Yet it's Sammy's next words that nearly make my head explode.

"Because that's the only way she could be sure you and DJ would come. However, she didn't know to account for me."

"This is done. I do my way." Misha seethes.

"I know. Your way is the one needed. I'll be with you, Uncle Misha. It's time to take care of her. She's in Mishutka Mishyenka's way."

"Jamie, where are ya?" Logan and I say in unison.

I groan when neither of us gets a reply. Tell me why I'm not surprised. Here we go.

Blue Collection Character Tree

Legally Bound 1

Bobby Mairettie and Paige Kemble-Mairettie.

Father and mother of:

Peyton and James Mairettie (*twin boys*)
Sydney Mairettie and Maria Lynn Mairettie (*twin girls*)

Legally Bound 2

Marcus Mairettie and Rita Briggs-Mairettie.

Father and mother of:

Daniel Mairettie
Hannah Mairettie

Legally Bound 3

Nathaniel (Nate) Briggs and Pamela (Pam) Kemble-Briggs.

Father and mother of:

Tiffany and Tracey Briggs (*twin girls*)
Nathaniel Briggs Jr.

Legally Bound 4

Jasper Briggs and Marie Mairettie-Briggs.

Father and mother of:

Clay Briggs

Legally Bound 5

Sam Mairettie, a.k.a. LaSalle Samuel Locatelli and Monique Natasha Gabriel, a.k.a. Tasha Locatelli.

Father and mother/stepmother of:

Jessica Mairettie Locatelli (mother, Ellen, ***deceased***)
Megan Mairettie Locatelli (mother, Ellen, ***deceased***)
Sammy Mairettie Locatelli (mother, Ellen, ***deceased***)
Elijah Locatelli
Paulie Locatelli
Karen Locatelli
Sunny Locatelli

The Mairettie Family

Grandpa Marcello Mairettie and Grandma Marie Ann.

Father and mother of:
Marcello Mairettie Jr.
Andrew Mairettie
James Mairettie
Jessie Mairettie
Lynn Mairettie
Gianna Mairettie

James Mairettie and Minnie Mairettie.
Father and mother of:
Bobby Mairettie
Sam Mairettie (Ellen Kensington-Mairettie, *wife*)
Marcus Mairettie
Marie Mairettie

The Briggs Family

Thomas Briggs and Raquel Marinos-Briggs (***deceased***).
Father and mother of:
Nathaniel Briggs
Rita Briggs

Earl Briggs (younger brother of Thomas) and Caitronia Marinos-Briggs (twin sister of Raquel).
Father and mother of:
Kelly Briggs-Fecteau (Alexie Fecteau, *husband*)
Jasper Briggs

The Kemble Family

Peyton Kemble and Davina Kemble.
Father and mother of:
Pamela Kemble
Paige Kemble

Other Important Legally Bound Characters

Camille (Cam) McWien-Carter (Seth Carter, *soon-to-be ex-husband*).

Father and mother of:
Seth Carter Jr.
Eddie Carter
Aiden Carter
Austin Mc Wien (*Camille's father*)
Baroness Olivia Kontos (Baron Kontos' widow, *ex-lover of Jasper/ Thomas Briggs's new love interest*)
Vanessa (Julissa) Smith-Mims (***deceased***) (Patrick Mims, *husband,* ***deceased***)
Czar Gabriel (Tasha's brother)
Brenda Gabriel (Tasha's sister)
Kurtrina Gregory (Tasha's sister)
Keisha Gregory (Tasha's sister)
Senator Roland Gabriel (Tasha's father)
Yolanda Gabriel (Tasha's mother)
Misha Krupin and Keisha Gregory (***deceased***).
Father and mother of:
Milanie Krupin
Faina Krupin
Pavel Krupin (***deceased***).
Logan O'Brien and Raven Johnson (***deceased*** *girlfriend of Logan*).
Father and mother of:
Shauna O'Brien
DJ, a.k.a. Desha
Phoebe Romaine (Ellen's grandmother, **deceased**)
Fifika Romaine (***deceased***)
Salvador Romaine (Ellen's uncle)
Uncle Alfanzo Locatelli
Marco Locatelli
D'Angelo Locatelli
Uncle Carlo Locatelli
Shura
Afanasy

Hush 1
Uri Donati and Valentina Caprisi-Donati.
Father and mother of:
Vita Khayla Donati

Nori Donati
Inzo Donati
Eva Donati

Hush 2
Luca Donati and Shannon Caprisi-Donati.
Father and mother of:
Carlo Donati (introduced in Ballers 2)

Hush 3
Michael Angelo Donati and Symphony Isabella Mansilla-Trovati-Donati.
Father and mother of:
Artemis Donati
Baby on the way

The Donati Family

Angelo Uri Donati (***deceased***) and Donatella Manzo-Donati~~Zuko.~~
Father and mother of:
Uri Donati
Nico Donati ~~Zuko~~
Annabella Donati ~~Zuko~~ (*Nico's twin sister*).
Michael Donati ~~Zuko~~

Uncle Nicholas Donati (brother of Angelo Donati) and Ava Donati.
Father and mother of:
Luca Donati

The Caprisi Family

Vincent Caprisi and Khayla Grant-Caprisi (***deceased***).
Father and mother of:
Valentina Caprisi
Lissette Caprisi (***deceased***)
**Shannon Caprisi (*Vincent's daughter*)

Other Important Hush Characters

Uncle Valentine Caprisi (*Vincent's Brother, head hitter*)
Iman Grant (*Khayla Sister, **Shannon's mother,* ***deceased***)
Roberto Donati–Zuko (*Donatella's husband,* ***deceased***)
***Posed as Dale, the accountant from Legally Bound 3*

Cole "Brooklyn" O'Brien
DJ, a.k.a. Deja

Ballers 1

Bradley Monroe and Tamara Hathaway-Monroe.
Father and mother of:
Brielle Monroe
Ashley Monroe and Ashton Monroe (twins)
Corey Monroe (*baby Tam is pregnant with at end of Ballers 1*)

The Monroe Family

Vernon Monroe and Gloria Monroe.
Father and mother of:
Trevor Monroe (Donna, *soon-to-be ex-wife)*
Bradley Monroe
Ann Monroe (Bradley's twin sister) (Tom, husband)
Trevor Monroe and Donna Monroe.
Father and mother of:
Jessica Monroe
Toby Monroe and Paige Monroe (*twins*)
Jonathan Monroe
Tom Rivers and Ann Monroe-Rivers.
Father and mother of:
George Rivers and Melissa Rivers (*twins*)
Amy Rivers

The Hathaway Family

Byron Hathaway and Fiona Hathaway.
Father and mother of:
Ellerie Hathaway
Tamara Hathaway

Other Important Ballers Characters

Stacey (Tam's best friend)
Reese (Tam's best friend, Nico's girlfriend in Ballers 1)
Alee (Tam's best friend)
Cyrus Pierson (Tam's boss).
Father of:
Tommy Pierson
Carey Pierson
Stephanie Pierson

Ballers 2

Nico Donati and Reese Bridges-Donati.
Father and mother of:
Nico Jr. Donati
Lanya Donati
Orso Donati
Santo Donati
Stefano Donati

Ballers 3

Cameron Perry and Maribel Amina Jones, a.k.a. Amina.
Father and mother of:
Cade Perry
Chance Perry
Cecilia Perry

Pieces of Trevor's Heart

Trevor Monroe and Lynn "Cakes" Galveston.
Father and mother/stepmother of:
Jessica Monroe (mother, Donna, ***deceased***)
Toby Monroe a.k.a Scoot and Paige Monroe a.k.a Snacks (*twins*) (mother, Donna, ***deceased***)
Jonathan Monroe a.k.a Bam (mother, Donna, ***deceased***)
Brooklyn Valentina Monique Monroe, a.k.a Twinkle
Brandon Moses Monroe, a.k.a Bird
Clifton Travis Vernon Monroe, a.k.a Doc

Other Important Ballers Characters

Tiberius Roman (Reese's ex-husband)
Symphony (Michael's right hand)

Brothers Black 1

Wyatt Black and Lanelle (Nellie) Bryant-Black, father and mother of:

*Nora Black

*Evan Black

The Black Family

Joseph Black and Cassidy Black, father and mother of:

*Wyatt Black

*Noah Black

*Johnathan Black

*Felix Black

*Toby Black

*Braxton Black

*Ryan Black

The Lockhart Family

Rob Lockhart and Faith Lockhart, father and stepmother of:

*Heather Lockhart

Steve Lockhart and Nora Bryant-Lockhart (deceased), stepfather and mother of:

*Lanelle (Nellie) Bryant-Black

Chase Lockhart and Jennifer Lockhart, father and mother of:

*Rebecca (Bean) Lockhart (Noah's best friend and love interest)

Other Important Brothers Black 1 Characters

Missy (Johnathan's ex-girlfriend, deceased)

Lucy (Heather's girlfriend)

Barry Coleman (deceased)

Brothers Black 2

Noah Black and Rebecca (Bean) Lockhart-Black, father and mother of:

*Brodie Black

*Connor Black

*Baby on the way

Other Important Brothers Black 2 Characters

Joshua (deceased)

Carmen (Nene) Nash (reporter; niece of Mariah Briggs from Yours Series; Ryan's new crush)

Logan O'Brien

Brothers Black 3

King Toby Black and Queen Ogeima Feechi (Kamara) Abi-oye-Black, father and mother of:

*Lulu Black

*TJ Black

*Baby on the way

Other Important Brothers Black 3 Characters

Missy (Johnathan's ex-girlfriend, deceased)

Lucy (Heather's girlfriend)

Barry Coleman (deceased)

King Elijah Abioye, a.k.a. Mr. Naidoo

Queen Ada Catherine Naidoo-Abioye

King Kwäzē Naidoo-Abioye

Celeste (Kwäzē's ex-girlfriend)

King Afafa (deceased)

Missy (Johnathan's ex-girlfriend, deceased)

Lucy (Heather's girlfriend)

Barry Coleman (deceased)

Joshua (deceased)

Carmen Nash, a.k.a. Nene (Reporter, Mariah Briggs, from Yours Series, Niece, Ryan's new crush)

Logan O'Brien

Dylan O'Brien

Jamie O'Brien

Cole 'Brooklyn' O'Brien

Uncle Jonah McGowan

Uncle Jack McGowan

Uncle Raymond McGowan

Uncle Ronan McGowan

Carrick McGowan

Malcolm McGowan

Graham McGowan

Jeremiah McGowan

Reilly McGowan

Brothers Black 4

Braxton Black and Heather Lockhart-Black, father and mother of:

*Riley Black

*Rowen Black

Other Important Brothers Black 4 Characters

Debbie Lockhart-Kline (Rob's ex-wife, Heather's mother)

Lucy (Heather's pretend girlfriend)

Amanda Kline (Heather's half sister)

Ernest Kline (Heather's Stepfather, deceased)

Eugene, a.k.a. Crooked Nose

Logan O'Brien

Dylan O'Brien

Jamie O'Brien

Cole 'Brooklyn' O'Brien

Uncle Jonah McGowan

Uncle Jack McGowan

Uncle Raymond McGowan

Uncle Ronan McGowan

Carrick McGowan

Malcolm McGowan

Graham McGowan

Jeremiah McGowan

Reilly McGowan

Nicholas Lincoln

Sephora Lincoln

Thomas Briggs

Brothers Black 5

Felix Black and Kaye Porter-Black, a.k.a. Kaye Blaze, father and mother of:

*Dashawn Black

*Second child unannounced

Other Important Brothers Black 5 Characters

Lakia Redding (Kaye's writer friend)

Dean (Kaye's writer friend)

Hayidah (Doll for Club Desire)

Pastor Wayne Porter (Kaye's father)

Danesha Porter (Kaye's mother)

Danny Porter (Deceased, Kaye's brother and Felix's best friend)

Grandma Reid (Kaye's grandmother)

Grandpa Reid (Kaye's grandfather)

Alberto Pérez (Felix's best friend)

Jacob McTavish (lead actor in Kaye's movie)

Mona Richards (deceased, a fan)

Logan O'Brien

Dylan O'Brien

Jamie O'Brien

Cole "Brooklyn" O'Brien

Connie O'Brien

Kate O'Brien

Ronan McGowan

Carrick McGowan

Brothers Black 6

Ryan Black and Carmen Nash, father and mother of:

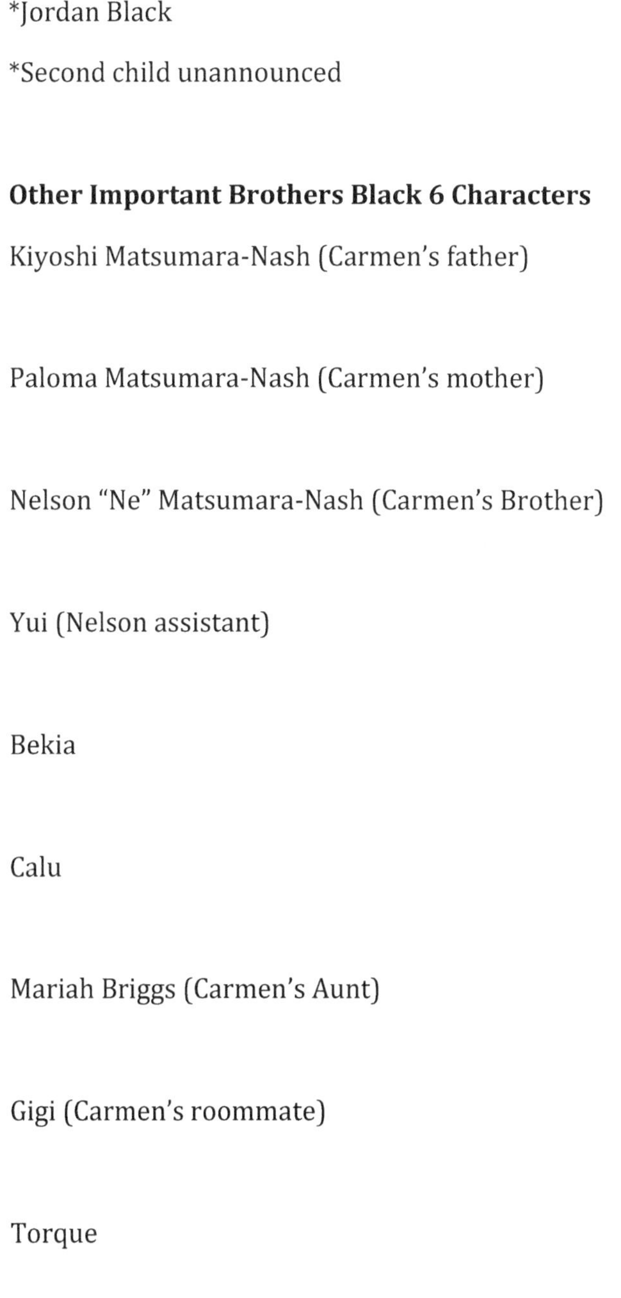

*Jordan Black

*Second child unannounced

Other Important Brothers Black 6 Characters

Kiyoshi Matsumara-Nash (Carmen's father)

Paloma Matsumara-Nash (Carmen's mother)

Nelson "Ne" Matsumara-Nash (Carmen's Brother)

Yui (Nelson assistant)

Bekia

Calu

Mariah Briggs (Carmen's Aunt)

Gigi (Carmen's roommate)

Torque

Alexander (oldest triplet)

Maximilian, a.k.a. Mil (middle triplet)

Tobias (youngest triplet)

Austin Mc Wien (deceased)

Logan O'Brien

Misha Krupin

Dr. Omid V-Shah

Connie O'Brien

Kate O'Brien

Don LaSalle Locatelli

Tasha Locatelli

Valentine Donati

Uri Donati

Brothers Black 7

Johnathan Black and Cherone "Roni" Pérez -Black, father and mother of:

*Mena Black

Other Important Brothers Black 7 Characters

Natasha "Indigo"

Grissel Pérez (deceased)

Eliam Pérez (deceased)

Irina Krupin (deceased)

Yours Series
Nicholas Lincoln and Sephora (Sophi, a.k.a. Soph, a.k.a. Lilla du) Emilsson.

Father and mother of:
Nicole Lincoln
Nadia Lincoln
Nicholas Lincoln Jr.

The Lincoln Family

Dean Lincoln and Shelly Lincoln (***both deceased***).
Father and mother of:
Nicholas Lincoln
Rick ~~Carbon~~ Lincoln
Gavin ~~Carbon~~ Lincoln

The Emilsson Family

Liam Emilsson *(was thought to be deceased)* and Faraz Emilsson.
Father and mother of:
Lucian Emilsson
Ettie Emilsson
Sephora Emilsson

Lucian Emilsson and Kimberly Ann Clove.
Father and mother of:
Lilla Emilsson

Other Important Yours Characters

Mark Fienberg (Sephora's best friend)
Ivana Graves (Nick's ex-girlfriend, deceased)
Bianca (Liam's mistress, missing)
Winton (Nick's driver and security)
Jillian Carver (Nick's ex-temporary PA, ***deceased***)
Harvey Carver (Jillian's father and Nick's family friend, ***deceased***)
Bailey Wilder (waitress, Mark's girlfriend)
Dylan O'Brien

Nick's crew

Wyatt Black
Kevin Briggs (*wife* Mariah Briggs, *Nick's PA*)
Craig Hilton
George Ligal
Lucian Emilsson
Andrew Connor (*Ettie's husband*)

Ronan Book 1: Kings of New York
Ronan McGowan and Dean Foxx, a.k.a. Danika "Danny" Peoples-McGowan.
Fur Dad and Mom of:
Bullet McGowan
Blitz McGowan
KD "Killer Doll" McGowan

The McGowan Family

Cianán McGowan and Laoise McGowan
Father and Mother of:
Jonah McGowan
Jack McGowan
Raymond McGowan
Cassidy McGowan-Black
Ronan McGowan

Carrick McGowan
Graham McGowan
Malcolm McGowan
Jeremiah McGowan
Reilly McGowan
Aunt Róisín McGowan (Jack's wife)

The O'Brien Family

Mick a.k.a Dougie O'Brien and Athena a.k.a Kara Black-O'Brien
Father and mother of:
Logan O'Brien

Connie O'Brien
Cole "Brooklyn" O'Brien
Kate O'Brien
Jamie O'Brien
Dylan O'Brien

Other Important Kings of New York Book 1 Characters

Lyric Hughes
Byron Hughes (*Twin killed in accident, **deceased***)
Myron Hughes (***deceased***)
Dayton Hughes
Marlow Givens
Percy Stratton
Den'Nisha Peoples
Uncle Freddie Philips
Rory
Lochlann
Bujar (*The Albanian boss, **deceased***)
Dalmat (*Bujar's brother, **deceased***)
Erjon (Bujar's cousin)
Oisín
Tadhg

Dylan Book 2: Kings of New York
Dylan O'Brien and Ciara Walsh, a.k.a. Cee-Cee Young

The McDougal Family

Grandpa Lennox McDougal and Grandma Orla Murphy-McDougal.

Father and mother of:

Archie McDougal
Ewan McDougal
Kenneth McDougal
Duncan McDougal
Adline McDougal-Walsh, *formerly* Adline Murphy-O'Brien

The Walsh Family

Bram Walsh and Adline McDougal-Walsh.

Father and mother of:

O'Shea Walsh (Adopted son)

Angus Walsh

Donald Walsh

Donald Walsh and Iesha Rogers-Walsh.

Father and mother of:

Ciara Walsh

Ciarán Walsh

Other Important Kings of New York Book 2 Characters

Daliah Gibson
Vega Stratton
Taegan Quinn
Simon Byrne
Cadla Sullivan
Theo Young
Sean Young
Lily Young
Laki Kalani
Amy Kalani
Iesha Roger-Walsh (*wife of Donald Walsh,* **deceased**)
Helen Walsh aka Léan Black aka Onyx (*wife of Angus Walsh*)
Queeny Walsh (*wife of Q'Shea Walsh*)
Eoghan Quinn
Dimitri
Nashawn
Ross
Aidan
Booker
Kary

Brooklyn Book 3: Kings of New York

Cole a.k.a. Brooklyn Patrick O'Brien and Deja Walsh, a.k.a. DJ:

Father and Mom of:
Cara O'Brien
Liadan O'Brien
Patrick O'Brien

Other Important Kings of New York Book 3 Characters

Callum
Blair
Aisling
Nakim
Emory
Arnez
Seán
Ewan McDougal
Kenneth McDougal
Duncan McDougal

ABOUT THE AUTHOR

Blue Saffire, award-winning, bestselling author of over eighty contemporary romance novels and novellas, writes with the intention to touch the heart and the mind. Blue hooks, weaves, and loops multiple series, keeping you engaged in her worlds. Blue writes for her own publishing company, Perceptive Illusions as Blue Saffire, as well as Royal Blue.

Blue and her husband live in a house filled with laughter and creativity in Long Island, NY. Both working hard to build the Blue brand and cultivate their love for the arts. Creative is their family affair.

Blue holds an MBA in Marketing and Project Management, as well as an MED in Instructional Technology and Curriculum Design. She is also an NLP Master Practitioner.

ACKNOWLEDGMENTS

Friend, this was a labor of love. The timeline work alone … listen, okay. This universe is so massive. Every time I dive in, I learn something new. Cole and DJ have lived in my head for so many years. It started with that baseball bat. LOL. All the pieces are starting to fit together perfectly.

Man, I love me some Cole. DJ was my girl, though and Onyx. I'm in love with this series. Two more brothers and so much more to reveal. This book put me in my happy place.

As always, my dear reader friends, thank you so much for your continued support and patience. I want you to know now how much I appreciate you. Each book is written in hopes you will find your happy place too. Thank you for allowing me to be the one to give that to you.

Thank you for the encouraging emails, videos, posts, shares, comments, and DMs. Y'all are the absolute best. Remember, sharing is caring. If you have a friend who reads, let them know about me, please.

To my person. Thank you for listening and cheering me on as I got this one right. Thank you for staying up with me for all the long nights. Forever grateful.

All praise and thanks be to God. Without you, I wouldn't be able to do this. My divine source, my connection, my healer. I walk by faith and not by sight. There is knowing and there is believing. I am thankful that I know. Thank you for your presence and your blessings. Unapologetically blessed and highly favored.

Next! It's complicated. You will see.

Wait, there is more to come! You can stay updated with my latest releases, learn more about me, the author, and be a part of contests by subscribing to my newsletter at

www.BlueSaffire.com

If you enjoyed *Brooklyn Book 3*, I'd love to hear

your thoughts and please feel free to leave a

review on my website. And when you do, please let me

know by emailing me TheBlueSaffire@gmail.com

or leave a comment on Facebook https://www.facebook.com/BlueSaffireDiaries or Twitter @TheBlueSaffire

Other books by Blue Saffire

Placed in Best Reading Order

Also available …

Legally Bound

Legally Bound 2: Against the Law

Legally Bound 3: His Law

Perfect for Me

Hush 1: Family Secrets

Ballers: His Game

Brothers Black 1: Wyatt the Heartbreaker

Legally Bound 4: Allegations of Love

Hush 2: Slow Burn

Legally Bound 5.0: Sam

Yours 1: Losing My Innocence

Yours 2: Experience Gained

Yours 3: Life Mastered

Ballers 2: His Final Play

Legally Bound 5.1: Tasha Illegal Dealings

Brothers Black 2: Noah

Legally Bound 5.2: Camille

Legally Bound 5.3 & 5.4 Special Edition

Where the Pieces Fall

Legally Bound 5.5: Legally Unbound

Brothers Black 4: Braxton the Charmer

Broken Soldier

Brothers Black 5: Felix the Watcher

A Home for Christmas

Doctor Feel Good

Brothers Black 6: Ryan the Joker

Brothers Black 7: Johnathan the Fixer

Wild Hearts

Pieces of Trevor's Heart

Ballers 3: His Team

Ronan Book 1: Kings of New York

Dylan Book 2: Kings of New York

Brooklyn Book 3: Kings of New York

Coming Soon…

King of Gods Book 4: Immortal Iron Brothers Series
King of Past Book 5: Immortal Iron Brothers Series
Jamie: Book 4: Kings of New York

Other Blue Saffire Series

Hold On To Me Series
My Funny Valentine
Be My Valentine

Hitter Squad Series
Remember Me

Work Husband Series
Unexpected Lovers
My Best Friend's Wish
The Ones Left Behind
The Last Ones Standing

The Lost Souls MC Series
Forever
Never
Always

The Moran Brothers Series
Love Notes
Stay With Me

The Ahole Club Series**
Pit Book 1: The A**hole Club
Ox Book 5: The A**hole Club
Kelex Book 6: The A**hole Club

Immortal Iron Brothers Series
King of Knights Book 1
King of Inferno Book 2
King of Tides Book 3

Check out Blue Saffire exclusives on the
BlueSaffire.com website

The Fixer
His Miracle Baby
Razor
Dane
Trip
Professor Jones
Room 112

Other books from Evei Lattimore Collection Books by Blue Saffire
Black Bella 1

Destiny 1: Life Decisions
Destiny 2: Decisions of the Next Generation
Destiny 3 coming soon…

Star

Other books from Royal Blue Gay Romance Collection written by Blue Saffire
Kyle's Reveal
Beau's Redemption

www.ingramcontent.com/pod-product-compliance
Lightning Source LLC
LaVergne TN
LVHW020041110826
845155LV00029B/581